Praise for *New York Times* bestselling author
Christine Warren

You're So Vein

"Filled with supernatural danger, excitement, and sar-
castic humor."   —*Darque Reviews*

"Five stars. This is an exciting, sexy book."
                                        —*Affaire de Coeur*

"The sparks do fly!" —*Romantic Times BOOKreviews*

Walk on the Wild Side

"A seductive tale with strong chemistry, roiling emotions, steamy romance, and supernatural action. The
fast-moving plot in *Walk on the Wild Side* will keep
the readers' attention riveted through every page,
and have them eagerly watching for the next in-
stallment."   —*Darque Reviews*

"There's no shortage of sexy sizzle."
            —*Romantic Times BOOKreviews* (4½ stars)

"Christine Warren is amazingly talented…*Walk on
the Wild Side* is undisputedly a masterpiece."
                                    —*Night Owl Romance*

MORE…

"A fully realized tale with amazing characters and intriguing plots."   —*Fallen Angel Reviews*

Howl at the Moon

"Warren delivers a rapidly paced tale that pits duty against honor and love. Populated with intriguing characters who continue to grow and develop, it is fun to see familiar faces in new scenarios. This is a world that is always worth visiting!"
                    —*Romantic Times BOOKreviews*

"A fantastic addition to the world of The Others…grab a copy as soon as possible. Christine Warren does a wonderful job of writing a book that meshes perfectly with the storylines of the others in the series, yet stands alone perfectly."   —*Romance Reviews Today*

"Warren weaves a paranormal world of werewolves, shifters, witches, humans, demons, and a whole lot more with a unique hand for combining all the paranormal classes."   —*Night Owl Romance*

"*Howl at the Moon* will tug at a wide range of emotions from beginning to end . . . Engaging banter, a strong emotional connection, and steamy love scenes. This talented author delivers real emotion which results in delightful interactions . . . and the realistic dialogue is stimulating. Christine Warren knows how to write a winner!" —*Romance Junkies*

The Demon You Know

"Explodes with sexy, devilish fun, exploring the further adventures of The Others. With a number of the gang from previous books back, there's an immediate familiarity about this world that makes it easy to dive right into. Warren's storytelling style makes these books remarkably entertaining."
—*Romantic Times BOOKreviews* (4½ stars)

She's No Faerie Princess

"Warren has fast become one of the premier authors of rich paranormal thrillers elaborately laced with scorching passion. When you want your adventure hot, Warren is the one for you!"
—*Romantic Times BOOKreviews*

"The dialogue is outrageous, funny, and clever. The characters are so engaging and well scripted…and the plot . . . is as scary as it is delicious!"
—*Romance Reader at Heart*

"Christine Warren has penned a story rich in fantastic characters and spellbinding plots."

—*Fallen Angel Reviews*

Wolf at the Door

"A great start to a unique paranormal series."

—*Fresh Fiction*

"This book is a fire-starter . . . a fast-paced, adrenaline- and hormonally-charged tale. The writing is fluid and fun, and makes the characters all take on life-like characteristics."

—*Romance Reader at Heart*

"Intrigue, adventure, and red-hot sexual tension."

—*USA Today* bestselling author Julie Kenner

BORN
TO BE
WILD

Christine Warren

St. Martin's Paperbacks

This is a work of fiction. All of the characters, organizations, and events portrayed in this novel are either products of the author's imagination or are used fictitiously.

BORN TO BE WILD

Copyright © 2010 by Christine Warren.

For information address St. Martin's Press, 175 Fifth Avenue, New York, NY 10010.

ISBN: 978-0-312-35719-1

Printed in the United States of America

St. Martin's Paperbacks edition / March 2010

St. Martin's Paperbacks are published by St. Martin's Press, 175 Fifth Avenue, New York, NY 10010.

10 9 8 7 6 5 4 3 2 1

CHAPTER ONE

Dr. Josephine Barrett had just flipped off the lights in her triage area when a low, heavy pounding thundered at the clinic's back door. So much for the novel experience of eating her pizza while it was still hot.

For a split second, she debated hiding behind the ultrasound cart and pretending the office was already closed, locked, and deserted; but that was just cowardly, not to mention irresponsible. No one would be trying to knock down the door on a Saturday night unless they had a genuine emergency. And it wasn't like this was Portland, where the next clinic down the road could take the case. In the tiny, rural town of Stone Creek, Oregon, Josie was the only veterinarian in twenty miles, and there was no way she could turn her back on a patient in need.

No matter how strong the urge.

Sighing, she flipped the light switch back up. *Fine, but if this is Mrs. Cowlitz's Persian with Dentu-Creme matted in its coat again, I swear to God I will not be responsible for the size of my bill.*

Grabbing her stethoscope, Josie strode to the rear of the clinic and pushed open the heavy security door. "The office is closed right now. Is this an emergency?"

The second sentence bounced off the back of a large and fast-moving male form that hadn't bothered waiting for her to step aside and let it in. The intruder shouldered straight past her and over to one of two surgical-steel exam tables at the far side of the room. Her subconscious barely had time to register recognition of the local sheriff in time to choke off an irritated threat about calling the police.

"Sheriff Pace, I'm not sure if you realize this, but it's after nine o'clock, and I've been—"

Whatever she'd been about to say died in her throat as the uniformed figure stepped to the side to reveal the ragged bundle he'd just deposited on the table.

"Jesus Christ!"

Josie bolted forward, shoved the sheriff out of the way, and peeled aside a corner of the reflective silver survival blanket. She pressed her palm hard against the bloody, matted fur beneath a limp forelimb. The beat she felt there was weak, but discernible.

"What the hell happened?"

"Your guess is as good as mine," the deep voice answered, sounding taut and . . . displeased, "as long as it involves at least one round from a .50-caliber hunting rifle."

"Where?" Now intently focused, she ran her hands over the rest of a shockingly still gray body, searching for wounds.

"Left flank."

Josie grunted, shoved the blanket entirely aside, and began probing the heavy muscle he'd indicated. Or rather, where that muscle should have been. Right now there was more blood than meat. A long, ragged trough of flesh had been carved out of the animal's leg just below the hip.

She swore again and grabbed a packet of sterile packing from the counter just behind the table. While she tore it open, she ran an educated eye over the rest of the still form. "Any others?"

"Bullet wounds? Not that I saw, but she's a mess. I didn't waste a lot of time checking her over. I thought I'd leave that to you."

Pressing the wad of cloth against the top of the wound where it bled sluggishly, Josie applied pressure and jerked her chin in the sheriff's direction. "I need to hold this in place for a minute, so I'll need your hands. You're going to take her rear paws in one hand and the front in the other and *gently* roll her over so I can check her other side. But first, you're going to grab that blue muzzle on the counter and slip it over her nose. When it's in place, you can tie it off at the back of her head."

"She's unconscious. I don't think she's in any condition to take a chunk out of me—"

"I don't care," Josie cut in. "You just brought me a critically injured adult female timber wolf. She might be too weak to fight, but I'm not taking the chance. And more importantly, you're not taking the chance in my hospital. Pain makes us all do strange things, and it's not like she's wearing a rabies tag." She scowled and nodded toward the counter. "Muzzle."

The sheriff obeyed, and since she didn't have time to wonder how he felt about it, Josie couldn't have cared less whether or not his macho sensibilities had tinged his movements with reluctance. She just concentrated on applying pressure to the bullet graze and waited for him to turn the injured wolf onto her other side. A quick assessment when he did revealed a few scratches, but nothing that looked nearly as serious as the wound she'd already seen.

She nodded. "Okay. Back over." When he had the animal resettled, she grabbed his right hand and pressed it down on the gauze packing. "Hold this. Firmly."

He didn't bother to protest, and Josie didn't bother to mention that she didn't care for being stared at, especially not when the injured animal opened her eyes and fixed Josie with a steady, amber gaze. That was an observer she'd deal with happily.

Josie's hands were already moving to the hole at the front of the muzzle and lifting the animal's lips to peer into her mouth. The fact that the wolf didn't even blink was making her nervous. As was the pale, pale sticky surface of the animal's gums.

"I'm sorry, girl," she murmured, her voice pitched soft and soothing even while her movements remained briskly efficient. "I know it hurts, but you're being so good. Just be good for a few more minutes, and I promise I'm going to do everything I can to help you."

The wolf didn't move, but she whined and the tip of her tongue flicked out the end of the muzzle, almost as if she understood. Josie repeated the promise to herself and shrugged her stethoscope into place, positioning the chest piece behind the animal's elbow and listening intently. Then she frowned.

Her hand went automatically to her pocket and pulled out her ophthalmoscope. When she peered into the wolf's dark golden eyes, she nearly dropped the instrument on the poor thing's nose.

"This is not a wolf," she blurted out.

The wolf whined.

The sheriff frowned. "What do you mean?"

"I mean that this"—Josie pointed, pointedly—"this is not a timber wolf. It's a human being."

The sheriff lifted an eyebrow.

"Okay, she looks like a wolf," Josie conceded, "but she's not. Or at least, that's not all she is. She's Lupine."

"How can you know that?"

"Because I went to school for four years and did another six months of internship and three years of residency to learn how to identify and treat members of canine species. This"—she pointed again, for emphasis—"is not canine. She only has a partial tapetum lucidum."

"Tapa-who?"

"A reflective layer of tissue behind the retina that helps to reflect light and enhance night vision. In canines, the tapetum lucidum lines the entire back of the eye's lens. Hers is concentrated just around the fovea. If she were a wolf, that would be really, really not natural."

The sheriff shrugged. "Okay, I'll take your word for it. But I don't think it matters all that much. She's still hurt, and you're still a doctor, so how about you give a comparative anatomy lesson later and just patch her up right now?"

"Didn't you hear me? She's *human*. I'm an *animal* doctor. I can't treat a human being."

"No, she's not. She's Lupine, but at the moment she's got more physically in common with Mr. Potter's springer spaniel than with Mr. Potter." He spoke slowly, as if she needed extra time for comprehension. As if she hadn't graduated at the top of her class from both Reed College and the UC Davis School of Veterinary Medicine. "Not to mention that Dr. Shad's office is closed until Monday, and I don't think it would be in her best interest to wait for an appointment. So what do you say? Why don't you take a shot at it? You know, as long as we're here."

Although the impulse to inject the man with a horse laxative tugged at her seductively, Josie's sense of responsibility and medical ethics won out. Turning her back on the sheriff, she placed her stethoscope against the wolf's belly and tried to hear any important sounds over the angry throbbing of blood in her ears. A soft *whoosh* immediately caught her attention.

Frowning, she shifted the scope a few inches caudally and listened again. Then she straightened up and pressed the tips of her fingers gently against the wolf's abdomen.

"Grab that phone and press the button next to the name ANDREA," she ordered, looking back up at the sheriff. "There's internal bleeding. She's going to need surgery."

"Andrea?"

"And tell her to hurry. Otherwise I'm going to have to teach you how to tube and anesthetize an injured Lupine."

Without a word, the sheriff turned and strode for the phone. Apparently he approved of Josie's decision to go into private practice rather than teaching.

Eli waited in the clinic for almost three hours, despite Dr. Barrett's warning that the surgery would be a long one and she'd be happy to call him with an update when it was finished. His shift was over, had been over before he'd stumbled on the still, bleeding form of the injured Lupine a little before nine o'clock. So he had nowhere else he had to be. At least, not for another seven or eight hours.

He supposed he could have gone home and tried to sleep—Gods knew his gritty eyeballs and the headache pounding at the back of his skull indicated a need for the unfamiliar stuff—but sleep wasn't going to cure the restlessness that had been crawling along his hide for the past couple of weeks. What he needed was the good solid prowl he'd had planned for the end of his shift, the one he'd had to abandon in order to get the wolf to the vet.

After nearly three weeks of double and triple shifts for himself and the two deputies he employed who hadn't succumbed to the latest flu that was going around, Eli thought he deserved a few hours to cut loose, shed his human skin, and let the beast inside him out to run. Instead, he'd barely gotten his uniform collar unbuttoned before he'd scented the blood.

He hadn't heard the shot, which was strange, but between the growl of his SUV's engine, the crackle of his police scanner, and the voice on the cell phone he'd held to his ear, he supposed there was a chance he'd just missed it. It had been another long shift, after all, at the end of another long week of them, and he'd been on the phone with Ramsey when he pulled into the gravel parking area at the edge of the forest, so he supposed he should forgive himself for his distraction. He hadn't realized anything was wrong until he'd stepped out of the truck and taken his first deep breath of the crisp spring air.

The sweet tang of fresh blood had filled his head and sent hunger momentarily stretching through him. Then he'd sniffed again and realized he wasn't smelling a fresh deer carcass or the remains of some coyote's rabbit dinner. The blood smelled heavier than that, with the curious bitterness of a predatory animal and the peculiar thickness of a large spill.

Something had been near death. Some *Lupine* had been near death.

It hadn't taken him long to find her. All he'd needed to do was follow his nose, and since he hadn't known precisely what he would find, he'd tracked the odor on two feet instead of four, with his radio in one hand and the other on the holster of his service revolver. His flashlight had stayed in his belt. After all, in the darkness he had the eyes of a cat.

She had fallen near the base of a huge pine tree, the kind of old growth that had always made the logging companies just a little bit nervous. A sniff and a quick touch had confirmed that she was still alive, so Eli had wasted no time in scooping her up and carrying her back to his truck, but he'd made note of where he'd found her so he could return in the daylight and go over the scene. Cat's eyes or no, some things could still be overlooked in the dark.

Now that he'd deposited the Lupine safely in the doctor's care, Eli couldn't stop thinking about the incongruity of the situation. Hunters rarely roamed the area around Stone Creek. The town's reputation reached too far for most people to feel real comfortable about shooting something that might or might not have passed them in the Home Depot a few hours earlier. Even the fundamentalists who liked to talk big about how Others were abominations who should be hunted down and killed tended not to like the odds of getting away with taking that kind of action in a place where two-thirds of the local population was something other than human.

Which meant that only locals tended to hunt in the local forests, and most of them did so the old-fashioned way—on all fours with their fur flying. The few who went out with rifles from time to time tended to respect the state-outlined game seasons, and right now the only things a body could legally shoot at were coyotes, cougars, and waterfowl. No one in Stone Creek hunted cougars or coyotes, and the middle of a dry pine forest wasn't exactly prime grounds for goose or duck.

So who had taken the shot that injured the Lupine currently stretched out on the vet's operating table, and what exactly had he been aiming at? Eli didn't imagine sleep would get any more appealing to him until he figured that out.

He rose from the doctor's stool he'd perched on when the door to the operating room opened at the other end of the short hall. When Dr. Barrett emerged in her stained green scrubs, Eli was watching.

"How did it go?"

She braced one hand against the small of her back and stretched wearily. "About as well as it could, all things considered. The bullet wound was the easy part. We got that cleaned out and stitched, but the internal bleeding was what had us worried. Thankfully, we caught it before she lost enough to require a transfusion, because I'm not sure how to go about finding a donor match for a Lupine. The bleeding was in her spleen, which we had to take out, but theoretically, she should do fine without it."

"Theoretically?"

"Canines and humans can both live fairly normal lives after splenectomy, and I've never heard differently about Lupines, but I'm far from an expert on their anatomy and physiology."

Eli heard both the doctor's words and the hesitation behind them. He could also see a certain shadow in her serious brown eyes that told him there was more to the story than she'd already revealed.

"But?" he prompted.

"But, I can't be sure," she admitted. "I'll do some research tonight, but even so, it's a little too late to worry about it. I can't go and sew it back in, even if it hadn't been irreparably damaged by something other than the bullet."

"What do you mean?"

"You nailed the cause of the wound on her flank. A .50-caliber bullet grazed the left upper thigh, no question. But that was a comparatively minor wound. It certainly didn't cause her internal injuries."

Eli frowned. "Then what did?"

"Some kind of blunt-force trauma, but I can't tell you what from. I'd have to shave her from her neck to her tail to check out the bruising before I could make a reasonable guess, and I'm not willing to do that. At this point, I don't want to cause her any unnecessary stress. Not to mention it will be a lot easier to keep her temperature up and out of shock territory if she keeps her fur coat."

"You really don't know a lot about Lupines if you think it wouldn't have grown back in a day or two," he murmured, his mouth quirking at one corner. Then his gaze fixed on the doctor's face, and all traces of humor fled. "What?"

Dr. Barrett hesitated. "I'm not so sure about that."

Why did that one short sentence give Eli such a bad, bad feeling?

"I might be human," she continued, frowning, "and

this might be the first Lupine I've ever admitted to my clinic, Sheriff Pace, but I grew up in Stone Creek. The Unveiling was no big surprise to me. I've been around shifters all my life. But this Lupine you brought me isn't healing like any shifter I've ever heard of."

"Meaning?"

"Were you not listening? She needed *stitches*."

That did sound odd. Most shifters had truly amazing healing powers. Wounds tended to knit almost while you watched, even faster during a shift. The fact that the Lupine had stayed in her wolf form had been one of the reasons Eli had known she needed medical attention.

"Serious wounds slow down the healing process," he said. "And I'm assuming whatever sedative you used is going to slow her down for a while, too."

"Probably, but I'll feel a lot better if that wound looks to be on a faster healing track tomorrow." A frown lingered on her face, creasing the smooth skin between her brows. "It worries me that the internal injuries didn't appear to have even begun the healing process when I opened her up."

"Like I said, the worse she was hurt, the longer it will take her to heal. She'll make a big step forward once she wakes up long enough to shift."

The doctor shot him a sardonic glance. "While I'm sure you meant that to reassure me, let me say that I hope it doesn't happen before morning, because that will be the earliest I can set up a recovery space suitable for a human. Before that, she's taking the risk of waking up in a cage. I don't imagine that would go over well."

Eli shrugged. "If she's anything like me, she's woken up in stranger places."

Dr. Barrett looked up while she tugged at the ties on the back of her surgical gown. "Stranger than a vet's office?"

"Try in the middle of a kennel full of sled dogs."

A grin flashed across the doctor's face and nearly knocked Eli back on his ass. If anyone had asked him to describe the local veterinarian before tonight, he'd have summed her up like any other subject—approximately five-foot-three, maybe 120, brown and brown, with an average build and an average face. But that smile was anything but average. The expression transformed her face from an ordinary if intelligent visage to the enticing, impish countenance of a sexy pixie.

Wasn't that a hell of a thing?

"Hey, if you didn't wake up harnessed to the sled, I'd say you were doing pretty well," she observed, stripping off her gown and tossing the bundle of cloth into an open hamper against the wall. The scrubs she still wore beneath looked limp and wrinkled but noticeably less bloody.

They also covered a body that was noticeably less average than he had always assumed.

Eli coughed to cover his astonishment and shifted away from the counter with the built-in desk he'd waited at during the surgery. "Tell that to the frostbite I nearly got on my butt. It was February, and the dogs slept in the snow caves they dug for themselves. Well, they slept until they caught my scent. Then they mostly lunged around on the ends of their tie-outs and barked at me."

He saw the flash of curiosity on the vet's face and saw how she just as quickly pushed it aside. He'd heard that she'd grown up in Stone Creek, so it shouldn't surprise him that she had her Others etiquette down pat.

"Feline," he explained, since she was being too polite to ask. "Lion. The dogs weren't wild about my natural cologne."

Her next expression, he couldn't read so clearly. Nor could he figure out why that should bother him.

"What's a lion doing out here? We don't have much savanna in western Oregon."

"I noticed that. No pride, either." He shrugged. His family hadn't understood his choices, either, but he'd made them for himself, not for anyone else. "There are only four prides in the United States right now, and last I heard none of them was looking for a Felix. If shifters stayed exclusively in the habitat of their animal forms, we'd have overpopulated those areas and died out a long time ago. I've lived in a few interesting places over the years."

"Well, our Lupine friend might not have lived as adventurous a life as you have," she said, and she looked away from him to a desk full of office supplies. Pulling out an empty manila folder and a pre-printed form, she began to make notes in a new medical chart. "No doubt both of us would feel better if we at least knew who she is and if anyone out there is missing her."

Eli stared at a pair of hands that looked too small and delicate to dig around inside a living body, then caught himself and forced his gaze back to her face.

Her ordinary face, he reminded himself.

"Right. I'll contact Richard Cobb and see if he knows anything. Even if he doesn't, he'll make sure word gets out."

The doctor nodded, acknowledging that the Alpha of the local Lupine pack was the proper person to consult on this. "I'd appreciate it if you could have someone from her family contact me as soon as possible. I really don't think it's appropriate for her to stay here for very long. Especially not once she loses the tail."

"Once Cobb hears about this, he won't let any grass grow under his feet. Trust me."

Eli had to fight against the urge to look for an excuse to linger, which didn't sit well with him, so he compensated by being perhaps a bit to brusque in making his farewells.

"Let me know how she does," he grumbled, already striding for the back door. Clearly something in this room had begun to affect his sanity. Or maybe all those extra shifts were catching up with him. Either way, he figured the best thing for him to do was go. Quickly. "I'll make sure Cobb finds out who she is by tomorrow, latest."

"Thanks," the doctor began, but she never finished.

Or if she did, Eli didn't hear it. He was too busy executing one of the first strategic retreats of his life and wondering why it felt so much like running away.

Exp. 10-1017.03
Log 03-00119

Dosage administered to test subject
(TS-0024) via intramuscular injection.
Resistance made use of force necessary.
Technician reported a struggle and inju-
ries, both blunt force and penetrative.

Subject released post-administration
and will remain under covert observation
beginning after the twenty-four-hour
estimated incubation period.

Remain hopeful that recent modifications
will reduce incubation by 6-12 hours in
secondary host. Must wait and see what
contact test subject achieves with control population.

CHAPTER TWO

Josie slept poorly that night. Whether it was because she spent the time on a hastily inflated air mattress next to the Lupine's cage, or because she couldn't get her mind off her first real encounter with the local sheriff, she couldn't quite decide.

Well, okay, she could decide, but that didn't mean she was ready to admit to anything. Far from it, though what there was to admit to was another question. A slightly awkward encounter with a relative stranger? It wasn't like that had never happened to her before.

A quick glance into the cage near her head assured her that the Lupine remained calm and furry, quite possibly because she was doped up on more pain meds than Josie had ever prescribed before—shifters metabolized drugs so fast that they required much larger doses than humans or animals in order to achieve the same levels of relief. Once Josie began to taper the dosages, hopefully her patient would regain the ability to answer some questions. Along with regaining her opposable thumbs.

With a groan, Josie rolled to her knees and then pushed herself reluctantly into a standing position. Somehow sleeping on an air mattress positioned on a linoleum-tile-covered concrete floor was a lot less comfortable at thirty-two than it had been at twenty-two. It hardly seemed fair. Nor did the amount of money she would have been willing to pay at this point for half an hour to herself with a cup of coffee and a very hot shower. Unfortunately, given that it was Sunday, the clinic was closed, and her staff had the day off, she'd be lucky to get her wish within the next four hours.

It was days like this when she began to seriously consider taking on an associate. Providing she could find an associate willing to work for beans and relocate to the most remote northwestern corner of Oregon.

Josie grimaced and forced herself to begin making the rounds of all of her currently hospitalized patients. In addition to the Lupine, she had George Carpenter's Irish setter, Jenny, who had taken her pursuit of a grouse a little too seriously and broken her leg in a rabbit hole she hadn't seen coming. The bone had been set on Saturday afternoon, but given Jenny's age—eight on her last birthday—Josie had felt more comfortable keeping her overnight before sending her home.

Then there was Clovis, Mrs. Patterson's cantankerous Siamese cat, who just couldn't seem to keep his nose out of anything, including a spilled bottle of Bailey's Irish Cream liqueur. Clovis had been, to put it politely, three sheets to the wind when his owner had rushed him in yesterday convinced this his unsteady gate meant that he'd suffered a stroke and consequently would be permanently brain-damaged.

Josie had valiantly resisted the urge to observe that the brain damage might very well have preceded the alcohol poisoning.

Judging by the yowls currently emitting from Clovis's cage, it sounded as if the activated charcoal and IV treatments had done their job overnight. Chalk up another victory for the good guys.

Still wishing violently for coffee, Josie grabbed a pen and began making notations in everyone's charts until her brain woke up enough to begin her actual examinations. Without caffeine, that could take a few more minutes.

She was just reaching for the latch on Jenny's cage when the door from the front office opened and a familiar figure bowled inside.

"Morning, Doc," the young man said, looking much too cheerful for six thirty on a Sunday. "Andrea gave me the heads-up that we had a new patient as of last night, so I thought you might be able to use an extra hand this morning."

"A blessing on your house, Benjamin Broder," Josie said with feeling. "Remind me to pay you overtime for this."

"You got it!" The youngest of her vet techs peered around her into the Lupine's cage. "Is that her? Is she really a werewolf?"

"Yes, and don't call her a werewolf. It's considered insulting. She's Lupine. Or a shifter."

"Right. So right now, she looks like a wolf, but she's actually human some of the time?"

"Yes."

"So why's she here and not over at Dr. Shad's office? His practice sees humans and Others, doesn't it?"

Josie didn't mention how much she'd prefer to trade her patient with the local physician, but she thought about it. She'd actually been thinking about it for a good many hours now.

"Because it was an emergency, and the sheriff didn't want to take the time to drive her all the way into Astoria to the hospital while she was bleeding pretty badly," she explained, proud to hear that her work at sounding calm and reasonable seemed to be paying off. "Plus, it's one of Dr. Shad's 'Gone Fishing' weekends, so it wasn't like he could have been called in on an emergency basis."

"But are you even qualified to treat a huma—er, a human*ish* patient?"

Josie glared at her employee. "Does she look very human to you at the moment?"

"Okay, fair point."

"Gee, thanks."

Ben shrugged. "I didn't mean to say you *couldn't* treat a person, just that I wasn't sure if you *should,* if you know what I mean. I mean, with liability and all that."

"Please, do not mention that word in this clinic." Josie shuddered. "Imagining the look in my insurance agent's eye is enough to make me reconsider joining a convent."

"Old Dr. Barrett would probably be all for that idea," he teased.

Josie thought of her father, the one who had sold her his own veterinary practice when he'd decided it was time to retire, and of the way he still called her his baby girl and glared at her every time she mentioned a date. "Yeah, well, he's already had to adjust to the idea that he doesn't set my curfew anymore, so I'm sure he'll be able to adjust to me shelving that idea again."

Before Ben could start asking more questions, Josie piled the day's patient charts into his arms and switched back to doctor mode. "Today we just have Jenny, Clovis, and the Lupine, knock wood," she said briskly. "Jenny can go home if Mr. Carpenter comes by to pick her up. Just make sure he has the broken-bone aftercare sheet, and remind him to call if he has any concerns, or if she seems to be in pain. It was a simple closed fracture, and we got it aligned really well before we put the cast on, but I'll give him a day or two worth of pain meds, even though she may not need them. Make sure you set him up with an appointment for four weeks from now, though, for follow-up."

She went over Clovis's situation briefly, then turned and frowned into the Lupine's cage. "I'm going to call and leave a message for Dr. Shad in a minute, but until either she shifts or we hear from him, we're just going to manage her condition instead of her species." She outlined last night's procedures for Ben and reviewed her chart notes. "You'll need to check her incision and wound site and change the dressings, but other than that, at the moment we're just monitoring her. The biggest worry, of course, is infection, but it's also a little weird that she hadn't fully regained consciousness or tried to shift yet."

Ben hummed in agreement, his pen busy making notes of her instructions.

Josie pursed her lips. "Do me a favor and do a draw on her. I can run a CBC to check for any kind of underlying infection that might be compromising her system, and I'd like to double-check the concentration of her meds. I looked a dosage up online last night, but I'm a little paranoid about getting it right for her."

"Got it." Ben crossed a *t,* dotted an *i,* and looked up. "Anything else?"

"Nope, just the usual for the rest."

"No problem. I've got it under control. And since that's the case, why don't you go upstairs and get a shower or some coffee or something? You look like you could use it."

"Thanks, I will." She turned toward the door, then paused. "I have to feed Bruce first, though. He slept in the file room last night. I think he was mad that he didn't get the pizza I promised him."

Ben waved her away. "I'll take care of him. He's still asleep at the moment. I heard him snoring when I came in."

"Thanks, Ben. I really appreciate this. It's been a crazy weekend so far, and I really—"

"Need a shower. You still smell like Betadine," Ben finished for her, grinning.

Josie rolled her eyes, but she obediently made her way out the rear exit of the clinic and up the outdoor back stair to her apartment on the house's top floor.

Stripping off her worn scrubs made an instantaneous difference in her attitude, but it wasn't until she stepped under the steaming spray of her shower that she really began to feel something resembling normal again. She raised her face to the stream of water and slicked back her hair while her mind turned toward the next item on her agenda. Oddly enough, that item turned out to be not coffee, but the rather unexpected figure of Stone Creek's newest sheriff.

Newest, of course, was a relative term. From what Josie knew, Eli Pace had moved to town a little more than three years ago in order to take up his current position in law enforcement. If the small-town gossip mill was correct, he'd previously lived and worked in Seattle, having served as a detective on that city's police force. More than one resident of Stone Creek had wondered what would make a man in his thirties with a successful career in the big city move to their remote little corner of the Northwest, away from all the culture, nightlife, and eligible women a more metropolitan setting had to offer. A small betting pool had quickly been established, and word down at the tavern said the current odds favored a woman at the root of it, either divorce, death, or nasty breakup.

Personally, after last night, Josie felt she needed to lay her money on death, because she couldn't possibly imagine what kind of lunatic would deliberately end a relationship with the man who'd carried an injured wolf into her clinic in the dead of night. Had she been blind not to realize how hot that man was?

Josie blinked hard, sending drops of water flying back toward their source.

Wow, that thought had certainly snuck up on her. Had she honestly developed a case of the hots for a man she'd never spoken to before last night?

Rinsing the last of the conditioner from her hair, Josie reached for the faucet and shut off the water. A few twists of cloth and she had both hair and body wrapped in terry toweling and a frown still on her face as she padded back into her bedroom to dress.

Admittedly, there was nothing odd about her finding the sheriff attractive. She, after all, was *not* blind, and she would have to be not to notice the very fine physical attributes of a well-built, six-foot-tall man when one stood right in front of her. Josie had definitely noticed, everything from a pair of ridiculously broad shoulders and a correspondingly wide chest to callused, long-fingered hands to long legs and slim hips that somehow looked even sexier when slung with a heavy utility belt and holster.

And then there had been those eyes, green and glittering and fringed with surprisingly black, thick lashes for a man with sun-streaked, toffee-colored hair. The memory of those eyes stayed with her. She could picture them now, intent and unreadable, seeming to follow her every move without revealing a single thought of his own. How in the world had she missed noticing those eyes before last night?

Josie snorted and yanked up the zipper on her jeans. It had probably been quite easy, she acknowledged, scuffing her feet into a pair of battered loafers and heading back to the bath to dry her hair. She had never seen him in his animal form, and Josie had never been the kind of girl to notice much that wasn't covered in fur.

Whether it came from growing up in a rural community known for a population made up two-thirds of Others, or from growing up as the daughter of the only veterinarian for twenty miles, Josie couldn't be sure. Either way, according to her mother her first word had been *kitty* and the first birthday or Christmas present she'd ever asked for had been her own puppy. And a stethoscope. No one had ever doubted what the youngest Barrett girl was going to be when she grew up, least of all Josie. Unfortunately, at the age of five, she hadn't considered what a single-minded focus on her future career path would mean for her social life.

Or the lack thereof.

Bundling her mostly dry brown hair into its usual ponytail, Josie grabbed her keys and her wallet and left her apartment, thumping down the stairs to the small parking area at the back of the clinic. On the small patch of grass between the blacktop and the building, a familiar figure waited for her with inexhaustible patience.

"Morning, Bruce," Josie greeted cautiously. "Does this mean that you've forgiven me for the pizza thing?"

Chocolatey brown eyes blinked at her from beneath grizzled gray eyebrows, but Bruce's expression remained impassive.

"Oh, I get it. You've decided the only way I can atone for last night is to spring for breakfast this morning, is that it?"

Bruce's plumy tail wagged in response.

"All right, then. Come on. I'm headed to the bakery anyway. We'll see what Mark has on offer."

With a satisfied grunt, Bruce pushed up from his sitting position and fell into step at his mistress's side.

Josie rounded the corner of the clinic building and set off down the quiet, tree-lined side street toward the center of town. The walk would take less than five minutes, given the fact that Stone Creek didn't consist of much town, but with her thoughts still jumbled, likely the exercise would do her good. And at the end of it, there would be coffee.

The center of Stone Creek remained quiet at not-quite-eight on a Sunday morning, and Josie and Bruce made their way down Main Street without running into more than two or three acquaintances. None of them, thankfully, stopped Josie to ask a question about their pets.

She couldn't help casting a glance toward the historic

brick building that housed both the town hall offices and the police station as she passed, but the nineteenth-century facade offered no clues as to what might be happening inside. Still, it took a concentrated effort to pull her gaze away and focus it back on the clapboard front of the Sweet Spot Bakery & Café. As soon as she opened the door, though, the small shop received all of her attention. The seductive scent of coffee, yeast, and cinnamon lured her inside like a magic spell.

A quick command had Bruce settling with disgruntled grace in front of the plate-glass window while Josie made her way inside.

"Mark Hennessey, I swear to God, if I didn't love you with all my stomach, I'd report you to the Inquisition for practicing witchcraft."

A shaggy, sandy-haired figure stepped through an open doorway behind the tall glass counters, wiping his hands on an already smeared white apron.

"If you're referring to the Spanish Inquisition, it was formally disbanded in 1834. And the Roman one changed its name in 1908. But since I'm not Catholic, I don't think either one really has any jurisdiction over my baked goods."

Her eyes fixed on the trays full of gooey, doughy, sugar-laden treats already on display, Josie didn't even bother to look up to catch the local baker's smirk. She didn't need to. Their morning routine had been established years ago. "So you don't deny that you use unnatural means to create your confections."

"Josephine, baby, if you knew how I created my confections, you'd never look at another man again."

"What makes you think I look at any of them now?"

"You know, I had always assumed that you just *performed* de-sexing operations, not underwent them yourself. Then again, I could be wrong."

"You can be the queen of England if you want, as long as you give me three of everything and an extra-large coffee with cream before you leave to take up your royal duties."

Mark was already reaching for a stack of tall paper cups. "Nah. I mean, don't get me wrong; it's not like I haven't considered it as a career change, but I'd look funny in those little veiled hats."

"Not to mention the pantyhose." Josie handed her old high school buddy a packet of raw sugar off the counter, then leaned her elbows on the polished wooden surface while he diluted her beverage with enough dairy product for any five people. "So what's good this morning?"

He threw her a dirty look as he dumped in the sugar. "Have I ever made anything that wasn't good?"

Josie thought for a moment. "There was that first loaf of rye bread you attempted. The thing could have served as a boat anchor."

"I was thirteen. It was more than fifteen years ago. I think you need to move on. My breads have."

"Yes, but your breads are more evolved than I am."

The first sip Josie took had her eyes closing and her throat humming. No one made coffee like Mark. If she hadn't remembered the way he'd looked in his Peter Pan costume during their sixth-grade play, she'd have proposed to him the minute she turned eighteen. And that would have really pissed off his wife.

When she managed to pry her lids back up, she tried

again. "Okay, let me put it this way. What do you have today that will meet Sir Bruce's exacting culinary standards?"

"And not get your license revoked by the state veterinary board? I've got naturally sweetened organic carrot muffins. He liked those last time."

"Hm, give me two. He's pretty pissed at me."

Mark snapped open a folded sheet of parchment and reached for the tray of muffins. "What did you do this time?"

Josie made a face. "I reneged on pizza night. But it wasn't my fault. I had an emergency."

"As if that's any kind of excuse. A woman's word should be her bond."

"So he's made clear. I'm hoping this will at least get him to speak to me again." Accepting the tray he handed her, Josie headed toward the door and her grudge-holding pet. "How about you warm me up a cinnamon roll while I go beg for forgiveness?"

A moment later she left Bruce on the sidewalk under the bakery window, happily feasting on the warm muffins and bowl of bottled springwater that Mark had provided. When she stepped back into the shop, her friend was busy transferring huge chocolate chip cookies from a sheet pan to a bright red plate in the glass display case.

A huge, frosted cinnamon roll sat on a smaller blue saucer on the counter beside her coffee.

"You are a saint," she breathed, reaching for the roll with one hand and a stack of napkins with the other.

"Sarah tells me that all the time," he agreed. "'A saint among husbands' is how she likes to put it."

"I won't go there, but I'll totally vouch for a saint among bakers."

"Don't talk with your mouth full. Especially not when you're eating the very thing you swore last week that you were going to give up for Lent."

Josie swallowed a gulp of coffee and grinned. "I'm not Catholic, either. Besides, I deserve a cinnamon roll, darn it. I had to sleep in the clinic last night, and I swear you can feel how cold and hard that floor is even through the air mattress."

"Busy night?"

She shrugged. "Just one emergency, but it was pretty serious. Had to go into surgery."

"Anyone I know?"

Josie started to shake her head, then hesitated. In a town with fewer than three thousand residents, most everyone in Stone Creek knew most everyone else, including their pets, but a wolf wasn't a pet so her initial reaction was to deny that Mark might know her patient. Then again, her patient wasn't actually a wolf, was she? And since Josie still had no idea of the Lupine's human identity, how did she really know if Mark knew her or not?

"We're still waiting to contact the . . . owners," she finally said, looking away and busying herself carrying her breakfast over to one of the three small tables in the corner of the shop. "I probably shouldn't say anything until I've talked to them."

Mark shrugged his agreement, but his brow quirked up as he repeated, "We? I thought you played the saint and gave your entire staff Sundays off so you could martyr yourself on the altar of overwork."

"Funny. As it happens, Ben came in to help me out today, but I wasn't talking about my staff. I meant me and the sheriff. He's the one who found my patient and brought her in."

"Eli brought you an injured animal?"

"Why not? Sheriffs are supposed to be like grown-up Boy Scouts, right?" Josie pulled off another chunk of soft, sticky dough and eyed her friend. "But when did you get to be on a first-name basis with the local fuzz?"

"This is the closest thing to a doughnut shop in thirty miles," a new voice answered, and Mark and Josie both looked toward the door to where the man in question stood, wearing a crisp blue uniform and an amused expression. "Mark was the first local resident I introduced myself to."

Gasping with a mouthful of cinnamon roll nearly caused Josie to choke. She grabbed quickly for her coffee and took a healthy swig to wash down the bite and used a napkin to wipe her eyes when they started to water.

"Dr. Barrett, are you all right?" the sheriff asked, focusing his bright green gaze on her. "Do you need some help?"

Josie waved a hand at him and shook her head. "No. Sorry." She gasped for air. "You just startled me. I'm fine."

"Oh, good," Mark said mildly. "Deaths on the premises are really bad for business. For some reason, they seem to upset the customers."

"Speaking of customers," Eli broke in, "I was wondering if one of yours might belong to the fellow loitering out front."

Josie wiped her fingers on a stack of napkins as she struggled to regain her composure. Why did she always seem to be at her least cool and collected in front of a good-looking man?

"Bruce is my dog, Sheriff," she said, striving for a mild tone. "Is there a problem with him?"

Eli shook his head. "Not at all, Doctor. I was actually just going to compliment whoever had trained him to sit and wait like that without even tying him to anything. I've never seen a more well-behaved dog. You should be proud."

Mark snorted. "It's Bruce who should be proud. Josie had very little to do with it."

Josie shot her friend a glare, but she shrugged when she turned back to the sheriff. "Mark is unfortunately right. I really haven't done much training with Bruce at all. I think the reason he doesn't wander has more to do with the fact that he's one of the laziest animals on the face of the earth than that it's what I told him to do."

"Last year I watched him sleep through the entire July Fourth fireworks display," Mark agreed. "And we were only sitting like fifty feet from where they were setting them off. Most people had to lock their dogs inside their houses. Bruce lay down on our blanket in Kirkland Field and snored through the whole thing."

"And, trust me, his snores were almost louder than the explosions."

Eli grinned. "That's some dog. Where did you get him?"

"He got me," Josie corrected, her fingers pulling idly on the rim of her coffee cup. "I was working late one night, running labs, and I heard a noise coming from the parking lot behind the clinic. When I opened to door to look out and see what it was, Bruce strolled in and made himself at home. He was only about four months old at that point, but he already had paws the size of dinner plates."

"Yeah, I noticed that. What is he, do you think? Part Great Dane?"

Josie shrugged. "I usually go with mostly Irish wolfhound and mastiff, with maybe some Saint Bernard thrown in, but that's purely a guess."

"He does like brandy," Mark agreed, "so it's a good guess." He dropped the sheet pan onto the counter behind him and smiled at the sheriff. "So what can I do for you, Eli? I don't do doughnuts on Sundays, but I've got the cinnamon rolls, and I think the scones came out pretty well today."

"I'll take a bribery box to go," Eli said. "And coffee for three. If I go back to the station empty-handed, I'll end up locked in one of my own cells. But believe it or not, I didn't actually come in here for pastries. I was just walking by when I looked through the window and saw Dr. Barrett. She's the one I've been looking for."

```
Exp. 10-1017.03
Log 03-00122


Unable to locate TS-0024. May be required
to adjust staffing if performance does
not improve.


New dosages to be administered immedi-
ately to new subjects. Goal includes
TS-0025 through TS-0029. At least three
new subjects required for sufficient
data.
```

The early methodology will be adjusted.
Clearly more than one subject will be
required in order for sufficient levels
of transmission to be achieved.

Looking into radio tracking equipment
for Stage 4. Remain optimistic as to
ultimate project success.

CHAPTER THREE

The one I've been looking for.

Something inside Josie sprang to life at the sound of those words, but that something wasn't entirely comfortable. Exciting, but not comfortable. The sheriff made it sound more like a sacred prophesy or a statement of personal intent than the matter of business she assured herself it had to be.

It *had* to be.

Josie ignored the surge of fluttery butterfly wings in her stomach and took a casual sip of her coffee. "You were looking for me? I hope I'm not wanted for questioning in anything."

"Not at all. I just wanted to ask you about your latest patient. How is she doing this morning?"

"About the same as she was when you left, unfortunately. I had hoped she'd be a bit more alert this morning."

Mark passed a fat white pastry box tied with white butcher's twine into the sheriff's hand, along with a tray containing three enormous take-away cups of coffee. While he made change, Eli kept his attention on Josie. She fought momentarily against the urge to fidget, then gave up and stood to drop the remains of her cinnamon roll into the trash.

"She hasn't changed then?"

Josie shook her head. "Not as of about ninety minutes ago, but I should be getting back to check on her again." She turned toward the counter, even while her body began inching toward the door. "Mark, delicious as always. I left a ridiculous yet appropriate fee on my table. Tell Sarah hello for me and I'll see her tomorrow morning."

"Hold on and I'll walk with you," Eli said, pocketing his change and picking the coffee tray up again. He gestured toward the door.

Josie wasn't sure if the surge of adrenaline in her veins signified excitement or panic. Either way, she figured it meant danger.

She forced a smile. "Don't be silly. I'm going in the opposite direction from you. I don't want to take you out of your way."

His expression hinted that he found her dithering amusing, but he was polite enough not to mention it. He just followed her out the door with a last nod for Mark and fell into step beside her as she made her way back down Main. Bruce abandoned his final inspection of his crumb-free tray to follow at their heels.

"It's not like there's much way to go out of in Stone Creek," he observed evenly. "It won't be much more than five extra minutes. Besides, I'd like to look in on your patient for myself."

Josie clung to her coffee cup like a life rope and tried for a casual tone. Since the sheriff hadn't given any indication that he suffered from the same heightened awareness around her that she felt around him, letting him see her discomposure would inevitably lead to humiliation, she was sure.

"I take it that you haven't heard anything about her identity yet," she said, watching the steam curl up from the hole in the rim of her cup. It kept her from staring at his shoulders. "Since you haven't mentioned anything."

Eli shook his head. "I left Rick a message last night, but he hasn't called me yet. It's still early, though. Trust me, as soon as I know, you will."

"I'd appreciate that. I did the same with Dr. Shad. I'll feel a lot more comfortable when I can turn her over to his care. It doesn't seem right somehow, having her in a cage in a veterinary office, no matter what she looks like at the moment."

Out of the corner of her eye, Josie saw his mouth quirk up in a smile. "Speaking as someone who can imagine what that would be like, I feel compelled to thank you for being so conscientious. But no matter who she turns out to be, I'm sure our Lupine will be too grateful to you for saving her life to hold a grudge over her accommodations."

Josie shrugged uncomfortably. "Still."

Just as the sheriff had implied, the distance between Main Street, where his office and the bakery were both located, and her clinic on Pine Street took all of two more minutes to cover. Stepping through the back door into the open space of the triage area, Josie took a deep breath of the disinfected air and felt her nerves settle just a bit. Being back in her element made her feel more like a competent, professional woman and less like a junior high school girl with her first crush.

"Oh, good, you're back," Ben greeted, leaning down

to scratch Bruce's ears as the huge mutt ambled past on the way to his fluffy, padded bed behind the reception desk. "Sheriff Pace. Did you come to check on the Lupine? Dr. J said you were the one who brought her in last night."

Eli nodded, setting his parcels down on the nearest section of free counter space. "I did, even though I'm told there isn't much change."

"Not so far." Ben looked back at Josie. "While you were gone, though, I did start running those tests you asked for."

That effectively managed to pull the last straggling bits of her attention off the sheriff and back onto her work where it belonged. "How do things look?"

"Interesting."

"And that means?"

"You're the doctor. You get to tell me, as soon as you take a look at them."

"Right." Her fingers itched to get ahold of those test results, and she actually took a couple of steps toward the CBC machine before she remembered the sheriff standing near the door behind her. Cursing to herself, she threw him a smile and gestured toward the kennel room. "Why don't I take you to see the Lupine first, Sheriff? I'm sure you must be anxious to get back to work yourself."

His mouth curved again in that smile Josie was convinced meant he wanted to laugh at her but was too polite to actually do. As if that made some sort of difference.

"No, I can see that you've got another busy day ahead of you, Dr. Barrett. And your assistant says there hasn't been any real change since last night. I can wait until she's more alert. I always find it easier to take statements from witnesses when they're actually awake."

"In this case, you might also want to wait until she rearranges her hyoid bone."

Josie blushed at the sharp tone of her comment. Clearly she needed to avoid the sheriff in future if he was going to send her emotional reactions into such turmoil. There could be health risks.

She formed a smile to soften her explanation. "The bone people have in their throats between the jaw and the spine. Its form and placement are requirements for human speech. Wolves have it up high under their tongues and use it more for breathing and swallowing than vocalization."

"Good to know."

He picked up his coffee and baked goods, and this time he sent Josie a full-fledged smile, which should have been a relief after all those secretly amused half smiles of his, but it really wasn't. Instead it sent her blood pressure through the roof and had the butterflies in her stomach forming a very enthusiastic conga line.

"I'd appreciate a call as soon as the Lupine wakes up, and I'll definitely shoot one to you when I hear back from Rick." Eli nodded at Ben, smiled once more at Josie, and shouldered open the door. "You two have a good day, now."

With that, he was gone, and Josie had to lock her knees to keep from dissolving into a heap on the linoleum tile.

"Um, wow. Wasn't expecting that," Ben ventured after a moment of buzzing silence.

"Expecting what?"

He looked at her with patent incredulity. "Was I not supposed to notice that the sparks you two were shooting off each other nearly trigged the fire sprinklers? Because I like my job, and I can pretend if I have to, but I'd like it noted in my next performance evaluation that I'm not actually that stupid."

Josie glared. "I don't know what you're talking about. The sheriff and I barely know each other."

"Okay, then. One oblivious idiot coming up." He pulled out a chart and flipped it open. "Do you want to take a look at the Lupine's CBC then?"

Her lips pursed. "Yes. Why don't we do that?"

He shuffled a printout to the top of the file and held it out for her, his mouth silent and his expression carefully blank. Josie rolled her eyes and then focused them on the test results.

She had wanted to run a complete blood count for a couple of different reasons. One was simple curiosity. She had never treated an Other before, but she had grown up around them, so she had heard all about their remarkable healing powers. The scientist in her couldn't resist seeing if evidence of that ability would show up in their blood work. But for the same reason, the very fact that the Lupine in her clinic wasn't showing much evidence of accelerated healing had her a bit worried, and she wondered if there might be some sort of infection or unknown medical condition underlying her traumatic injuries. If so, that could help explain things. If the Other's body was preoccupied with trying to heal an acute or chronic condition that had preceded the shooting, maybe it didn't have the energy to spare to speed up the mending of her wounds. A look at her CBC results, and specifically her white blood cell count, might shed some light on that mystery.

Josie scanned the numbers on the lab report and blinked. Then she scanned them again. Then she frowned at Ben. "Did you look at these?"

The vet tech nodded. "Three times. Then I recalibrated the machine and reran the test. Then I looked at them another three times. The results are valid. Wacky as all get-out, but valid."

"And you rechecked her vitals?"

"Twice."

"No sign of fever or anything else?"

"Nada."

"This is totally weird."

"Tell me about it."

Josie read the numbers again and shook her head. "I need to find a reference where I can check these against Lupine normals. Maybe we're just using the wrong comparatives."

"I've already pulled something up." Ben waved toward the laptop computer that sat open and running on the desk built into the counters lining the inside wall of the triage room/lab space. "That was the first thing I did after running the second test. The numbers I circled are the ones that *still* look funky."

Mumbling to herself, Josie hooked an ankle around the wheeled physician's stool and pulled it out from the desk, perching on it as she peered at the computer screen. Her finger followed the numbers on the printout as she compared them over and over against the values on the screen.

"This is just crazy."

"I know. If I weren't so darn good at what I do, I'd have wondered if I managed to screw up the tests twice in a row. But the second time, I double-checked myself every step of the way. The results are real."

She looked up at her technician—the best one she'd ever worked with, even while interning at one of the best veterinary school clinics in the nation—and shook her head. "Any living being with a white cell count this high should already be dead of the infection that caused it. How can her temperature not even be elevated?"

Ben snorted. "I was hoping that as the brilliant veterinarian you are, you'd be able to explain that to me."

"I don't have a frickin' clue." She glanced at the clock. "Has Dr. Shad called, by any chance?"

"Nope."

"Damn it. He's at least treated Others before. Maybe he's seen something like this."

"From the quick look I did while you were out, I don't think anyone has ever seen anything like this."

"Thanks, that's comforting."

He shrugged. "Sorry. I think the question, though, is what are we going to do about it in the meantime? With numbers like those, we can't just wait for Dr. Shad to decide he's had enough trout for the weekend. If that really is an infection, like you said, she should already be dead. And I'm assuming we're trying to prevent that."

Josie sighed. "All right. First I want to make up some smears to look at under the scope, so if you used everything from the last draw, you'll need to take some more blood. Then as soon as we have samples—lots of samples—let's switch her antibiotic to a penem and see if a broader-spectrum med will make a difference."

"You got it."

"Oh, Ben," she called when he moved immediately away to follow her instructions. "Did you get time to look at her painkiller concentration levels?"

"Yeah, that was the one test that came back normal. According to the literature I found, her dosage is right where it ought to be. Whatever is keeping her under, it's not the meds."

"Thanks." She watched him head for the kennels and groaned. "Just what I always wanted. A medical mystery in someone else's field dumped in my lap with no consult in sight. Why did I want to be a vet again?"

From the other side of the door near her stool came the comforting sound of Bruce's familiar snoring.

Josie closed her eyes and leaned over the desk, burying her face in her arms. "That's really not a good enough reason."

Indulging in a brief moment of self-pity, Josie clenched her fists, released a small number of pithy but potent curses aimed at precisely no one, then lifted her head, blew out a deep breath, and got back to work. She might not have asked for this case, but it was hers now, and she'd be darned if she didn't find a way to cure it.

Exp. 10-1017.03
Log 03-00127

Technicians out at this moment inoculating new test subjects. Have chosen dosing

site near suspected subject population
center in hope of tracing transmission
from first- to second-generation subjects.

New data monitoring equipment definitely
becoming higher priority.

CHAPTER FOUR

By the time Eli was ready to call an end to his shift about twelve hours after leaving the veterinarian's office, he estimated that he'd caught himself thinking about her approximately seven hundred times. Which was only about once a minute, he figured. Wasn't that about as often as men supposedly thought about sex? He couldn't remember, but he did have to admit that sex factored into more than a few of those seven hundred thoughts.

Part of that, he recognized, had to do with how obviously the surprisingly attractive doctor had reacted to him. Whether or not she might also be thinking about sex, he didn't know, but he'd bet that on some level she had developed a very physical awareness of him. What else could account for all those blushes he'd seen creep up her cheeks while they talked? It was October in the Northwest, so it couldn't be the weather, and he knew for a fact that Josephine Barrett was way too young to be having hot flashes. She smelled nothing like a woman in menopause. She smelled warm and sweet and ripe and absolutely delicious.

A sudden tightening in the fit of his uniform trousers made Eli shake his head and push away from his desk.

There he went again, mind wandering back to the vet when it ought to be focusing on the job. At least now he would have the excuse of being off the clock when it happened again. And Eli had absolutely no doubts that it would.

Locking his office door behind him, he shrugged into his jacket as he walked through the open area that housed the desk of the part-time secretary-dispatcher and the cubicles used by his two full-time and three part-time deputies. At the moment, one of the part-timers, Tim McGann, sat behind the gray fabric dividers filling out the never-ending paperwork that went with a job in law enforcement. If Eli had once thought there might be less of it in a town as small as Stone Creek than there had been in a city like Seattle, he'd been doomed to disappointment.

"I'm heading out, Tim, but I've got my pager," he called, lifting a hand when the deputy's sandy-red head popped up from behind the cubicle wall. "Here's hoping you'll have a quiet night."

"I imagine I will," the younger man grinned. At twenty-three, he was the rookie in the department, but he had been born and raised in Stone Creek and knew every resident and every square inch of the town. That and his mellow, amiable disposition made him an asset to their small force. "After all, it's a school night, so most of our favorite hooligans should be under curfew. Thank God."

Eli snorted and stepped out into the brisk autumn night. It was true that most of the crime in Stone Creek had more to do with teenage delinquents and bar fights than gangs, drugs, or career criminals, but that only made the situation with the Lupine that much more puzzling. The hunters out here knew what game was in season during which part of the year, and they sure as hell knew that wolves still appeared on the state's endangered species list. Since a good portion of them were just as likely to hunt on four legs with teeth and claws as on two with rifle and shot, they were also not inclined to shoot at any game they thought might end up being a neighbor out for a breath of fresh air. The idea that a hunter had shot at a wolf and then left her in the woods to die just didn't make sense. There had to be more to this story, and Eli intended to find out what it was.

One of his first orders on arriving at the office this morning had been to send the deputy on duty out to the site where he'd found the Lupine. Initially, he'd planned on going out there himself, but a surprise visit from the town's mayor had nixed that idea and tied him up for most of the morning. Even after Ed Whipple had finally left, his reminder of the upcoming town council meeting had forced Eli to put his curiosity on the back burner while he dealt with the paperwork and reports he needed for the meeting. As much as he wanted to go over the shooting site himself, that was the kind of thing his deputies were paid and trained to do; they weren't paid or trained to do his more tedious administrative tasks.

He still planned to go out there himself, especially since his deputy had reported finding nothing suspicious in the forest. The other man had taped off the area to deter people from mucking around there, but Eli wanted to see it for himself. He had a better nose than most of his officers, and he had more experience than all of them. He wouldn't rest until he double-checked that—literally—no stone had been unturned. Solving this shooting case had jumped to the top of his list of personal priorities.

In fact, he decided, shrugging against the restlessness that had plagued him all day, there was nothing stopping him from going out to the shooting site right now. It wouldn't be any substitute for a daylight walk-through, but even without the benefit of light to guide his eyes, his nose might pick up something interesting.

And prowling through the woods might burn off enough of this restless energy to keep him from planting himself under a certain veterinarian's window and cater-wauling a few Feline mating calls later tonight. He'd heard they lacked the desired effect on human women. Especially ones who weren't completely tone-deaf.

Decision made, Eli changed direction and strode back toward the front of the sheriff's office. Climbing into his black SUV, he carefully backed into the street and pointed the hood toward the spot where he'd discovered the wolf the night before.

The drive took less than twenty minutes, but even that short spell of enforced stillness had tension crawling up the back of Eli's neck like a poisonous spider. By the time he pulled to a stop and parked at the side of the road precisely in the same spot he'd used last night, he had concluded that getting out of town had been a very wise choice. In his present state, yeowling outside of Josie Barrett's window seemed less likely than crawling straight through it and into her bed. And subsequently into her.

Slamming the truck door shut, Eli pocketed his keys, checked his service revolver's position in its holster, and headed into the forest. Then he took his first deep breath and swore.

Smoke.

Quickening his pace, he stepped away from the path
that led to the spot where he'd found the Lupine and
headed south in the direction of the sharp, bittersweet
scent of burning wood. While the wildfire danger in October might be less than it had been during summer's dry
spells, it never took much for small fires to break out in
the woodlands surrounding Stone Creek. Given the abun-
dant trees and dried pine needles for kindling, one care-
less camper could place the town in a precarious position.
It was why all fires built outdoors within three miles of
the city limits required a permit from the Stone Creek
sheriff's office.

Eli hadn't signed any permits in more than a week.

He expected that he'd have to lecture a bunch of teen-
agers on the laws and responsibilities of building fires in
the woods and maybe even confiscate a few illegally ob-
tained six-packs. Then another quick lecture on under-
aged drinking—he had that one down so pat, he could
recite it in his sleep—and he could get back to the real
reason he'd come out here tonight. At least, that was the
plan until the smell of the smoke changed from acidic
to acrid, wood fuel and pine kindling suddenly over-
powered by the stench of burning fur and charring flesh.

He broke into a run.

Within a few hundred feet he began to hear voices, not
the boisterous sounds of partying delinquents, but adult
voices filled with the deep, thick rumble of anger. His
hand moved immediately to the top of his holster and he
slowed his pace, deliberately softening his footfalls until
even he could barely hear them over the muffled sound of
conversation.

His fingers tightened when he neared the edge of a

small break in the trees and saw the bright glow of fire-light seeping into the surrounding dark of the forest. Within the space of several long strides, he could make out the size and shape of the fire and begin to feel the heat against his face.

It was a bonfire, more than four feet in diameter, with flames that leapt at least ten feet into the air. In the center, Eli could see a dark lump resting atop a bed of logs, and around its perimeter at least three or four men circled, continuing to add more fuel to the already raging inferno.

Catching sight of one particular face, Eli swore under his breath and took his hand away from his weapon. He stepped forward into the clearing.

"What the hell is going on here, Cobb?" he demanded.

The face that turned in his direction was taut and set with visible fury. Above the square, clenched jaw, Lupine golden eyes blazed nearly as bright as the fire.

"I'm taking care of my dead, Pace," Rick Cobb growled, his body turning into a confrontational angle. "I'm going to advise you not to interfere."

Eli's gaze flicked again to the dark form atop the blazing fire, and he felt himself scowling. "Who?"

"Sammy Paulson. He was found out here this morning by another member of the pack. He had collapsed at the foot of an old-growth pine and was cold by the time we stumbled across him."

The name rang a bell, and it took only seconds for Eli to connect it to a tall, lanky teenager with fair hair and a decent head on his shoulders. He hadn't stuck in the sheriff's memory because of past misdeeds, but because he'd been a good kid from a good family whose members always did their part to help out the community.

"Shit. I'm sorry. What happened? Was he sick?"

"We don't get sick."

"You know what I mean. I'm not talking swine flu; I'm talking cancer."

"No, he was a normal Lupine kid. Chris Meadows is the one who found him." Rick gestured toward the two men tending the fire. "He came out here for a run and almost tripped over . . . it. He came and got Lucas and me immediately. Of course, we assumed he'd had an accident or been attacked, but from what the three of us can tell there wasn't a mark on him. His neck wasn't broken; hell, his claws weren't even chipped. So we have no fucking clue why he's not out catching footballs instead of catching fire."

Eli's gaze flicked to the funeral pyre, and he winced as he saw the young wolf's limbs begin to curl back on themselves from the heat of the flames. "If you'd ease up on tradition for once, we might be able to find out. We could have an autopsy done. Or we could have had."

The Stone Creek tradition of burning the dead dated back far enough that no one knew when it had started, or precisely why. Some speculated about a possible connection to pre-Columbian Viking explorers, and some pointed out that in a forest, it was easier to burn than to dig; either way, the practice was an old one, and a deeply honored one.

Rick shook his head, firelight glinting off the light brown strands. "No. He wasn't a cub anymore. He deserved to be treated with dignity. He deserved to have his smoke spread to the stars. It's what his mother asked us to do."

It didn't take great empathic abilities to read the rage

and bitterness in the Lupine's voice. Rick Cobb might have been Alpha of his pack for only a few years, but he took his duties to heart. Eli suspected, actually, that duty to the Stone Creek Clan *was* Rick's heart, and he knew that the loss of any pack member wounded. Which made the next words out of his mouth taste so damn bitter.

"Normally, I would agree with you, but the current circumstances aren't what I would call normal," he said, catching the Alpha's gaze. "You really should have returned my calls before now, Rick."

The flames that flashed in the Lupine's gaze had nothing to do with the reflection of a bonfire. "Well, excuse me, but I was a little busy today, Sheriff," he snarled. "You see, I had to find a member of my pack dead on the forest floor for no known reason, and then I had to break the news to his mother that her only cub wouldn't be coming home again—ever—and ask her what arrangements she wanted to make for his *corpse,* so you might say I had a lot on my plate."

"And you might say that I'm about to serve you another helping."

"What are you talking about?"

"That's why I called you last night, and left you three more messages today. Sammy Paulson isn't the only member of your pack who's gone down in the woods lately."

The Alpha's response to that news didn't bear repeating, but it did prompt Eli to quickly and quietly outline the situation with the unconscious Lupine he'd delivered into Josie's care. "Any idea who it might be?" he concluded.

"No, but give me ten minutes and you can be damn sure I'll find out." Pulling a cell phone from the pocket of his jeans, the Alpha flipped it open, then looked back at the sheriff. "You don't think they're related, do you? Sammy and the female you found last night?"

Eli hesitated, waiting to see who would win the war between his head and his gut. Stalemate.

"I don't see how," he finally said, forcing out the reluctant conclusion. "The female was shot, either accidentally or on purpose, and we have no way of knowing that Sammy didn't have some kind of heart defect or something that caused him to collapse. Shifters might be immune to a lot of contagious diseases, but we aren't immortal, and there's a lot of leeway between a germ and a congenital anomaly."

Rick looked as dissatisfied to hear that as Eli had been to say it. "Maybe, but I wouldn't exactly call myself a happy camper right now."

"Me neither."

The Lupine sighed. "I need to make some calls."

"Right. Do you plan to come to Dr. Barrett's office? Take a look at the patient yourself?"

"Not tonight. There are still things that need to be done here. But as soon as I find out who she might be, I'll send someone over."

"I'm sure the doctor will appreciate that."

"Tell her she can expect me tomorrow, though. Whoever she's got in her office, I'm going to want to see for myself."

Eli nodded. "I wouldn't expect anything else." He took a step back and nodded toward the fire. "If you or Mrs. Paulson needs anything, you know where to find me."

Rick's mouth twisted ruefully. "You know, that's your biggest problem, Eli: Everyone always knows where to find you."

Turning away, Eli snorted and started back into the forest. His search through the shooting site could wait until daylight. With the area taped off by his deputy earlier in the day, he was reasonably comfortable that no one would tromp through it tonight, especially not with Rick and other members of his pack out. The Lupines would prove an effective deterrent to passersby. And they deserved their privacy. All mourners deserved to be left in peace.

Despite the Alpha's half-joking words, Eli had the very uneasy feeling that his problems were about to get a whole lot bigger. The thought sank its burrs into him and clung, riding him all the way back to the road, refusing to be shaken even as he climbed behind the wheel of his truck. It needled him as he started the engine and followed him all the way back to town, as persistent as the lonely, heartbreaking echo of howling wolves that carried sharp and poignant on the cold night air.

CHAPTER FIVE

Josie kept the door to the kennel area propped open so that she could hear if any of her patients made a sound indicating that they required attention, but so far the evening was proving as tedious as the paperwork she filled it with.

Sighing, she rubbed a hand over her forehead. If she were honest with herself, Josie would have to admit that the only sound she cared about at the moment was one indicating that the Lupine in the other room might be waking up. And the only reason she had no patience for any other part of the job she loved was that her mind couldn't stop chewing on the problem of this particular case.

All her life, Josie Barrett had known that she wanted to be a vet, and she had pursued her goal with a single-mindedness bordering on compulsion. She had all but coasted through her training, not due to any particular academic brilliance or inherent intellectual genius, but simply because she spent all her spare time reading and studying a subject that fascinated her. She found the mechanics of animal physiology riveting, and nothing satisfied her so much as puzzling out the solution to a problem with only the clues provided by careful observation and testing. Human physicians could ask their patients questions if they needed guidance for a particular problem, but all Josie could do was watch and feel and test and treat until she found the right answer. And in return, she got to see a creature who had been ill or in pain recover and thrive. She couldn't have asked for a greater sense of personal satisfaction.

Except in the rare case when the right answer completely eluded her.

Biting back a growl of frustration, Josie reached for the cup of coffee on the exam table before her, then grimaced as she realized it had long ago gone cold. She'd poured it for herself nearly two hours ago, just before she brought her stool and stack of charts over to the large, clean surface of the exam table to work. It had seemed like a good way to simultaneously catch up on the backlog of paperwork that never went away and keep an eye and ear tuned in to her latest puzzle, but now the caffeine kick had begun to wear off and she'd made little noticeable headway in either the paperwork or the Lupine case.

It frustrated Josie to no end to find herself faced with a patient she couldn't even diagnose properly, let alone treat. For a woman who prided herself on her credentials, this felt like failure, and failure didn't sit well on her narrow shoulders.

"This is starting to get to me, Bruce," she said, slipping one foot out of its battered loafer and using it to rub the belly of the dog currently sprawled beneath the table in front of her.

Bruce obligingly cocked a hind leg and twisted his torso to offer her better access.

"She should be awake by now. Every reference I've

consulted so far agrees on that. Lupines do not remain unconscious for this long unless there's something seriously wrong. And in Others terminology, a minor gunshot wound does not count as serious. So what the heck else is going on?"

Bruce grunted and rolled completely onto his back.

"Not a big help, frankly. So far everything but that white count is normal, which means there has to be an infection somewhere, but nothing is showing up in culture."

Another grunt, following by a sneeze-like exhalation.

"If I run one more test or set up one more culture, I'm going to run out of both blood samples and culture media, and I suspect all I'm going to get are the same results I've gotten for the past twenty-four hours." She sighed. "I could really use a clue here."

For a second, Josie almost thought Bruce intended to give her one. The enormous hound jerked his head off the floor, pendulous flews dangling, and stared intently at the rear door of the clinic. With a soft, whooshing woof, he flipped back onto his stomach and eyed the heavy metal exit portal with steady intensity.

Reaching down, Josie scratched behind one floppy ear and slid off her stool. "Really? Company at this hour?"

She'd barely gotten the words out when a crisp tap at the back door was followed by the click of the latch. The panel swung open a few inches and a familiar head poked in through the opening.

"Dr. Barrett. I saw your light on and thought it was probably you still in here. Has anyone ever told you that you work too much?"

Bruce scrambled to his feet and stood beside his mistress, watching the scene calmly but closely.

"Sheriff Pace," Josie greeted, her hand moving out of habit to rest atop her dog's heavy head. "I can't say I was expecting to see you again today. What can I do for you?"

Eli stepped fully into the room and pulled the door shut behind him. He held up a large white bag and offered a casual smile. "I was hoping we could put our heads together again about this situation with the Lupine. I even brought dinner as a tool of bribery. Don't tell the town council."

Before Josie could decide what to make of the unexpected gesture, or how to react to her unexpected visitor, Bruce made up his mind for both of them. He inhaled half a dozen times in rapid succession, then crossed the floor between him and the sheriff in two exuberant leaps, skidding across the slick tile to finish in a perfect, attentive sit at Eli's feet.

She couldn't help laughing. "Let me guess: You brought Laura Beth's meat loaf, didn't you?"

Laura Beth Andrews worked at Joe Schmoe's Café, the most popular—and only—dedicated dining establishment in Stone Creek. Unlike the Stone Creek Tavern, which supplied mediocre snacks and average pub food to help soak up its alcoholic offerings, Joe's prided itself on a small but satisfying menu featuring seasonal local ingredients presented in both traditional home-cooking favorites and more adventurous rotating specials. It also happily catered to the children and families who felt so out of place at the tavern.

"I'm amazed they even hand out menus on meat loaf night," Eli said, grinning at her over Bruce's head. "Personally, I can't imagine ordering anything else."

"Neither can Bruce."

"So what do you say?" He shook the bag a little and raised an eyebrow. "Have you two eaten yet?"

Josie pursed her lips. She hadn't, but Bruce had. Still, she'd never known her dog to turn down an extra meal, and she found herself battling a strange reluctance to turn away the sheriff's company. She told herself it was just because she needed a distraction from her paperwork. It had nothing to do with his broad, muscular shoulders, or the way his green eyes sparked at her from between thick, dark lashes.

Nothing at all.

She waved him forward with small snort of surrender. "While it might make a difference if *I* had, Bruce clearly fails to see why that matters. Come on in and sit down."

Turning to fetch a second stool for her guest, Josie watched out of the corner of her eye as the sheriff turned his attention from her to her huge, lumbering dog. Well, normally Bruce lumbered; at the moment, he simply sat in front of Eli, quivering from nose to tail with the anticipation of his favorite human food indulgence. For some reason, though, the sheriff looked mildly wary of her pet.

"Don't mind Bruce," she assured him. "He's pretty mellow with strangers. Mostly he just ignores them. Are you afr—er, do you not like big dogs?"

"Oh, I like them just fine, but sometimes I find that they're not all that wild about me."

Josie recalled his story last night about the sled dogs and grinned. "Well, like I said, you don't need to worry about Bruce. Even if he'd decided to hate you this morning, he can't bring himself to do it anymore. A man who comes bearing meat loaf is his best friend for life. You probably just made it into his will."

"I'm going to remember that trick," the sheriff said, laughing. He stepped around her dog, wisely holding the bag of food up against his chest as he crossed to the exam table. He waited for her to shuffle her files back into order and move them to the counter before he set it down and settled onto the stool across from hers.

He removed disposable dinnerware and plates from the bag and set them neatly before each of them. "Has there been any change in the Lupine's condition?"

Josie shook her head. "I wish I had something new to tell you, but her condition is still the same. It's starting to worry me, especially since I don't know who she is. Without any kind of medical history on her, figuring out the problem is that much harder. Have you heard from the Alpha yet?"

"I spoke to him briefly." Eli took two round foil containers from the bag and set them on the table. "He hadn't heard of a missing female from his pack, but he was going to make some calls and ask around. He was in the middle of something fairly important when I saw him, but he said as soon as he's free, he'll come down here himself to check her out. And in the meantime, if he hears from anyone he expects might know more, he'll send them over immediately."

Josie nodded and helped herself to the food. "Good. I'll feel better when I at least know her name. Not that I expect it to make much difference in her condition. Mostly it will make me feel better." She made a face. "I had my vet tech run some tests today, though, just to see if we missed anything, and her white blood cell count was really high. So it does look like she might be fighting off some kind of infection. I'm wondering if maybe that's hindering her recovery somehow. I really thought she would have shifted by now, or at least regained full consciousness."

"That is odd. Most shifters have pretty amazing immune systems. We're practically immune to most human infections. You won't see a Lupine with mono, for instance. And personally, I've never been sick a day in my life, unless I ate something bad. Even that's a rarity."

"I know. That's what I've been reading for the entire day. The Lupine shouldn't be able to contract any kind of serious infection. But I can't think of another explanation for her white cell count. It's astronomical, even for an Other. And her stitches and surgical incision look good, but they're not healing much faster than I'd expect in a normal wolf." Josie shook her head and stabbed her mashed potatoes with unnecessary force. "There's something going on there. I just haven't been able to figure out what it is."

"You will."

She felt the Feline's eyes on her and looked up. His mouth quirked as he glanced from her face to her plate. Following his gaze down, Josie realized she hadn't taken more than a bite of her food. Mostly, she'd just hacked it into little bits and pushed it around her plate until it resembled a multicolored mess. She flushed.

At her feet, Bruce moaned at the tragic waste.

"Thank you for bringing dinner, Sheriff Pace," she said hastily, feeling her cheeks flush with color. "I guess I'm more distracted than I am hungry. How much do I owe you? I can't let you pay for my little art project here, since I didn't even have the decency to enjoy it."

"Eli," he corrected, his cajoling even as he watched

her face with a kind of subtle intent. "And sure you can, since I invited myself to join you for it."

"Thank you. Eli," she acknowledged, slipping a bite of meat loaf under the table to a heartily approving Bruce. It gave her an excuse to look away until the butterflies in her stomach settled down. "Frankly, though, I think you're charging yourself too high a penalty. Trust me when I tell you I've dined with less pleasant companions. Of course, most of those have been patients . . ."

He grinned. "Well, I'm glad to know I rate higher than a sick Pekingese, anyway."

"Oh, much. First of all, unlike most Pekingese, you're not a mouth breather, and that kind of thing always counts with me."

His grin turned into a laugh, and raw electricity danced along her skin until she had to clench every muscle in her body to prevent a visible shiver from coursing through her. So much for calming those butterflies. This man made her react in ways she hadn't since she was a teenager.

Or even *when* she'd been a teenager, come to think of it.

"So, Dr. Barrett," he said, bracing his forearms on the table and leaning toward her. "Tell me, what made you decide to become a veterinarian?"

"Please. Just Josie," she said, jumping to her feet before she could give into the urge to meet him halfway across the expanse of surgical steel and see if her assumption that kissing him would send her into immediate cardiac arrest was accurate. "I'm going to grab myself a soda. Can I get you one? I'd offer you a beer, but I don't keep any in the clinic."

He smiled, a crooked, knowing sort of grin that only served to make her walk toward the fridge even faster.

"Soda is fine," he said, "Josie."

The way his voice dropped on those last two syllables almost made her drop the soft drinks. As it was, she wasn't sure her walk back to the exam table would have passed a sobriety field test. His company was going to her head faster than the beer she hadn't drunk.

"I'm not all that sure I had a choice," she continued, setting both cans on the table and sinking back into her seat. "About being a vet, I mean. My father started this practice back in 1972, so I literally grew up in a vet's office. Not that my dad pushed me into it—I think he secretly hoped I'd go into human medicine so I could make decent money one day—but it just always fascinated me. I used to practice wound dressing on my teddy bears and apparently had to be earnestly talked out of performing exploratory surgery on the neighbor's cat to find out why it wouldn't stop meowing one summer when I was seven."

Josie knew she was babbling, but at the moment babbling seemed safer for her than any of the alternatives she could think of.

"It turned out the cat was in heat, which I didn't really understand, but my mom said the only way to distract me was to let me help out in Dad's office." She grinned sheepishly as Eli chuckled. "Not with surgery, of course, but with cleaning the kennels and the exam rooms and alphabetizing charts. Things like that."

"I'm impressed. Not many people know what they want so young and manage to go after it."

"I like to say I was determined. My mom usually

changes that to obsessed." She looked up and met his eyes, and she could have sworn she saw a reflection of her own hyper-awareness mirrored there. She hurriedly took a sip of her cola. "What about you? Did you not grow up wanting to be a cop?"

Eli shook his head. "I wanted to be a professional hockey player. Or an astronaut. And I had a brief desire to be in a rock band, but that was mostly because Mary Pressman had a thing for guys with long hair and guitars."

Josie fed Bruce more meat loaf and smiled. "Somehow I have trouble picturing you as the long-haired type."

He ran a hand over his closely cropped hair, the length almost militarily severe. "Yeah, so did my mom. Mary ended up dating Eric Bosky, until he went to juvie for breaking and entering."

"Poor Mary. But what killed your dreams of sports glory and space exploration?"

"Well, I gave up hockey because I realized I really sucked at it. I was fast and coordinated, but I had no real sense of the game. At least that's what my coach told me right before he cut me from the team. And I abandoned the astronaut idea when I had my first change."

Josie blinked in surprise. "Why? Are there no Others working at NASA? I find that hard to believe."

"There are Others in the space program, sure," he said, slipping her dog a bite of his own dinner. "But you won't find them being sent up. Everyone is afraid of what might happen if they got trapped up there over a full moon."

"But that whole full moon thing is a crock. Even before the Unveiling, everyone in Stone Creek knew that the moon can't force shifters to change their forms. Sure, there are Lupines and Others out there who like to take advantage of a nice, well-lit night to do some hunting, but it's not like something out of a Lon Cheney movie."

Eli toasted her with his soda can. "Ah, but the people of Stone Creek have always been an enlightened bunch when it comes to the Others. Most of the human population still doesn't really understand that much about us."

"I so don't get that. Is that why you took the sheriff's job out here, though? Because you'd heard we were a haven for the things that go bump in the night?"

"Not really. I just wanted a change of pace. I'd started to feel a little crowded in Seattle. The work was exciting, but it's possible to have a little too much excitement, you know?" He finished the last bite of his mashed potatoes and speared a broccoli floret. "I was ready for something different, and I knew I wanted to be somewhere more rural. More like where I grew up. Though I will admit that the idea of living in a place where the human and Other populations were so well integrated did have a certain amount of appeal."

Josie pushed her plate away and picked up her drink. "That's our claim to fame, all right."

"Oh, I wouldn't say it's the town's only appeal."

"No?"

Eli held her gaze and shook his head, his green eyes glittering brightly. "Not by a long shot."

She leaned forward slightly, as if drawn to him by some magnetic force, which she supposed was as good an explanation as any. How else could she describe the attraction that seemed to be building between them?

CHAPTER SIX

Eli watched the object of his fascination sway toward him and bit back the urge to reach out and haul her across the table. For most of the last twenty-four hours, he might have wondered whether Josie Barrett felt even a fraction of the attraction for him that he had developed for her; but if that slightly dazed look in her eyes and the smell of her sweet warm skin were any indication, his question had just been answered with a resounding yes.

He might actually have thrown caution to the wind and eaten her alive if her dog hadn't chosen just that moment to switch his allegiance from his clearly neglectful mistress and drape his huge, drooling muzzle on the thigh of Eli's jeans. Clamping his teeth together, Eli pulled back and sent the mutt an only half-joking glare. Somehow, the feel of canine saliva soaking through denim proved to be a real mood killer.

"What?" he growled at the dog, hoping Josie would assume he was teasing. "Are you trying to tell us it's time for dessert?"

The veterinarian blushed scarlet at that question and reached for the dog's collar. At least, he hoped it was from the question and the knowledge that each of them would like very much to have the other for dessert, instead of from the embarrassment of having a hungry hound assault her guest.

"Bruce!" she scolded sharply, grabbing her half-eaten dinner with her free hand and hauling both food and dog toward another room of the clinic. "You know better than to beg from company. Come on. You can finish my leftovers in the file room, if you can't be trusted to behave yourself."

Frankly, the only one whose behavior Eli distrusted at the moment was himself. He'd been about three seconds away from ravishing the pretty veterinarian on her own exam table, so what did that say about his company manners?

Josie returned a second later, already apologizing. "I'm so sorry about that. He doesn't normally do that to people he's just met, but I'm afraid that when it comes to Laura Beth's meat loaf, the idiot just has no self-control."

"Don't worry about it. I understand about the futility of resisting that kind of temptation."

Believe me, I know.

"I should thank you again for dinner," she said, beginning to fuss with the debris of their meal, balling up napkins and dropping them into the discarded take-out sack. "It was very nice of you to bring it over so late."

"Is that what it was?" Eli growled. He crushed his empty soda can in his fist and tossed it into the recycling bin under the counter. "I didn't buy you dinner to be nice."

Josie blinked up at him, her eyes wide and wary. "You didn't?"

"No."

"Then why did you?"

"Because I wanted to. I wanted to get to know you better. I still do."

She didn't say anything at first, just kept her eyes fixed on the shiny surface of the exam table as she sprayed it with disinfectant and wiped it with a wad of paper towels. Eli almost found himself wishing for the first time that he were a vampire, so he could get an idea of what was going on in that head of hers.

"There's really not that much to know," she said finally. "I've already told you most of it. I grew up here in Stone Creek. I became a vet. I took over my dad's practice when he and my mother decided to retire to Arizona. My older sister lives there, too, with her husband and two kids. And you already met Bruce. That's pretty much the full story."

They bumped shoulders when each of them reached to deposit their litter in the trash bin at the same time. Josie seemed to withdraw from the brief contact, and that pissed Eli off. He didn't want her trying to get away from him.

He didn't want her getting away.

Maybe he would have reacted differently if he hadn't seen that he intrigued her just as much as she did him. He could read it in her eyes, in the rhythm of her breath. And he could smell it on her skin. This was a mutual fascination they had going between them, and he refused to let her ignore it.

Grabbing her gently by the elbow, Eli turned Josie to face him and softly tightened his grip. She lifted her chin, her gaze skittering away from his to settle somewhere in the vicinity of his left earlobe.

"That's not what I meant, Josie," he murmured quietly, but her shivers told him he heard. It wasn't that cold inside the clinic, no matter how chilly it had gotten outside. He reached up and tucked an escaped strand of shiny dark hair behind her ear, and the shivering intensified. "I think you know that."

She forced out half a chuckle. "Wow, wouldn't I sound like an arrogant so-and-so if I said yes to that."

"I don't think you'd sound arrogant. Just honest. You want to get to know me, too. Don't you?"

He could see that she wanted to deny it. He saw the impulse in her clear dark eyes, saw her wrestle with it, and saw when her conscience won out. She wouldn't lie to him, not about that.

"I . . . maybe," she admitted softly. "It's weird. I mean, we must have bumped into each other a hundred times over the last three years. Stone Creek just isn't that big. So how is it that this is happening now?"

"I don't know. I'm just glad it is."

A soft breath sighed from the softness of her mouth, and Eli could almost feel it part for him as he leaned down and brushed his lips against hers for the length of a stuttering heartbeat.

She tasted better than the scone he'd devoured that morning along with his coffee. Sweeter and richer and altogether more intoxicating. But what struck Eli wasn't the way she tasted, but the way she made him feel. Just that gentle touch of lip to lip, skin to skin, made his heart pound as if he'd sprinted up the side of a mountain. His head spun, and his fingers literally itched and flexed with the need to touch her. It didn't matter where. He just needed every bit of connection he could forge between them. He needed to convince himself that she was real.

He stepped closer. There was still space between

them—he didn't want to scare her off—but now he could feel the heat of her all along his front from his collarbone to his toes. He could feel the pulse of energy between them, and even without body-to-body contact the closeness soothed him. It calmed his restlessness even as it ramped up his desire, and he marveled that one woman could cause such conflicting reactions within him. She aroused and calmed, excited and comforted at the same time. He'd never experienced anything like it.

Never experienced anything like her.

Without thought he lifted a hand, cupped it along the curve of her jaw. His thumb swept across the baby-soft skin of her cheek, and his mouth swallowed the soft hitch of her breath as she shivered in response. She felt as much as he did; Eli could sense it.

The animal inside him urged him to grab her, pull her closer, devour her and assuage his hunger. It roared and snapped inside him, made his throat clench and his muscles tighten. But Eli instinctively knew that Josie meant too much for that; she was too important. He needed patience, needed to court her.

If only that could be done as easily as if she were Feline, too. If Josie were another Feline, he would find her in their cat forms, call to her from the dim cover of the trees. He would take her out on the hunt and trail her across the rocky hilltops, help her bring down their quarry and leave her the choicest bites.

That sounded so much simpler to him than the alternative. Since she was human, he'd have to settle for dinners and movies and conversations. She would expect them to talk and share their thoughts, compare opinions, and learn each other's tastes.

Damn, why did humans have to make everything so complicated?

Of course, if there would be more of these kisses, Eli supposed he could take the strain of it.

His other arm reached out, intent on wrapping around her, pulling her closer. He wanted her leaning against him until he could feel her weight and the soft, feminine curves of her body. He wanted to see how they fit together, even if it meant he would get no sleep tonight because he'd be imagining the fit unencumbered by clothes or inhibitions.

The sound of heavy knocking on the clinic's back door alerted him to an intruder.

Instinctively, he tore away from the embrace and turned, placing himself between Josie and any potential threat. For a moment he remained all snarling animal, tensed and waiting for an attack, his eyes scanning the horizon for threats. Then the door hinges creaked, and he caught the familiar scent of Lupine. Blinking away a thin haze of his animal self, Eli refocused on the sight of a short, sturdy male form peering around the edge of the heavy, metal security door.

"Pace, are you in there?" the man asked, and the sound of his voice let Eli put a name to the still-shadowed face.

"It's me, Bill." He took a casual step forward and gritted his teeth against the loss of Josie's warmth. It didn't matter that he was plenty hot on his own; he wanted to keep touching her. "What can I do for you?"

Bill Evans stepped inside the clinic and frowned anxiously up at him. "I just got a call from the Alpha. He said you found an injured Lupine last night and brought her back to town. To the vet, since Dr. Shad was away."

Eli nodded. Bill was a member of Rick's Stone Creek Clan, and if the man was coming here ahead of his Alpha, it meant the local pack leader suspected Bill knew the identity of Josie's patient.

"I did. A female. Do you know who it might be?"

The man ran a hand through a shaggy mess of light brown hair and drew in a shaky breath. "Lady, I hope not," he said. "Rick said she sounded like she was hurt pretty bad. But—it's just . . . my Rosemary didn't come home last night. We had a real stupid fight just before suppertime, and she took off. She does that sometimes when she needs to cool down. She says it's that or rip my balls off, so I didn't think about it at the time. But then she didn't come home. I went out this morning to look for her, but I didn't find nothing, and then the Alpha called and told me about the one you found. But it can't be my Rosie. Can it?"

Eli had a very bad feeling that's exactly who it was. He searched for some way to break the news to the obviously distraught Lupine, but Josie stepped forward and spoke with a note of sympathetic professionalism.

"Bill? I'm Dr. Barrett. I can't say for sure who I've been treating, since there wasn't any identification on her, but I can tell you that her condition is stable. Either way, I'm sure you'll feel better if you can see her for yourself. She's resting in the other room right now. Why don't you come with me, and I can let you see the patient, and you can tell me whether or not you know her."

Josie spoke softly to Bill as she led him through the back of the clinic to a small room with cabinets on one wall, sophisticated-looking equipment on another, and a third lined with assorted sizes of clean metal cages. Eli could see that most of them were empty, but in the bottom row, the largest of all the cages was nearly hidden by a monitor and IV stands. A twin-size air mattress complete with pillow and rumpled blanket lay a little to the side. Behind the wire door, the still form of the injured Lupine lay on a thick fleece blanket, her eyes closed but her side rising and falling steadily with her breathing.

"Oh, Goddess, no. Not my Rosie," Bill groaned, throwing himself to his knees beside the cage. He made distressing little whimpers as his hands fumbled for the latch. "Rosie, baby, come on. Look at me. It's Billy. Rosie! Rosie, can you hear me, sweetheart?"

Josie bent down beside him and gently brushed his hands away so she could open the cage herself. "She had a minor bullet wound on her flank, Bill, but we stitched that up with no problem. The more serious issue was some internal bleeding. I had to operate to see where it was coming from and to get it stopped. I had to take out her spleen, but she should do just fine without that." She opened the door and laid a hand on the man's shoulder. "She's probably still sore, so you'll need to be gentle with her."

Bill nodded frantically, but his eyes stayed locked on Rosemary. As soon as the barrier between them shifted, he lay down next to her, half in and half out of the cage. One elbow propped up his torso beside her, while he reached for her with the other, his shaking fingers tenderly ruffling the fur just behind her jaw.

"Aw, Rosie, baby. Look what you've done to yourself. My poor girl."

Josie looked over her shoulder at Eli and grimaced, a sentiment he wholeheartedly shared. It was almost painful to watch the Lupine's obvious grief and concern. But as touching as Bill's reunion with his wife might be, they really needed him to answer some questions. Like, who might have wanted to shoot at Rosemary? Why were her injuries not healing? Why was she still unconscious? What kind of infection could a Lupine have contracted without showing any of the usual signs of illness?

Eli cleared his throat.

"Bill, we're so sorry that Rosemary was hurt," Josie said before he had a chance to speak, "but we are taking very good care of her—"

"Then why is she in a cage?" Bill demanded, glaring up at her through watery, red-rimmed eyes. "She's not an animal! Why are you treating her like an animal?"

Eli saw the look of hurt that flashed across Josie's face and felt a snarl of irritation tickle the back of his throat. He wanted to smack the Lupine for talking to her that way, but sheriffs weren't allowed to go around assaulting people. Even the ones who showed disrespect to their mates.

"Dr. Barrett isn't treating your wife like an animal, Evans," he bit out, his voice low and perhaps a bit snarly. "She's treating her like a patient. In case you haven't noticed, her clinic isn't exactly fitted with beds and TVs."

Josie shot him a glare, then softened her expression for the Lupine. "Mr. Evans, I feel just as bad about where I've had to put Rosemary, I assure you. I would love to see her in a real bed at the clinic, but unfortunately, Dr. Shad has been out of town this weekend, so he hasn't been able to take over her care. I've done the best I could, but she does need to be kept quiet and still while her body heals."

"She should be healed already. What did you do to her?"

That time, Eli did step forward. "I'm going to suggest you watch your tone, Bill. Dr. Barrett hasn't done anything to Rosemary that didn't need doing. She has taken excellent care of your wife, and I'm sure she will continue to do so. Neither of us has been able to explain why Rosemary hasn't healed, or why she hasn't shifted. In fact, I think the doctor was kind of hoping you'd be able to help us figure that out."

Bill deflated at those words and shook his head. "I—I don't know. I can't think why not. I mean, it's instinct. If you get hurt, the first thing you do is shift. It usually feels like hell, but it also takes care of most of the problem. That's kid stuff. She should have done it as soon as she was hit."

Josie frowned. "Was Rosemary sick at all in the last week or so, Mr. Evans? Did she have a cold or the flu? Anything like that?"

"Lupines don't catch colds, Dr. Barrett. We're immune to them. We're immune to almost everything that makes humans sick. And I haven't seen Rosie sick a day since I've known her. That's been twelve years now."

"Because if she was already sick, if her immune system were somehow compromised, that could explain the slow healing," Josie insisted. "It might even explain the lack of shifting, if she just felt too weak to go through that."

"I'm telling you, she wasn't sick. Not ever. She's as healthy as I am."

Eli took hold of Josie's arm and pulled her back from the cage. "All right, Bill. We had to ask. Would you like to spend a few minutes with Rosemary?"

"I'd like to stay with her. Stay the night. She might

wake up. She might need me. I don't want her waking up all alone in a cage. It's just not right."

"I understand how you feel, Mr. Evans," Josie began, "but I just don't have any place to put you. I slept on the air mattress last night, but believe me when I tell you I wouldn't wish that on my worst enemy. I'd be happy to call you—"

The Lupine's expression turned mulish. "No, I have to stay with her."

"Mr. Evans, I honestly—"

"I can crawl into that cage with her," Bill interrupted. "I won't mind. It's big enough for the two of us in wolf form. And I promise I'll be careful of her tubes and stuff. We don't get stupid just because we change shape. I can be careful."

"I'm sure you can, but—"

Eli nudged her with a knee. "C'mon, Doc. Let him stay. He can keep an eye on her so you won't have to sleep on the floor again, and maybe his presence will help bring her around. You never know."

"It's totally unorthodox—"

"Please."

Josie gave in with a sigh. "All right, but you're going to have to promise not to touch her monitor or her IV. She's on an antibiotic in case there is some kind of infection, and until I know for sure that there isn't, I don't want the treatment interrupted. The last thing she needs is to develop an unknown resistance to an unknown bug."

"Sure."

"And you have to be up, out of the cage, and dressed by six o'clock. I don't want my staff finding you still here in the morning and freaking out."

"I promise!"

The vow barely made it through his teeth before Bill scrambled to his haunches, bowed his head, and shifted, shaking off layers of cloth to reveal thick fur. It happened so fast that Josie looked dizzy from the change. She made a strangled sound of protest when Bill the scraggly, buff-colored wolf climbed carefully into the cage with his mate and curled up against her back. He nuzzled her ear and gave a tender lick to the neat line of stitches on her flank before laying his muzzle gently over her shoulder with a heartfelt groan. Even the veterinarian in Josie didn't try to stop him, though, and Eli thought that was the important part.

He tugged at her sleeve and nodded toward the door. "Come on. Let's give them some privacy."

He could see her medical training and her emotions warring inside her, their battle plans broadcast in those chocolate-dark eyes of hers, but in the end she sighed and followed him back through the swinging door to the triage area.

"Well, at least we know who she is now," Josie said, sounding as if she lacked a certain amount of the excitement she thought appropriate.

"There is that," Eli agreed, but his mind was already flipping through a million questions that Bill hadn't been able to answer.

He wanted to talk to Rick some more, so that was a third call he'd have to make, and tomorrow morning, when he was ostensibly off duty, he could finally head back out to the scene of the shooting to see if there was anything worth seeing. His deputy hadn't turned anything up, but if Eli got lucky, maybe his sharper Feline senses would help him find some tracks that belonged to the shooter, or even a bullet casing. Josie could deal with the medical mystery and puzzle out the reason for Rosemary's delayed recovery, but Eli wanted to know why the Lupine had been shot in the first place.

Josie cleared her throat, tugging his attention back to her, and shifted her weight from foot to foot. "Well, um, thanks again. For dinner, I mean."

The look on her face matched the hesitation in her speech, all uncertain and female and vulnerable. It made Eli's mouth twitch and his chest swell.

His chest, and other things.

"We'll do it again," he told her, reaching up to tuck back a strand of silky dark hair that had slipped free from her ponytail. Then he couldn't resist rubbing the pad of his thumb over the full center of her bottom lip. He'd never felt anything so soft, not in his life.

"We will?"

"Soon."

He bent his head and took her mouth before she could stop him. Judging from the way she melted against him, though, stopping him didn't number among her top priorities. He knew it was a fierce kiss, not the kind he'd planned on. Not right away. He'd meant it to be a good-night kiss, soft and sweet and a little bit seductive, but instead his beast had seized control, and it wanted to gobble her up like a Christmas cookie.

It took a serious expenditure of willpower to pull away, and even more to step back from her. When she looked at him like that, with her lips pink and swollen, her lids heavy, her eyes all soft and unfocused, it was all he could do not to carry her down to the nearest horizon-

tal surface and show her exactly how she affected him.
But this wasn't the time.

It wasn't the time.

He ended up repeating that to himself all the way
home. It was the only thing that kept his feet headed in
the right direction.

Exp. 10-1017.03
Log 03-00128

Technicians report three doses success-
fully administered, however one subject
appears to have suffered a reaction and
must be removed from the experiment.
Have instructed techs to leave the remains. Will use them as unplanned aside
to study if current product has any
native mutation abilities that could be
passed on through consumption of contam-
inated material.

Tomorrow will have technicians dose a
replacement subject along with three new
subjects for Stage 3C. New product will
be ready by morning. Optimism remains
high.

CHAPTER SEVEN

He couldn't help wishing his time in the woods had a different purpose, but at least he got to actually spend time in them. As he made his way back to the area where he'd picked up Rosemary, Eli remembered how much he'd been looking forward to the end of his shift on Saturday for that very reason.

He'd worked a lot of doubles and a lot of overtime in the last few weeks while half of his staff—the human half—dropped like flies from this year's merciless strain of flu. Saturday, he'd finally had enough coverage to give himself the night off, and he'd intended to spend it furry. In lion form, ghosting through the forests and hillsides on the outskirts of town. Unfortunately, he'd barely managed to shift before he'd caught the scent of blood and ended up following his nose right to Rosemary.

Eli stopped three feet from the base of the tree where he'd found her. To the naked eye, there was little indication that anything unusual had happened here. There was no huge pool of blood, no chalk outline, but he didn't need those to know he'd found the right spot. He could smell it. He could smell the blood that had soaked into the soil beneath the litter of pine needles, twigs, and fallen leaves. He could smell Rosemary's scent, now that he recognized it, and he could smell the lingering odor of something else. Faint and fading, it barely registered as a whisper among the aromas of the forest, but Eli could smell the last think traces of it. It smelled almost . . . human.

Eyes narrowing, he dropped into a crouch and ran a sharp gaze over the spot where Rosemary had lain. The disturbance in the forest carpet showed him precisely where it had been. Only a very talented and highly trained tracker could pick out those kind of signs, but Eli was both. And he was Other. Tracks had a damn hard time hiding from him.

He scanned the area to the north, and within a few seconds he saw the first of Rosemary's tracks. Or rather the last of them, the last staggering steps she'd taken before she'd fallen and lain still beneath the massive fir.

She had run to this spot, then. The shooting had happened elsewhere. Eli would find out exactly where.

He stood, but kept his eyes on the ground. Moving silently more out of habit than intent, he began to follow the trail of paw prints leading away to the north. It was slow going. There hadn't been rain since early last week, so while moist, the soil hadn't formed the kind of mud that captured prints as perfectly as photographs. The tracks Eli followed had more to do with broken sticks, a drop of blood on the fronds of a fern, or small spots where a fast-moving paw had kicked away the loose debris and left a bare patch of dirt exposed to the world.

He walked for several yards, making note of the way the Lupine's gait had grown gradually slower and more uneven. She'd started out running, he could see, but she'd been getting weaker toward the end. Her strides looked to be longer the farther he went from the site where she'd fallen.

Moving deeper into the woods, he could feel the temperature dropping. The cover grew denser here, and less light penetrated all the way to the ground. On the plus side, less breeze penetrated, too, so when Eli lost sight of the Lupine's trail, he could turn to his nose to keep him pointed in the right direction. He could still smell Rosemary fairly clearly, but the faint whiffs of the other person he'd caught before still came and went, maddeningly elusive.

A few more feet and he halted, head jerking up. The smell of blood was stronger here, and with it Eli detected a sharp bite of fear. He'd bet money that this was where the bullet had struck. Picturing Rosemary in his mind, he estimated the height of her flank and trained his gaze on that level before he began carefully examining the surrounding fauna. Finally, after five tense minutes, he turned to face northwest and he saw what he was looking for—a rough-barked hemlock tree, thick around with age, with faint, dark speckles along the eastern face.

He hunkered down beside the broad trunk and inhaled deeply. The scent of the wood and the leaves nearly overwhelmed the trace of copper, but Eli caught it anyway. The tiny spots on the coarse lumpy bark were blood. Rosemary's blood.

Bracing his forearms across his thighs, he crouched down near the height of the Lupine's back and looked back in the direction he'd come. He could see which way Rosemary had been heading, and he'd found the spatter that marked the place where she'd been standing when the bullet hit her. Since the shot had only grazed her, that meant the bullet should still be out here somewhere. The question was whether Eli could find it.

He spent a frustrating forty minutes searching. He pawed through mulch, shifted leaves, and ran his fingers over more bark than a troop full of Boy Scouts, all to no avail. If that bullet was out here, it was hiding from him very effectively. If he really wanted to get his hands on it, he'd just have to come back with a metal detector.

A quick brush of his hands dislodged the remains of the last hole he'd scraped in the forest carpet. Since he hadn't found the bullet, his next step would be to look for a casing, which meant calculating the most likely spot where the shooter had stood when he'd aimed his rifle at a lone Lupine and pulled the trigger.

Growing up Feline in the middle of the Rocky Mountains had taught Eli a thing or two about rifles, bullets, and trajectories, but more than that, it had taught him about hunters. While he might have preferred to take down game the old-fashioned way—with teeth and claws and a breathless, adrenaline-surging chase through the trees—most of the human hunters he'd met had liked what Eli privately referred to as the La-Z-Boy School of Depredation.

Adherents of the La-Z-Boy method went out into the woods days in advance of the planned hunting trip, toting with them heavy tool kits, camouflage paints, and thermoses of coffee laced with alcohol. They then spent the better part of several days scouting out the perfect location to build a hunter's blind. Sometimes on the ground, sometimes partway up a tree, LZBs picked their spot and them commenced complicated construction projects wherein they harvested saplings and fallen branches and wove or nailed the suckers together to erect "natural" screens that they could use for cover on the day when they eventually started "hunting."

Even Eli had to admit that some of the things ended up as works or art. In the same way that abstract smears of paint thrown randomly onto a blank canvas counted as art. The blinds themselves occasionally involved paint, as the LZB would dab on a touch of black here, some olive there, a bit of dark green on the other, all so that on hunting day he could park his ass behind it and wait for the animal of his choosing to wander unsuspectingly into the sights of his .50-caliber rifle.

Call him old-fashioned, but Eli just didn't think that kind of thing was very sporting. But then, neither was shooting at a single gray wolf at least sixty miles from the nearest sheep herd, and more than that from the closest dairy farm. In a state where the animals had never made their way off the endangered species list. Could the shot have been a mistake? Eli would like to think so— that the hunter had been after deer, or even elk, although the season for them was still a couple of weeks off. He'd certainly rather deal with an overeager elk hunter with bad aim than someone who'd come out specifically to bag a wolf.

With that in mind, Eli began scanning the tree line looking for the telltale signs of a blind.

He had to admit, this hunter had done a better-than-average job. It took almost an hour before Eli spotted it, set off from the path Rosemary had taken by nearly a hundred feet and set back amid a tangle of thorn and mountain ash. It owed less to construction than most of the structures he'd seen and more to rearrangement and strategic accentuation. The hunter had used the profusion of the nearby bushes and supplemented their conceal-ment with dozens of thin branches from other plants in the area, some of which still bore foliage for additional concealment. Nothing looked like it had been trucked in from outside the forest, and no canvas or paint had been added to create one of the little huts that occasionally sprang up. This blind appeared to be entirely utilitarian, constructed solely for the purpose of concealing a shooter without standing out from the environment in any way. To a passerby—or an unsuspecting deer—it looked like just a particularly overgrown thicket in a forest full of them. No wonder it had taken Eli so long to find it.

Circling around behind the irregular five-foot wall of vegetation, he found himself in what felt like an alcove in the forest. The screen of the blind curved around in a rough semicircle to provide nearly 270 degrees of con-cealment. The shade cast made the interior noticeably cooler than the surrounding woods, but the cleverly tan-gled and woven branches left plenty of small gaps through which to monitor the path outside. Eli imagined a hunter sitting or kneeling here, probably dressed in full camouflage, and—if the expertly constructed blind was any indication—knowing enough about game to keep still or to make any movements slow and smooth. Such a man, he realized, would have a nearly perfect opportu-nity for a kill.

His mouth compressed into a straight line, Eli stepped forward and peered more closely at the front of the screen where it faced the blood-spattered hemlock. Depending on the hunter's position, there were several spots that would have served as decent peepholes, but only one, he judged, would be at the right level and position for the path of the gun barrel. Matte-finished, he imagined, so that light wouldn't catch on the metal and create a glint to alert the prey.

Gods, he thought, disgusted. This wasn't hunting. It was fishing with bullets. How could anyone possibly find it entertaining? Where was the challenge? The excitement?

Eli supposed that just went to show that he'd never really understand humans. They simply baffled him.

Stepping back toward the entrance of the blind, he lowered himself into a crouch and began to quarter off the enclosed area of ground in his head. If the hunter had left anything behind, he intended to find it.

The space wasn't large, maybe six feet in diameter, but Eli worked slowly and methodically. He searched with his eyes and nose first, then followed up with his hands, running his fingers through the soil and organic detritus for anything his other senses may have missed.

The first thing he noticed was the smell of the hunter, that elusive scent that had been teasing him all morning. It had coalesced here, in the spot where the hunter had sat and waited, perhaps for hours, until his quarry wandered into the trap. It smelled human; Eli was certain of that. But it didn't seem as strong as it should for being less than forty-eight hours old. Instead it smelled as if it had gotten all muddled up with the smells of pine and oak and dirt and moss. He could smell all of those things, could even smell the musky, meaty scent of rabbit and the old and musty smell of owl. He could smell the mice that scurried through the underbrush and the bitter tang of

metal and gun oil, and all of them smelled stronger to
him than the living breathing man who had sat here and
taken aim at one of the citizens under Eli's protection.

You know, that kind of pissed him off. How the hell
had the bastard managed it, first of all. And second, if he
could disguise his scent enough to nearly hide from Eli
here, would he be able to slip by undetected if they met
each other on the street? The thought made the sheriff
want to scream his frustration, but he just clenched his
teeth and continued to pore over the ground cover.

He had nearly reached the end of his search without a
single clue—which wasn't doing much for his mood—
when his fingers bumped into something foreign wedged
half under the root of an ash bush that made up part of
the natural screen. Freezing, he moved his hand again
and felt something cool and slick, like glass. He ducked
his head to look, but the plants blocked his vision too
well. Closing his fingers around his find, he tugged gently and emerged with a dirty lump about the size of a
large peach pit.

Eli frowned at the dirt-encrusted lump and brushed the
soil away with his thumbs. The dappled light coming
through the screen glinted off a small glass vial that was
topped with a ring and seal of silver foil. It looked like the
kind of thing doctors stuck needles into to draw out the
doses of vaccine they used before sticking you in the arm.
Or the ass.

What the hell was it doing here?

He barely had time to think the question before the
radio he habitually more clipped to his belt shattered the
quiet with a crackle of static.

"Patrol unit, this is dispatch, 10–49 to Pine Street,

number Seventeen. We have a . . . an 11–12. Or a 203. Ah, a-a-a . . . 240. Oh, shit, is that a 597? Oh, hell! Jimmy, just get over there! Do you copy?"

Eli didn't wait to hear if Jimmy copied or not. He was already sprinting to his Jeep, heart pounding. Seventeen Pine Street was the address of Josie's clinic, and 203 and 240 were the dispatch codes for mayhem and assault. It was no wonder Cindy had sounded so confused. Those weren't the kind of codes they heard much in Stone Creek.

And if someone was assaulting Josie, Eli knew he'd probably never hear them again. The town probably wouldn't want to keep a sheriff who'd just committed a bare-handed murder.

Exp. 10–1017.03
Log 03–00130

The largest challenge facing this project remains the difficulty in locating competent technicians to carry out the necessary tasks. Obtaining radio equipment has become of paramount importance as techs seem unable to effectively track test subjects once dosages have been administered. This makes it impossible to accurately observe and record the effects of the newest version of the product.

Extrapolations can be made from data existing re: source materials and from

observations of early in vitro and in
vivo studies, however this cannot substitute for firsthand data.

Will send techs out to attempt to locate
and gather data beginning tomorrow.
However, will begin tapping contacts for
discreet source of radio tracking tags,
preferably nanotech for easy concealment.

CHAPTER EIGHT

"Mr. Evans. Bill. I need you to take it easy, okay? No one here wants to hurt you. We're all on your side. We just want to help you. Both you and Rosemary. I promise."

Josie spoke in her calmest, most soothing, please-don't-bite-me-while-I-give-you-your-shots tone of voice, but Bill Evans didn't appear to be listening. At least, that was the impression she got from the bared fangs and pinned-back ears he had aimed in her direction. She could be wrong.

Behind her, Ben and Daisy stood perfectly still, their eyes fixed on the snarling wolf currently planted posses-sively in front of his mate's cage. Inside the cage, Rose-mary Evans continued to lie still and silent. Frankly, Josie thought that probably wasn't helping to calm Bill down.

Ben's hand still held the phone receiver poised half-way between his ear and the cradle, which was as far as he'd gotten after calling 911 and before the three of them had decided that anytime one of them moved so much as a muscle, the wolf who had been Bill only got angrier. They didn't like him when he was angry.

"Cindy said she'd send Jim Cooper straight out. He's the deputy on duty."

Josie gave a barely perceptible nod. "Okay. Did she say how long it would take?"

"He's out on patrol, so it depends on where he was when she made the call."

"I see." What Josie saw, though, was her own gruesome death flashing before her eyes. "I don't suppose you asked her to have him hurry?"

"Oh, no," Ben sniped, "I said to take her time."

"Right. Sorry."

"We could try tranquilizing him," Daisy offered. The fifty-something veterinary assistant sounded almost as calm as Josie, but Josie put that down to having raised twin boys all the way through their hell-raising teenage years before turning them over to the military with a sigh of relief. The calm tone wasn't fooling anyone, though. Out of the corner of her eye, Josie could see how pale Daisy was under the rosy sweep of her blusher.

"We could," Ben agreed, "but that would require one of us to walk over to the drug cabinet, unlock it, choose the correct sedative, draw it into a syringe, walk up to the crazy werewolf, and stick a needle in his ass. Who's going to volunteer?"

"I don't think sarcasm is helpful at the moment, Benjamin," Josie said. "Nor is insulting Bill."

Daisy shifted. Very, very slightly. "We have a tranquilizer air gun, don't we?"

"Again, someone has to go get it. It's in the wildlife kit in the storage room."

"Well, doesn't the wildlife kit have sedatives for large animals in it? I thought we kept it equipped for bears? And why is the wildlife kit in the storage room when we've had a wolf as a patient for two days now?"

"Because our patient isn't a wolf." Josie spoke through gritted teeth and decided that if the deputy didn't come soon to keep Bill from killing them all, she might just have to kill her staff all on her own. "Bill Evans is not a wolf. They are Lupine, and that means that at least part of the time, they're just as much people as you and me."

"They sure look like wolves at the moment," Daisy sulked.

Josie made a mental note to look into muzzles designed for human faces. "They're not."

"Besides," Ben broke in, "even if the kit has sedatives dosed for bear, I doubt that would be enough for the wer—er, the Lupine. Their metabolism is unreal. It would take a dose for an elephant to knock him unconscious. Especially since he seems to be pushing a decent amount of adrenaline at the moment."

"Can we forget about dosages and wildlife for the time being?" Josie snapped. "We can't get to the sedatives at the moment, so I think our first order of business is to come up with a plan about what we *can* do to get out of this situation."

There was a brief moment of silence.

Josie cherished every second of it.

Well, except for the menacing snarl that continued to vibrate from Bill Evans's throat.

"I got nothin'," Ben finally admitted, blowing out a slow breath, "but I'm all ears to hear what you ladies came up with."

"I'm assuming plans for murdering and/or firing veterinary technicians aren't exactly what you were hoping for," Josie muttered under her breath.

"Sorry, I didn't catch that."

Daisy sighed. "I'm still thinking."

Josie took a deep breath. "Well, if we split up, he can't go after more than one of us at a time, right?"

"Dr. J, don't say anything you—or *I*—might regret." Josie could practically feel Ben's glare piercing a hole in the back of her skull. "None of us needs to make the noble, yet insanely suicidal gesture of throwing herself into the teeth of the wild beast to give the others a chance to escape. That's just crazy talk."

"I was thinking less about letting the others escape than letting the others haul ass to the drug cabinet. And I think we'd better use the succinylcholine. I don't want to take chances."

"Right. Why take chances that the werewolf won't be completely tranquilized from the shot? I mean, it's not like there's any risk involved in, you know, *administering* it!"

"What did I tell you about sarcasm, Benjamin?"

"Damn it, Josie—!"

Before either of them could argue their point, the back door of the clinic flew open with such force that the bang of the metal hitting the brick wall outside made the teeth rattle in Josie's skull. It also made Bill Evans howl in rage and throw himself toward the exit in a snarling blur of fangs and claws.

Josie spun around just in time to see a look on Eli Pace's face that would have made the avenging angel Michael proud. Her glimpse lasted only a fraction of a second before the air around him seemed to bend and twist, and in the time it took her to blink, an enormous tawny, black-and-gold-maned lion stood in his place.

Or rather, leapt from the place where he had been standing.

The wolf and the lion met in midair, colliding like opposing storm fronts and sending a thunderous noise into the atmosphere. From Bill came a deafening roar of rage and hatred and from Eli an earsplitting scream of righteous fury. Each snapped forward with lethal white teeth and each dug razor claws into his adversary's flesh, further escalating the heat of battle.

Josie wasted about two and a half seconds in openmouthed astonishment before the wolf shifted his massive head and sank his fangs deep into Eli's shoulder. Fear and anger welled up in her chest and she realized that she'd kill that Lupine herself if he did anything to seriously harm Eli. Not before they'd had a real date, damn it!

She bolted for the drug cabinet like both the Others were after her instead of each other, shoving Ben and Daisy out of the way. They seemed happy to comply and ducked under the desk, huddling together as they watched the bloody battle play out in the center of the room.

Hands shaking, Josie thanked the powers that be that she trusted her staff enough to leave the drug cabinet unlocked during business hours when someone was in triage to monitor it. She threw open the doors and began pawing through the shelf where she knew the sux ought to be. She pushed aside the small vials of dilute injections and nearly screamed in frustration before she spotted the right label. She didn't usually order the 100 mg/mL concentration because there were so few situations where it was required, but she had been meaning to change out the vial in the wildlife kit the last time she ordered it from the supplier. Thank God she'd been too busy for real efficiency.

It seemed to take hours to uncap the syringe and draw two mils out of the vial, but she knew it was only seconds. She didn't care. Seconds counted. She just had to pray she'd picked the right dosage. Two hundred milligrams would kill a wolf of Bill's size, and was probably enough to kill a similar-size human, but with a Lupine's metabolism and drug resistance, she was hoping for a result of quick paralysis rather than death. She didn't want to see anyone here die.

Especially not herself.

A resounding thud nearly shook the room. Josie looked up to see Eli and the wolf hit the hard tiled floor in a tangle of fur and limbs. Each had his ears pinned straight back against his skull and his lips pulled back to expose powerful jaws full of gleaming wet fangs. Neither looked very happy, and neither looked close to giving up. Eli had blood trickling from the bite wound in his right shoulder, but Bill sported a long gash along his ribs that looked like it Eli had put it there with a swipe of huge, lethally sharp claws.

The lion certainly outweighed the wolf, and he had the advantage of size, as well. Close to seven feet long in animal form, Eli made an impressive sight, and his angrily swishing tail probably added another three feet to his length. Unfortunately, the wolf didn't look intimidated. He just focused his pale amber eyes on his enemy's throat and lunged forward, teeth snapping.

Swearing, Josie began to edge carefully to the side, looking for her chance to administer the injection. She needed a clear shot at a large muscle mass, but the last thing she wanted to do was to incapacitate the wrong animal. No need to make a bad day worse. And at the moment the shifters were wrestling so closely and moving so fast, she couldn't risk it.

God*damn* it!

With a great rumble of sound, the wolf wedged his shoulder and head and neck against the lion's chest, high up beneath his throat, and strained to push the other animal backward. Josie could see muscles shifting even under his dense coat, and she could hear the painful scrabbling of his nails against the slick floor as he struggled for purchase. To her horror, she saw him find it and watched while he began to raise himself up on his hind legs in an attempt to overbalance Eli.

She stepped forward—she had to *do* something!—but froze when she realized that if she approached from her current position, she risked coming up on the space between the two combatants. Either one would be able to track her movements and adjust his position out of her way. She needed to get behind Bill in order to have a clean shot.

A scream rent the air, a horrible high-pitched sound of fury and desperation with the static undertone that made no one doubt it had come from a very angry lion. Josie echoed it with a cry of her own as she watched Eli tumble backward under the determined force of the wolf. She saw him attempt to twist out of the way, but Bill sprang even as he felt the change in resistance, and he was on the lion faster than a heartbeat. His back feet dug into the insides of the cat's thighs, pinning them down, and he braced both front paws on the larger animal's chest.

The Lupine leaned forward, baring his teeth in a snarl

that now somehow took on a hint of triumph. He pressed his muzzle into the lion's face and Josie could almost feel that hot, moist breath on her own skin, feel the drop of saliva that slowly descended from the tip of a razor-sharp canine. She wanted to scream again; she did shudder, but Eli just bared his own teeth and hissed at the adversary pinning him to the floor.

When Josie saw the wolf's head snake backward, she sprang into motion. Darting to the right, she placed herself in line with the Lupine's flank and threw herself forward, the hand holding the needle poised close to her side.

It struck home with a satisfying *thwack,* and Josie reflexively hit the plunger, sending the massive dose of paralytic coursing into the cells of the wolf's muscular thigh. It might not be an IV infusion, but it would have to be enough.

The wolf yelped when he felt the needle pierce his skin, and he rounded on Josie with a howl of rage. His quick movement threw her off balance. She landed on her ass less than four feet away from the snarling animal and immediately began scooting backward as fast as she could across the polished floor.

He tried to leap after her, but already his movements had begun to grow clumsy, and his back feet slid out from under him, sending him tumbling onto the site of the injection. He growled in a way that make Josie think of vicious curses and struggled to right himself, but Eli was already on him. The lion twisted to his feet in a lithe motion and threw himself onto the wolf's back. Weakened by the drug, the smaller animal collapsed, all four limbs splaying out to the side, his jaw shutting with a snap as it banged into the hard tile. He made a yelping sort of whimper, then his eyes rolled back in his head and his muscles went limp.

Josie nearly broke out in a hallelujah chorus.

She rushed forward and immediately began probing at Eli's shoulder. "Ben, get me some saline in an irrigation bottle and some clean dressings. I want to flush this out right away. I'm not about to risk infection here."

The muscles under her fingers shifted, and suddenly she was touching not fur but smooth, warm skin. Her gaze shot up and she found herself looking into a slightly bemused expression on the face of a very human Eli.

"Sorry about that," he rumbled, his voice sounding lower than usual with an intimate note that made her stomach clench. "I was going to give you until the third date before I took my clothes off. I didn't want you to think I was cheap."

Reflexively, Josie looked down and saw that the sheriff wore that bemused expression along with precisely nothing else. His clothing had ripped to pieces in the haste of his transformation.

Her cheeks flamed, and she snatched her hand back from his now uninjured shoulder as if it, too, were on fire. Apparently, that "shifting heals" thing really worked.

"Uh, why don't I see if I have a pair of sweats or something in the break room that I can lend you, Sheriff?" Ben offered, his lips suspiciously pursed below madly twinkling eyes. "You know, to protect your reputation."

"I'd appreciate that." Eli nodded to the vet tech then turned back to Josie, seemingly unconcerned with his nudity. Even though Daisy's eyes were currently fixed on his ass like it was spread across the pages of *Playgirl*. "What did you give him?"

"Huh?"

"What did you give Bill?" he asked, clearly fighting back a grin. "To knock him out. I saw that needle you had."

Josie's blush deepened, and she cleared her throat. "Oh, um, succinylcholine. It's a tranquilizer. Well, a paralytic, really. It's mainly used for short-term muscle relaxation, like when we have to insert a breathing tube or get X-rays on a fractious patient. Some people have used it as an anesthesia induction agent, too."

As always, talking about her work calmed her, and her hands were only mildly unsteady as she reached for her stethoscope.

"I had to totally guess on the dosage for a Lupine, though, and it has been used as a poison in the past." She knelt down beside the unmoving Lupine and pressed the instrument against his side. "Thank God, he's still got a heartbeat. Daisy, can you go get me a trach tube? Better safe than sorry. His breathing does seem a little shallow."

When she heard nothing but silence, Josie looked up to see her assistant still frozen in place, her eyes glued to the sheriff's admittedly fine and thoroughly naked ass.

"Daisy!"

The woman jumped about a foot in the air, turned beet red, and rushed over to a cabinet against the wall. "Trach tube," she babbled. "Right. I'm on it."

Josie shook her head and looked up at Eli, her eyes deliberately avoiding all the things he wasn't trying to hide. Seriously, did the man have no shame?

"Sheriff, I appreciate the help here, but I have to say it: You're bad for my business."

"And I have to say, Dr. Barrett, that you're about to become bad for my image."

"What are you talking about?"

"Take a listen."

Josie stood still and listened intently, but it was several more seconds before she heard the sound of a siren coming closer. She cocked an eyebrow. "When you were growing up, did any of the other kids ever call you Radar?"

His grin was a bold slash of teeth. "Never more than once."

Josie humphed.

Ben trotted back into the room carrying a wad of folded cloth, which he tossed in Eli's direction. "Here you go. They're going to be tight, but at least you should be able to get them on. I thought about just handing you a pair of scrubs, but we don't stock them in the 'lion-slash-imposing-giant' size."

Eli just nodded and bent to step into the navy sweat-pants. "No shirt?"

"Not unless you have a thing for looking like a cheap, gay hooker. Dude, you're like three or four sizes bigger than me. At least. And I've never gone for the ghetto baggy look."

"Right. Well, thanks for the bare minimum, then. It doesn't do for the sheriff to be caught by his own deputies breaking the public indecency statutes."

Josie accepted the handful of sealed packages of sterile equipment that Daisy handed her and stood. "Since you boys are firm friends now, would you mind lifting Bill here onto an exam table? Ben, I want to get him trached, put a few stitches in his side. And then we're going to want to dose him with a milder—but hopefully long-acting—sedative. At least until we decide what to do with him."

"I vote we neuter him while he's under," Ben grumbled as he bent down to grab the wolf's front paws. "It's supposed to help prevent aggression, right?"

Eli frowned, his eyes dropping to the sullenly bleeding wound on the Lupine's side. He helped Ben deposit him on the surgical-steel exam table, then leaned in for a closer look.

"That looks like it just happened."

"It did." Josie shouldered him out of the way and began to flush the wound with a squirt bottle full of sterile saline. "Don't you remember? You're the one who did it."

"I know, but that was during the fight, and he's been out for almost five minutes. Resting. It should at least have stopped bleeding by now, if not started to scab over on the ends."

She pressed a thick, absorbent pad against the wolf's side to catch the dripping saline and continued to clean the gash. "Really? You guys can heal that fast?"

"You saw my shoulder."

"Well, yeah, but you shifted. I thought it was the shifting that made you heal so fast."

Eli shook his head. "Only part of it. Some of it's metabolism. And the rate we heal at depends on other factors, just like a human. It goes faster when we're relaxed and not doing anything to strain the injury."

The subject fascinated Josie, but she didn't have time to pump him for information on it right now. First, because the sirens had reached a crescendo directly outside the back door and then gone silent, signaling the arrival of the cavalry. Better late than never, after all. And second, because the real implication of what he'd just said had begun to sink in.

Josie looked from the Lupine on the table to the door of the kennel area, as if she'd be able to see Rosemary's cage through the door and walls separating them. Her lips parted, and she ducked her chin in disbelief. "You don't think . . . you can't mean that this is related to Rosemary?"

"Why can't I? Something is keeping Rosemary from recovering from her injuries, and keeping her from shifting. What if it's some kind of infection? And what if it's contagious? Have you seen Bill in human form since he got in the cage with her last night?"

"No, but—"

"And there's something else you need to know," he said. The grim tone in his voice made her breath catch in her throat. "When I spoke to Rick Cobb, the Stone Creek Alpha, last night, the reason he was too busy to come see Rosemary himself was that he was busy cremating another pack member who'd been found dead in the forest near where I found Rosemary. The kid they were burning had been found in his wolf form as well."

A rush of dread rolled through Josie like sickness. "Why did you wait until now to tell me this?"

"Because until just now, there was no reason to think the Paulson case and Rosemary's were related in any way. Rosemary's injuries could all have been due to being shot—"

"Theoretically," he stressed, when she tried to interrupt.

She gave a reluctant nod.

"And there wasn't so much as a mark on Paulson's body, from what Rick told me. Until Bill started showing symptoms similar to Rosemary's, there was no reason to think that whatever she had might be contagious, and those symptoms only showed up just now. But our patient count just jumped from one to two, and possibly three. That gives me a lot more faith in the contagious disease theory than I had yesterday."

Josie shook her head, but her brain whirled as she struggled to process the possibilities. She probably looked like a moron to the deputy, who cautiously peered into the room through the back door.

"Sheriff's department!" the man called. "Everybody okay in here?"

"We're fine, Jim," Eli replied, stepping forward and waving his co-worker inside. "Dr. Barrett had a little incident, but we've got it under control."

"Well, what kind of incident?" Jim Cooper asked as he stepped over the threshold. He didn't seem fazed by the sheriff's shirtless state, but he looked confused as his gaze traveled around the rest of the room. "I don't mind admitting I'm pretty curious. Did you hear that call on the radio? One of those codes was for loose livestock!"

"Yeah. We might need to update that, so there's a separate code for wildlife."

"Wildlife?" Jim caught sight of the injured animal on the exam table and his eyes went as wide as dinner plates. "Is that a wolf? Is that what this is all about? A wolf got into the vet clinic! How the hell did that happen?"

"It's a long story, Deputy Cooper," Josie said, setting aside the saline and ripping open the packaging around the endotracheal tube. "And frankly, we don't have a lot of time at the moment to tell it."

Eli put a hand on Jim's shoulder and guided him diplomatically toward the exit. "I've got things under control here, and I witnessed the event, so why don't I write up the report for you? You're on call for another eight hours. You don't need to waste any time here."

"You sure, Sheriff? I know this was supposed to be your day off—?"

"It's fine. This won't take long, and then I'll still have the rest of the day."

"All right, then. I appreciate it. I've already responded to two reckless driving calls from folks who live out on Seven, so it looks like it's going to be a pretty busy day."

"Have fun with it."

"Thanks, Sheriff." He nodded to the others. "Dr. Barrett. Folks. You all have a good day."

Ben placed a roll of tape in the wolf's mouth to keep it from closing around the trach tube Josie had just positioned, and began wrapping his muzzle with tape to secure it.

"Right," he muttered, just loud enough to be overheard. "Because it's been a peach so far!"

CHAPTER NINE

Despite all evidence to the contrary, Josie did have a practice to run and other patients waiting to see her, so she had to veto Eli's suggestion that they meet with Rick Cobb over lunch to talk about the situation regarding Bill and Rosemary. And possibly Sammy Paulson.

From what Eli had said, it sounded like Rick Cobb had intended to show up at the clinic first thing this morning to see his packmates for himself. Eli had insisted that he wait to talk to Josie first. If this little problem of Rosemary's was contagious, as Josie now had no choice but to suspect, she couldn't let any other Lupines into the clinic and risk exposing them. Bringing the local Alpha into the site of a possible infection wouldn't do anyone any good.

Meeting at Josie's apartment for dinner was a better idea all around. The middle of the day was when Josie normally caught up on her charting and returned phone calls, and she couldn't spare the time. Besides, there had been no change in Rosemary's condition, and Josie had pumped Bill full of enough sedatives to keep an elephant unconscious. In fact, she'd be happy to keep the Lupine tranquilized into the next decade if he planned to act like a rabid wolverine when left to his own devices.

Yes, she probably would be holding a grudge for a while over this morning's incident.

Either way, she had to tell Eli she couldn't spare any time for anything until after the clinic closed at six. And that really meant seven. At the earliest. So he suggested he bring Rick to her apartment upstairs, along with a pizza, at seven thirty.

She stepped out of the shower at precisely seven twenty-four, dried herself hurriedly, scraped her hair back into a soggy ponytail, and was pulling a UC Davis T-shirt on over her yoga pants when her doorbell sounded at exactly seven thirty, sending Bruce into a fit of barking. Breathless, she jogged across the apartment to answer the door.

She grabbed the pizza boxes first. Bruce, clearly no fool, shot one last disgruntled glance at the intruders, then followed the pizza.

"Come on in," Josie invited over her shoulder, already halfway to the living room. She'd laid out plates and napkins on the coffee table before her shower.

"Hungry?" a male voice drawled, and since Josie didn't recognize it, she figured that would have to be Rick Cobb.

Had he been holding the pizzas when she snatched them out of his hands? She hadn't really bothered to check.

"Starved." She dropped the boxes on the end of the coffee table, flipped open the lid of the one on top, snagged a slice of what looked to be topped with half a farmyard, and took a huge bite. A pointed glare at Bruce had him settling himself like a sphinx on the floor directly in front of the warm, fragrant boxes. Taking a minute, she chewed, swallowed, uttered a happy sigh, and then looked up at her guests. "So, you guys want something to drink? I've got diet soda, milk, juice, wine, or beer."

Both men eyed her with respect.

"Beer," they chorused.

"Coming right up. Make yourselves comfortable."

Josie continued to munch as she padded into the kitchen and pulled open the refrigerator. She knew her mother would keel over dead if she could see this display of bad manners, but Josie had missed lunch. Too many phone calls and an emergency involving a six-month-old basset hound, a porcupine, and a lesson well learned. She really had been starving.

She snagged three bottles of beer by the necks and balanced them against her hip so she could continue to devour pizza on her way back to the living room. When she got there, she saw that Eli and the man she assumed to be Rick had taken her at her word. They each sprawled in a corner of her chocolate microfiber sofa—which meant they took up the whole thing—with their mouths stuffed full of pizza. Neither had bothered to take a plate, and the stack of napkins appeared untouched. She really had set a bad example.

Figuring it was never too late to remember the social niceties, Josie passed out the beer and took both a plate and a napkin for herself before sinking into the over-stuffed armchair across from Eli. "Thank you, guys, for bringing dinner."

Like a professional waitress, it appeared she'd caught both of them mid-chew. Amused, she twisted the cap off her beer and took a sip while they exercised their jaw muscles.

"You're welcome," Eli said, finally grabbing a napkin

as a dribble of olive oil snaked down his chin. "Thanks for letting us share and not running away with both pies."

"My mother raised me better than that. I wouldn't have run; strolling is more lady-like." She ignored the flutter in her belly caused by his quick grin and turned to the other man. "I'm Josie Barrett, by the way. Since the sheriff hasn't seen fit to introduce us."

Rick Cobb wiped his fingers on a napkin as he extended his hand across the table toward her. "You can't rely on him. Cats never think about anything but themselves. I'm Rick. I think we've run into each other before, but this is the first time we've actually met, which seems like a shame to me."

The grin he flashed was both charming and wicked, and Josie liked him even more when he took the napkin he'd soiled with him on his hand's trip back to the sofa.

"I'm thinking about something other than myself right now," Eli grumbled, but the Lupine just grinned and took a swallow of beer.

"I think you're right." Josie ignored Eli completely and flicked her denuded pizza crust through the air toward Bruce. The dog snapped it up with the grace of a ballet dancer and the ferocity of a starving crocodile.

Reaching for a second slice, Josie blinked when she realized that in the time she'd been in the kitchen grabbing beer, each of the men had apparently inhaled one slice and gone for a second. Either that, or they'd started eating in the car on the way over.

"It's amazing in a little town like Stone Creek how you can still not get to know everyone," she continued, settling back into her chair. "You didn't go to school here. I'm sure I'd remember if you had."

"My parents sent me to private school in Portland. For all the good it did them. I still turned up back here, like a bad penny." Rick grinned. "But even if I had gone to the local schools, I'd have been years ahead of you, sweetheart. I'm sure you wouldn't have even known I was alive."

"Oh, you're not that old," she said, laughing. "You're . . . what? Thirty-seven? Thirty-eight?"

"Good guess. Thirty-seven."

"And you won't make thirty-eight if you don't cool it," Eli snapped.

Josie raised a brow in his direction. The sheriff sounded almost jealous. Of a little flirting? Because it was clear to her that flirting was Rick Cobb's stock in trade. He had that air about him, like a man who had never met a woman he didn't like. Josie knew better than to take a guy like that seriously. And besides, she and Eli hadn't even been on a real date yet. He had no right acting jealous.

Which was why she stomped hard on the tiny little part of herself that tingled over the fact that he had.

She took another sip of beer. "I've only been back in town a few years, so forgive my ignorance, but when did you take over the Clan? When I was growing up, the Alpha was Ed Tarbridge."

Rick nodded. "My uncle. He died about ten years ago now. A heart attack. I stepped in for him right away."

"I'm sorry to hear that. I don't remember him well, but I know my dad thought highly of him."

"Thank you."

Eli cleared his throat at a conspicuous volume. "So I told Rick a little bit about what's been going on over the last couple of days," he offered.

The pizza had put Josie in a generous mood, enough

so that she allowed the obvious attempt to pull her attention away from the other man and fed Bruce a second crust. "Really? What parts did you leave out?"

He frowned. "Mainly your professional opinion as to what the hell is going on."

"Right. Well, since I really don't have the slightest idea, I'm sure he has a pretty complete picture."

"I hope you'll accept my apology on behalf of my pack member for what happened, Dr. Barrett." Rick's face and tone were serious now. "That's never the kind of image we want to present of ourselves."

"Please, call me Josie. And I don't blame your pack at all. I might specialize in treating full-time animals, but Stone Creek is my hometown. I've met enough Others not to have some crazy idea that they're monsters. Clearly there's something going on here that we haven't figured out."

"That's why I wanted the three of us to get together and talk," Eli said. "We need to know if you have any idea what might be behind all this."

The Lupine made a face. "This would be easier if I could take a look at Bill and Rosemary, of course, but off the top of my head? I can't think of a damn thing."

"What would be easier would be if we knew a little more about Sammy Paulson and whether his case was definitely related to Bill and Rosemary." She saw the flash of pain behind Rick's calm facade and sighed. "I didn't mean it that way. I know that the pack always burns its dead, but did anyone see him in his last twenty-four hours? Was he acting normally? Did he look ill?"

"No. According to his mother, when she saw him last night, he seemed just fine."

"I think we have to assume that everything is related at this point," Eli said. "I'd rather be wrong and paranoid than wrong and responsible for a disease outbreak we could have prevented."

Rick nodded his agreement. "The problem is that I haven't heard anything about pack members being ill or anything else out of the ordinary. Until this afternoon, I would have said everything was fine. Things have been pretty quiet lately. It's nothing like last summer."

"Last summer?" Josie almost felt her ears pricking forward. Unlike Bruce, who had decided to digest his pizza bones via a good long nap.

"August before last. Don't you remember?" Eli tilted his head in inquiry. "There were some anti-Others demonstrations in Seattle and Portland. Skinheads, mostly, looking for one more group to hate. Well, a bunch of them rented at the campground out on Seven because they thought it would get them a bunch of press and win them some support if they spread the hate to the 'most famous mixed-species community in America.'"

"No, that must have happened while I was away. I went to two veterinary conferences back-to-back that August. My dad even came up from Arizona to fill in for me at the clinic, because I had to be away so long. I was gone almost three weeks."

"That explains it. But compared with a mystery virus and a Lupine being shot, that summer was a walk in the park. We had lots of yelling and sign waving, a couple of shoving matches, but no real violence." Eli nodded at Rick. "And I still owe you for helping make that happen. Without the volunteers from the pack agreeing to serve as temporary deputies, things could have been a lot worse."

Rick grinned, the expression suddenly less charming and more . . . feral. "The boys enjoyed it. Especially the parts where they got to break up those shoving matches."

"I appreciate that you did it without breaking bones." He turned back to Josie. "Anyway, it was a tense time for the pack—for all the Others in the area. Somehow it always seems that as soon as the unrest over the Unveiling starts to die down, something happens to stir it all up again."

"It's almost enough to make you a conspiracy theorist," Rick agreed. "But like I said, this year had been quiet. No protestors, not death threats, not even any poisoned-meat traps left in the woods. I'm starting to think that no one loves us anymore."

"Well, I'm happy to hear that—not that you're not loved, Rick, since I'm sure that's nowhere close to the truth," Josie said, "but I don't see what anti-Other activists or the lack thereof has to do with Bill and Rosemary. They have an illness. I mean, what else could explain what's going on? They have physical problems that, at least in Bill's case, can't be explained by poison or some kind of attack."

"Why don't you give Rick the complete picture on their condition?"

Josie shrugged helplessly. "They're both sick. I just can't figure out why. Rosemary presented—unconscious—approximately forty-eight hours ago with an external wound and extensive internal bleeding. Eli brought her in and said he'd found her like that, so we have to assume the injuries predated my seeing her by at least a couple of hours. There was no evidence of healing at the wound site, and the bleeding was still active when I took her into surgery. I had to remove her spleen to get it stopped. Since I first saw her, she hadn't regained consciousness. She had minimal awareness when I first evaluated her, but since we knocked her out, nothing. We took her off all sedatives and knocked her pain meds back to the minimum that I'm comfortable giving her at this point, and still . . . nothing. I'm thinking that's not exactly normal, right?"

Rick's brows came together in a deep furrow of concern. "Far from it. The first thing a wounded Lupine does is get out of danger and shift, especially one who's seriously injured. It's almost reflexive. Not to mention the best health insurance program in the world."

"That's what Eli told me, and it makes sense to me. The only thing I can think of is that the injuries left Rosemary too weak to shift. I mean, I imagine that takes a lot of energy, a lot of strength."

"It does, but still . . ." He paused. "Could you tell from your examination whether the gunshot wound and the internal injuries happened at the same time?"

"If you mean did the bullet cause the internal injuries, the answer is no; that's not possible. But if you mean did she get kicked in the stomach and shot at precisely the same moment, there's no way to tell. Judging by the amount of blood in her abdomen and the time line pieced together from Eli and Bill, I can estimate that they happened at roughly the same time, but roughly could mean simultaneously, or it could mean within fifteen to thirty minutes of each other. I suppose they could be unrelated incidents."

Eli held up a hand. "Wait. Back it up a minute. Kicked in the stomach? What makes you think someone kicked Rosemary?"

"It's just an example of what could have caused the internal bleeding. I told you when you brought her in that it was related to a blunt-force trauma. A kick is an example of that, but so is a baseball bat, the front end of a car, a bongo drum, and a comet hurtling down from the sky. It could be almost anything."

Rick looked at Eli. "You think whoever shot her also took time out to beat her?"

"I don't know, but it's possible, isn't it? I still can't figure out why anyone would have taken a shot at her in the first place. If someone was crazy or stupid enough to do that, who's to say he wasn't crazy and stupid enough to stomp on her some before he left?"

Josie saw a glimmer of tightly controlled fury in the Lupine's eyes and suddenly felt very thankful that she hadn't done anything to harm anyone in his pack. She watched very cautiously as he visibly reined in his temper and worked to form a reasonably level sentence.

"Is there any way that you would be able to tell how she sustained the injuries that caused the internal bleeding?"

"Like I told Eli, not without shaving her down, which I'm hesitant to do." She wrinkled her nose. "The bruising under her fur might tell me what kind of weapon was used, but then again it might not, and I don't want to stress her out if I don't have to."

"If we can't think of anything else that will point us toward finding who did this—"

"If it comes down to that, I'll do it, but at the moment I'm more concerned with making Rosemary and Bill well than I am with finding out who shot her. Because I seriously doubt that it was that bullet that's been keeping her unconscious."

"No, that would be kind of a stretch," Rick admitted. "She should have turned as soon as she felt the bullet."

"Maybe by the time she felt it, she was already being kicked." Eli caught Josie's glare and corrected himself. "Already experiencing the effects of blunt-force trauma."

"It would have to be a hell of first blow to keep her down." Rick sounded skeptical.

"That's why I wanted to ask about the last few days," Josie said. "Bill told us that he hadn't seen Rosemary acting at all unusual before the shooting, but if she was already sick before she was shot, her body could have been so busy fighting off an infection that she just didn't have the strength to shift after the bullet hit her."

The Lupine shook his head. "Lupines don't get sick."

"Never?"

"Nope."

"Never in the history of Otherkind?" she insisted.

Rick looked exasperated. "No, of course there have been incidents, but they're rare. The illnesses that Lupines are susceptible to aren't infections. They're things like cancers and genetic disorders. The occasional poisoning. We don't just catch colds."

"What about insect-borne diseases? Things like Lyme disease, or West Nile?"

He shook his head.

"Parasitic infections? Malaria?"

"Nope."

"Tapeworm?"

"Nope."

"*Fleas?*"

That at least got a laugh. "Sorry, Doc, but Lupines have immune systems that make hospital clean rooms look like incubators of the black plague. We just don't get human diseases."

"What about canine diseases?"

"What do you mean?"

"What about rabies?"

Rick jerked back in surprise. "You think Rosemary might have *rabies*?"

Josie slumped back in her chair. "No, the symptoms don't fit. Well, Bill's episode this afternoon might, but Rosemary's don't at all. I just had to ask because you were starting to piss me off."

"Well, I hate to be the bearer of bad tidings, but I've never heard of a Lupine with rabies, either."

"You know, I could really get to hate people like you."

"Have you considered the possibility that Rosemary doesn't have an infection? Maybe it actually is some kind of poison. Or cancer."

"I've considered it, but it doesn't make any sense. All of her organs are working normally, which pretty much rules out poisons. They generally work by shutting down one or more of those. And poison wouldn't explain her astronomically high white blood cell count. That's the leading indicator of infection in all living species that I know of. I mean, sure, cancer can do the wacky to your blood cells, but I've run the ultrasound over almost every inch of her over the last couple of days, and there's not a tumor in sight. And again, cancer generally likes your organs, your lymph nodes, or your bone marrow. All of Rosemary's are just fine."

Rick drained his beer and set the empty bottle on the coffee table. "There is one other possibility."

"I'm all ears."

"There could be some kind of magic involved."

Eli looked at the Alpha. "Like a curse?"

Rick shrugged. "It's worth thinking about."

"But I'm sure I would have smelled that. She didn't smell tainted, and I carried her in my arms. I drove her in my car. I definitely would have smelled it if there were black magic involved."

"Why? It's not like you have a nose like a Lupine. Can you think of anything else that would do this?"

Josie leaned forward. "If it were a curse—and I have no idea how a curse would do that, since I know less about magic than I do about shifters—how would that explain Bill's symptoms?"

"You're certain Bill has the same symptoms?"

Eli nodded. "I think we have to assume it. He shifted last night so he could stay with Rosemary at the clinic, but he promised Josie that he'd shift back and leave before her staff arrived for the morning. And that clearly didn't happen."

"Instead he went a little crazy and tried to attack anyone who got near Rosemary's cage."

"Plus, when I had to restrain him later, I scratched a hole in his side, and it showed no signs of healing until Josie sewed it up."

Rick's eyes widened. "He had to have stitches?"

"Did we leave that out? Yeah. Fifteen of them. I counted while I put them in."

"That's . . . unsettling. It was strange enough when it was just Rosemary, but to hear that it's happened to two members of the pack . . ."

"Right," Josie agreed. At the moment, she agreed heartily. She didn't like the current situation at all. "So would a curse be able to do that? And could it explain Sammy Paulson, too? I mean, I didn't think that magic was contagious."

"If you've ruled out illness . . ."

"But I haven't ruled it out," Josie protested. "I just can't figure it out."

The Lupine ran impatient fingers over his short, dark hair. "Well, I'm as baffled by the idea that it could be some sort of contagious illness as you are that it might be black magic. I can't wrap my mind around it."

"So what do we do now?"

"I said I didn't smell magic," Eli said slowly, clearly as confused as the others, "but that doesn't mean it wasn't there. Maybe I missed it. Somehow."

Rick shook his head. "I doubt it, my friend. As much as I enjoy poking at you, I trust your senses. If you didn't smell magic, either it wasn't there or it was something neither of us has any experience with."

"And that leaves us where?"

"I'm not entirely sure, but maybe we should consult with someone who's more of an expert than either of us."

"You mean bring in a magic user?"

"I'd suggest a witch. They usually have more experience with curses, and a generally broader knowledge of unpleasant wishes directed at others. The plus side to that, of course, being that they also know a great deal about getting rid of those kinds of wishes."

"Is there anyone in town here who could help?" Josie asked. "I know we have a couple of magic users, but of all the witches I can think of, none of them seems to fit the bill. I mean, Mrs. Harrigan has been around the longest, but I thought she mostly played around with herbs and potions."

"She does." Eli pulled a small pad—a cop's notebook—out of his breast pocket and jotted something down. "No one local has the juice for this. I know a few people in Seattle, though. I can ask one of them. Or better yet, ask if they can recommend someone in Portland."

"Please." Josie pulled both her feet up into the chair with her and crossed her legs tailor-fashion. If she could have curled into an exhausted little ball, she'd have done that. She looked toward Bruce's slumbering form with envy. "I'd just as soon not have two possibly contagious not-quite-wolves locked in my kennel for very much longer." She grimaced at Rick. "It just doesn't seem right, you know? But I don't have anywhere else to put them."

"Well, I'd rather that kenneling Lupines didn't become a new trend," the Alpha said ruefully, "but if they're really that ill, they should stay where they are, under observation and where they can continue to receive care. Plus, we don't want any more incidents like the one with Bill this morning."

"True that. I'm crossing my fingers that a witch can figure this out, though. Figure it out and fix it."

Eli looked toward Josie, and his expression softened into something somehow comforting. "The call is my top priority."

Rick rose to his feet. "And while he does that, I'll go bother the pack elders. Ask a few questions. Like I said, I don't know of any contagious illnesses that infect Lupines, but maybe there's something floating around in our history that I don't know about. It's worth a shot. And just in case, I'll talk to some friends and family of Bill, Rosie, and Sammy. Maybe someone will remember noticing something odd with a little more prompting."

Josie nodded. She knew she should stand, too, but she just felt drained. "I appreciate that. Give a call if you find anything. The number for the clinic rings up here, too."

"I will." He smiled at Josie, offered Eli a brief salute, and let himself out the front door.

Josie watched him go, but it wasn't until the lock snapped closed behind him and silence descended on the apartment that she realized what his leaving meant: She was now all alone with Sheriff Elijah Pace.

Her stomach gave a low, lazy flip.

Hesitantly, she looked over at Eli, only to find his gaze already on her. He leaned back on the sofa in a lazy sprawl, arms spread on the cushions behind him, but the look in his eyes was anything but lazy. Those green, glittering pools fixed on her with an unnerving intensity, giving her the nearly overwhelming urge to touch her hair, her face, her clothes, to search for something off. What else could he be staring at with such focus?

Josie caught herself twisting her fingers together and jerked them quickly apart, shoving her hands under her legs and pinning them there.

"Um, would you like another beer?" she asked.

Eli shook his head and reached toward her, his palm up and open, a compelling invitation. "Come sit with me for a few minutes."

She thought about saying no. Or, to be more accurate, she thought about how she probably should say no. She'd only known him for a couple of days, after all. Okay, she might have known of him for a lot longer than that, and she might have occasionally had a thought here or there about the fact that he was the best-looking man she'd ever seen within an hour's drive of Stone Creek and how if he ever happened to trip while walking past her and land on top of her, she wouldn't have screamed for help. But that had all been hypothetical. The sexual tension crackling between them . . . that didn't feel hypothetical at all. It felt magnetic.

It might have been easier if she'd been able to say that she moved across the room to him in a trance, as if he were a vampire exerting some sort of mind control over her. That would have been a cop-out, though. Not to mention a lie. She was exquisitely aware of every movement she made as she uncurled her legs, rose from her chair, and walked slowly and carefully around the end of the coffee table toward him. She felt the wide hem of her yoga pants sway around her ankles, felt the nap of the blue-and-green area rug and then the cool smoothness of the wooden floorboards beneath her feet. She felt the way the thick sofa cushions gave beneath her as she sat beside him and the pull of gravity when his heavier weight made a deeper depression that her body rolled naturally into.

Then she felt the hardness of his muscular body beside her, felt his right arm slip off the back of the sofa to curl around her and urge her against his chest. She felt the warmth of his breath against her skin and the warm, firm pressure of his mouth pressing against hers.

And then she felt everything.

CHAPTER TEN

Eli felt like every wish he'd ever made while blowing out his birthday candles had finally come true. All at once.

While he was pretty sure this hadn't been his exact wish the year he'd turned five, he didn't really think that mattered. It sure as hell should have been.

Josie melted against him like warm chocolate. Since he thought of that precise image every time he looked into those dark velvet eyes of hers, he thought the metaphor was particularly appropriate. She almost tasted like chocolate, too. The good stuff, not an ordinary Hershey bar, or the cheap stuff you could buy at the local drugstore, but the rich, dark, exotic concoctions that made a person understand what had inspired the ancient Mayans to make blood sacrifices to the cacao plant. She tasted like a sacred nectar, spicy, fruity, complex, and beguiling. He wanted to consume her and protect her all at once.

His arm drew her closer until she had to lean across his chest to return the kiss. The pressure of her sweetly rounded breasts against him pulled a deep rumble of satisfaction from his throat. Josie jerked her head back and stared down at him, her expression bemused and her lips slightly swollen.

"Did you just *purr*?" she asked in astonishment.

Eli felt his mouth curve in a slow smile. "I can't help it. That's what cats do when a pretty girl curls up in their laps."

She laughed softly and her gaze dropped to his mouth. She licked her lips. "Somehow, I think you have that backward."

"I'm too big to sit in your lap." He touched the tip of his nose to hers, wrapped both arms around her, and lifted her off the sofa, resettling her across his thighs. "But you fit just perfectly in mine."

Josie gave a purr of her own, her eyelashes drifting down even as she raised her face to his. Eli had no intention of refusing the invitation. He took her mouth again, drinking deeply of her unique, intoxicating flavor.

He thought for a moment that he could kiss her forever. He had almost forgotten how such a simple intimacy could serve as an end in and of itself. When was the last time he'd savored the intricate dance of tongue against tongue, the sweet yielding of a woman's mouth? When had he last felt this peculiar tightness in his chest, this bone-deep knowledge that life and the universe would be just perfect if the woman in his arms would simply stay with him?

Never. He had never felt anything like this.

Itchy fingers sought relief in the cool, heavy silk of her hair. With a tug, he pulled out the elastic and tossed it away. The damp tresses slid away from her crown like dark flows of lava, slick and slow and just as fascinating. Eli slid his fingers under the thick curtain, sifted through the smooth strands, and cupped the back of her skull. The curve of her head seemed to fit his palm perfectly, and somehow his thumb felt right at home in the soft, tender hollow where the top of her spine emerged. It rubbed against the downy little hairs that clung to the skin there, eliciting a broken moan from the mouth of his mate.

His mate.

The word reverberated in his mind, opening door like a master key. It didn't matter that this was only the second kiss they'd shared, that they'd never spoken before he'd barged into her clinic Saturday night. It didn't matter that he was Feline and she was human. Josephine Barrett was his mate. It was what she would always be, what she had always been, even if neither of them had realized it before this moment.

It just was.

Eli shuddered when her small, graceful hands slid up the front of his chest, glided over his shoulders, and pulled herself tighter against him. Everything about her aroused him, but the feel of her touching him nearly drove him over the edge. His thumb pressed delicately against the depression at the base of her skull and she moaned again. He thrilled to know that such a tiny, simple movement had the power to unravel her, like a magic button he could push to have her melting and arching against him. He fought a fierce battle against the temptation to press again and again to see how high the innocent touch could take her. Another time, he might try it, but this, this first time, was for exploring. Later, he would learn to linger.

His free hand was already way ahead of him.

It had lingered on her waist after shifting her to his lap, then drifted slowly to her hip. Now it reversed the trip, sliding across the curve of her hip and up toward her waist. But this time, his fingers twitched aside the hem of her T-shirt and delved beneath, stuttering at the silky smooth texture of her skin. His palm urged him upward, but his fingers couldn't be budged. Not yet. They were enthralled by the feel of her, by the gentle curve of her waist, a sweet, lush valley between the slopes of hip and torso. It seemed like such an innocent place to touch, a place anyone might put a hand in friendship or to give direction; yet he felt the way her muscles jumped and her breath hitched when he rubbed that little patch of skin and all at once, the idea of anyone else touching her made him want to scream out a warning. No one else should ever know how soft she was, how tender, how perfect.

He could feel the rhythm of her breath changing, growing faster and shallower. He sensed the subtle tension invading her limbs and gave thanks that she seemed to be responding as eagerly as he. She pressed herself forward, flattening her breasts against his chest and twisting her hips until she faced him from neck to knees.

Impatiently, his hands shifted, the fingers at her nape falling away to curl around the back of her knee. The other followed suit and guided her to shift again, until her legs parted and her knees settled on the sofa cushions on either side of his hips. He winced as she pulled away and held his breath while he waited for her reaction. He searched her face for clues, watching as uncertainty, arousal, caution, and desire all flickered across her face like images on a movie screen. Then she smiled at him, and his heart squeezed in his chest at the sight.

Something else felt squeezed when she reached for the hem of her T-shirt and her smile turned wicked. "You won't think I'm cheap if you see me naked before the third date, will you?"

Eli shook his head and felt his mouth curve irrepressibly when she crossed her arms over her chest and pull the top off over her head.

"Promise?"

His hands returned to her waist, lighting there like homing pigeons. "I promise."

Her hair swung forward when she bent toward him, falling around him like a curtain, and Eli groaned helplessly. When her lips settled on his, the groan turned into a purr. His hands slid up her back, pulling her toward him and tracing the graceful curve of her spine with impetuous fingertips.

Josie leaned into the kiss for a moment, then pulled back again and reached for the buttons that ran down the front of his dark cotton shirt. "Fair is fair," she whispered.

How he kept his hands off her while she unfastened that endless row of buttons, he would never know. He managed it, though, even when she made him lift his hips so she could tug the tails out of his jeans and spread the plackets wide over his chest. He didn't even flinch when she sat back on his thighs and ran her gaze over his chest like a child inspecting a long-anticipated Christmas present. He just hoped it would make her happy.

She stared for a moment longer, then gave a tug and finished stripping the shirt from him, dropping it to the floor behind her to join her own. Then she answered every prayer he'd ever uttered.

Wrapping her slender fingers around his wrists, she pulled his hands away from her back and guided them to her breasts, using her own fingers to wrap his around the soft mounds.

Eli thought he might even have thanked the Gods. Aloud.

Josie just grinned and smoothed her palms over the hair-roughened surface of his chest. When she leaned forward, his fingers tightened around her breasts, and she only sighed and pressed herself deeper into his grasp. Her lips brushed his like butterfly wings, once, then twice. Then her tongue swept out to tease the corner of his mouth.

"Eli?" she breathed, even though it was all he could do to remember that simple act.

His only response was a muffled groan.

"Eli," she murmured, her tongue darting to the opposite corner of his mouth. "I want you."

He squeezed his eyes shut, then dragged them open again when the horrible thought occurred to him that this might possibly turn out to be some kind of dream.

"Eli." More kisses, this time strung together with a series of nibbles along the curve of his lower lip. The woman was obviously trying to drive him absolutely out of his mind. "Eli, would you make love to me? Pretty please?"

Tomorrow, he might learn that the shriek Josie uttered when he bolted off the sofa with her clasped against his chest had been heard two miles away, but at the moment it didn't matter. In fact, the idea never occurred to him. He was too busy running for the bedroom as if his life and libido depended on it. He had the horrible suspicion that in this case, they just might.

The trip from the living room to the bedroom happened so fast that Josie only realized she'd missed it when her back bounced against her queen-size mattress with a dull thud. Eli Pace, it turned out, didn't believe in wasting time.

Well, that was all right, she decided, because at this particular moment, Josie decided that she didn't, either.

She'd never done anything like this before, but she didn't intend to let a little thing like that stop her. Oh, she'd had sex before—duh, she was thirty-two years old, and this was 2010, not 1810—but her experiences with the act before had all been in the context of relationships. The kind with more than forty-eight hours under their belts.

And actually, she hadn't really had that many lovers. There had been her college sweetheart first—Jeffrey— and that had lasted three years, until he realized that she really intended to follow through with that whole vet school business, and that it would mean another four whole years of classes and studying and exams and other things that she would refuse to blow off just to spend time with him. He'd dumped her the day after she'd gotten her acceptance letter from Davis. Next had come William. He'd been more of a friend than a lover, but they had fallen in and out of bed during most of veterinary school, when neither of them had been able to spare the energy to sustain a real romantic relationship. And after that, there had been Ian.

Ian had had possibilities. She'd met him during her residency in California, when he'd brought his cat to the emergency room after it swallowed a piece of string with a needle on one end. The needle had gotten lodged in Kitty's stomach, and one of Josie's mentors had performed the surgery to remove it. Ian had taken Josie out for breakfast to celebrate. They'd dated for a while and ended up living together for a year. Then they'd just ended.

Since then, she'd been too busy for a relationship, and after moving back to Stone Creek she'd realized that the idea of having anything else in her hometown just skeeved her. After all, a good percentage of the population had known her when she'd been in diapers, and at least a few of those had her parents' phone number and would be happy to call with reports on what little Josephine was up to *now*. No thanks.

The clinic had kept her busy enough that she hadn't missed having a lover all that much. She had always enjoyed her own company, always felt complete in and of herself, whether she happened to be in a relationship or not. She might miss having someone to come home to from time to time, but she never felt really lonely. She never got worked up over it.

But one look at Eli Pace and something inside Josie had gotten very worked up indeed.

She let herself sink back into the softness of her downy bedcover as Eli shifted over her like a heavy, heated shadow. She couldn't contain the slow shifting of her lips or the anticipation-filled smile that settled there. She didn't particularly want to. This moment, she had decided, was meant to be seized, to be grasped by both hands and clung to for all she was worth. When Eli looked at her with hungry green eyes and an expression of mingled awe and debauchery, she felt as if she were worth quite a lot. A jewel beyond price.

Letting one arm rest against the pillow above her head, Josie lifted her other hand and cupped the back of his neck. She drew him to her slowly, a journey he hardly resisted, savoring the anticipation, the quiver-inducing knowledge of the power and pleasure of his kiss. When their lips met, she could barely decide which she enjoyed more, the kiss itself, or the moment just before it, when his eyes went dark and hazy and unfocused with desire.

Then his tongue surged forward and Josie forgot about every moment except this one.

Her hand slid from his neck to his shoulder, kneading her way across thick ropes of muscle and sinew. She adored the size and strength of him, the way he could *be* so intimidating and yet not intimidate her at all. The only thing she felt when he loomed over her like a conquering barbarian was a surge of arousal. And, unexpectedly, of joy.

She stroked his shoulder, his back, the ridge of his collarbone, and back again. A hum of pure pleasure welled up inside her and vibrated against his lips, into his mouth. He caught the sound and swallowed it, returning it was a raspy purr.

God, she would never look at a happy house cat the same way. Ever. Again.

His torso arched away from her, out of reach of her embrace, and she protested with a little moan, then realized he had no intention of breaking the kiss and returned her hand to the back of his neck. She wondered if he felt the same pleasure that she did at a teasing pressure just there, so she tried it and felt the increased ardor of his kiss. Not quite the same, she decided, but hardly what she would term a failure.

He distracted her then with busy nimble hands. His fingers hooked in the waistband of her trousers and tugged at the stretchy cloth, easing the fabric down over her hips as if he meant to take his time. Whether he intended to savor the moment or hoped to keep from startling her, Josie didn't care. She canted her hips up to help, and once the waist cleared her hips, she used her feet and legs to kick the garment free.

She felt Eli's surprise, then his satisfaction. His kiss deepened and roughened for the space of a few breathless heartbeats before he pulled away and smiled down at her with those hypnotic cat's eyes. Her gaze locked with his, followed it as it slid from her to her lips, her throat, her breasts. Lingered. Moved on over the tiny curve of her belly, the round sweep of her hip. Lingered again on the neat little thatch of curls at her mound. Traced the line of her legs all the way down to the cotton-candy polish on her dainty bare toes.

Her breath caught and held, the most feminine part of her waiting for his approval. He gave it with a sigh of utter satisfaction.

"Glorious," he breathed, and bent to her mouth once more.

Josie welcomed him and returned his kiss with ardent fervor, but the kiss was no longer enough for her. She wanted more, wanted him to touch her, to take her, to move inside and become part of her. And she didn't want to wait any longer.

He responded to the urging of her hands at his sides and shifted, pressing her legs apart with a denim-clad knee and sliding between them. The touch of the rough fabric against her skin made her shiver, made her feel somehow more naked than she had when he'd looked at her, but there was no embarrassment. She felt like his description of her—glorious. She felt powerful and feminine and more than a little wicked. She felt like a little piece of seduction itself.

When he settled his weight above her, she welcomed it, wrapping her arms around his back and hooking one leg over the back of his. The action brought his hips into perfect alignment with hers, and they both froze at the sensation.

Grasping his face in both hands, Josie pulled back far enough to catch his gaze and whispered, "Okay, jeans have got to go. Now."

Oddly, Eli offered no protests.

He leapt off the bed, stripped, and levered himself back over her in three seconds, flat. This time when his legs slid between hers and their hips aligned, Josie didn't just shiver, she groaned, a long, drawn-out sound of unbearable pleasure. He felt so perfect, so *right,* lying above her. She didn't know how she'd be able to handle the pleasure of having him inside her, but she'd find the strength. God help her, she'd find it somewhere.

Her head tipped back when he lifted his mouth from hers and dragged it over the curve of her throat. She would give him whatever access he wanted, to whatever part of her he wanted to touch. When his lips skidded across the length of her collarbone, she sighed and kneaded the broad muscles of his back, but when his mouth closed over the tip of one breast and began to suckle, she arched like a drawn bow and cried out his name.

He grunted in satisfaction and scraped her nipple with sharp, careful teeth. The sensation made her vibrate, now less a bow than the perfectly tensed string of a cello, offering up a low, rich hum of sound. He reacted by thrusting more sensation upon her, every touch twisting the coil of arousal tighter, every caress designed to rob her of her sanity.

She couldn't say he played her body like an instrument, because she'd never seen a musician turn so suddenly ruthless. She had heard violins weep, but not like her body wept for him, moisture pooling in her core and spilling forth to beg him to join with her. A single, clear note of sanity somewhere far back in the recesses of her overheated mind urged her to turn the tables on him, to beat him at his own game, to touch and tease and tantalize until he lost all control. That was what he was doing to her, and sauce for the goose, after all . . .

But she couldn't. The minute spark of that thought drowned and gurgled under the onslaught of pleasure. The idea had barely formed when his mouth shifted to her other breast and sly, skilled fingers rounded the curve of her thigh to dive between, sliding within her on a stroke of ruthless giving.

Her body contracted like a pill bug, curling into itself as a mechanism of self-defense. She had to protect herself against this terrible pleasure. Against the way his fingers shifted and searched and uncovered her every intimate secret. She couldn't bear the need, the trembling, aching, yawning abyss of need that grew inside of her like a black hole, threatening to consume her from within.

Josie gasped. She screamed. She may have begged. In the end she couldn't remember. All she could remember was that she clawed at him with desperate hands, drew her legs open and up as if she could swallow him whole. She felt his touch, heard his deep, raspy voice attempting to soothe her, but her hunger controlled her, and it refused to be soothed. It wanted to be satisfied, and nothing else.

Finally, quickly, exquisitely, her granted her mercy. His fingers withdrew from her quivering sheath and he grasped her hips with both hands. His fingers dug into her soft flesh, biting hard enough to leave marks, if she had cared about such things. Panting, his hot, sweet breath like a blessing against her cheek, he jerked her hips up and plunged inside her, diving deep to her heart and shouting his pleasure to the ceiling.

Immediately and perfectly, they began moving together, the rhythm instantly finding them as if this weren't the first time they had been lovers, but the hundredth, the millionth. She yielded where he advanced, gained ground where he retreated. She clung to his back like the last steady handhold in a quaking galaxy, and he gripped her hips as if to release her would mean losing his own sanity.

Rising and falling together, they became one being, a single living thing made of heat and tenderness, pleasure and agony, heart and soul and mind and breath. Each lost all sense of self and a separate thing. They were only *us,* and as they threw themselves off the edge of the peak, hands and hearts joined, they knew they would never again go back to what they had been, alone and individual. Part of them had fused in that blinding moment of pleasure, and the bond that sealed it could never be undone.

Exp. 10-1017.03
Log 03-00133

Locating the proper radio tracking equipment proves difficult. Nothing has yet
met the high standards required for the
experiment. May have to proceed with
Stage 4 in absence of equipment and
recruit larger number of technicians to
perform subject tracking duties.

Stage 4 product will be complete within
the next 12–24 hours. Modifications to
the active strain appear in vitro to
provide hoped-for results. Laboratory
testing will be bypassed in favor of
active field testing. With the end goal
in sight and the tools for success at
hand, it would be a disservice to soci-
ety, to *humanity*, to withhold such an
important scientific advancement.

As an aside, the nonscientific partici-
pants involved in the project remain a
disappointment. Science will provide our
solution.

CHAPTER ELEVEN

Josie woke at three o'clock, suddenly and completely. One minute, she had been sleeping hard and deep, like a toddler after a day at the park, and the next her eyes flew open, her brain engaged, and the idea of any further sleep became instantly and completely ludicrous. She knew why it had happened, too, because she woke with the idea on the tip of her tongue.

Slides.

After seeing the results of Rosemary's initial blood tests, Josie had ordered Ben to make up some slides of the Lupine's so that she could examine it under the microscope, but things had gone so crazy since then that she'd never gotten around to viewing them. Those slides might hold an important clue about the Lupine's condition. Plus, if she prepared another set of slides with samples of Bill's blood, she could compare the two and confirm or disprove the idea that they were infected with the same illness.

Gah! Why hadn't she thought of this before?

Reaching for the heavy blanket draped at her waist, she began to lift it away so she could rise when she realized that down duvets didn't usually feel quite so . . . firm. Memory came flooding back—along with a blush—

and Josie knew exactly what had been keeping her warm half the night. Not her duvet, but a very special and efficient furnace named Eli Pace.

She subsided and turned her head to gaze at him, resting quietly on the pillow beside her. He looked more relaxed in sleep, but no younger. His face had too many ridges and angles to appear innocent, even while unconscious, but he did appear pretty content, the corners of his mouth curved just barely upward in an expression of satisfaction. Go figure.

Josie had to admit, she'd woken feeling pretty satisfied herself, at least as far as her body was concerned. Her mind still dwelled on the medical mystery before her, but every muscle in her body felt deliciously limber and stretched. By dinnertime, that would probably turn into overextended and aching, but for the moment she would just savor the pleasant sensations.

She had certainly savored them last night.

Blinking up into the darkness, Josie felt a smile curving her lips. She had absolutely no regrets about last night. How could she? She'd never felt anything like that. She couldn't even decide if it qualified as mere sex. Surely something that stupendous, that mind bending, had to have a less mundane title? She couldn't think what it would be, but it definitely deserved something more. Otherwise people would think it had been just the same as all her other experiences. They would think they might have had similar experiences themselves, and she couldn't allow the world to delude itself in that fashion. What had happened between her and Eli last night had transcended the realm of physical intimacy. It had turned into something else entirely.

Josie's smile slipped away as it dawned on her that she couldn't think exactly what.

Pushing the odd and unsettling thought away, Josie returned her attention to the question of the slides and realized that she was just too impatient to wait until morning to see them. Technically, she told herself, it was morning. The wee hours still counted as morning, otherwise they would have called them something else.

It took about ten minutes, a lot of excruciating slowness and incredibly gradual movements, to extract herself from Eli's grip without waking him, but Josie managed it. She slid from the bed with a sigh—was that relief, or wistfulness?—grabbed her yoga pants from the floor beside the bed, and padded silently back into the living room for her shirt.

From his position on the sofa, Bruce opened one eye, acknowledged his mistress's presence, then went back to sleep with a disconcertingly human sound of disgust.

Josie dressed quickly, shoved her feet into the fleece-lined rubber clogs she wore as cold-weather slippers, and was headed for the door when she realized that if Eli woke up while she was gone, her absence might give him the wrong impression. She didn't want him to think she'd run away from him, after all.

Taking a moment, she found a bright yellow sticky pad, jotted down a note, and affixed it carefully to the doorjamb between the bedroom and the living room. She even left it sticking conspicuously out into the doorway so that he couldn't miss it. Satisfied, she cast one glance at his sleeping form, then slipped out of the apartment and padded down the stairs to the back door of the clinic.

It took a few seconds to let herself in and deactivate

the alarm before she flipped on the lights. She tended to leave that for last since the buttons on the alarm pad glowed in the dark and she could see them just fine without the overheads. Once the lights were on, she dropped her keys on the counter and made her way to the slide prep area.

Conscience demanded that she make a brief detour to the kennels to check on Rosemary and Bill. They slept side by side in separate cages now, each still unconscious, their conditions unchanged. At least they had been able to extubate Bill just before closing last night. Once the sux wore off and they had weaned him onto a different sedative, the danger of having his breathing stop had lessened to negligible levels. She felt certain he was more comfortable breathing on his own.

Since he was unconscious, though, Josie decided to take advantage of the opportunity. She gathered up a needle and empty syringe and carefully drew a couple of milliliters of blood for some slides before she headed back into the other room. Although her impatience to see the slides Ben had created for Rosemary nagged at her, she took the time to prepare five new slides using the sample she'd just taken from Bill before she turned on the microscope and pulled out the small, blue plastic box beside it, carefully labeled with Rosemary's name and patient number, the date, and the number of slides it contained.

Josie's mouth quirked when she saw there were exactly five slides. Ben had been with her for almost four years now. He knew how she liked to work.

Pulling out the first small glass rectangle, she positioned it under the scope and fit on the slide clip. Then she chose a lens, peered through the eyepiece, and began to adjust the focus. When everything came into view, she would begin to scan the smear systematically, looking for foreign bodies, abnormal cells, or any other irregularities.

That was the plan, at any rate, but it turned out to be unnecessary. As soon as the cells came into focus, she found what she was looking for. She just couldn't quite tell what to make of it. Brows knit together, she stared at the slide until her temples began to throb. She fiddled endlessly with the fine-adjustment knob of the microscope, but the view never varied. Neither did it change when she swapped the first slide for the second. Or the third. Or the fourth. She had just inserted the fifth slide when a hand on her shoulder had her jumping out of her skin.

Josie spun around on her stool and glared ferociously at Eli. "Damn it, you nearly gave me a heart attack. Sneak up on me like that again, and I'm going to tie a bell around your neck. I swear to God."

The sheriff, dressed in nothing but his jeans, his feet bare, merely quirked an eyebrow and leaned forward, kissing her directly on her frowning lips.

"You know, if this is what starting work at three fifteen in the morning does for your temper," he drawled, "you might want to consider changing your hours."

"Ha-ha." Josie crossed her arms over her chest, but her expression softened. "I guess you saw my note."

"I did. I also appear to have pissed off your dog by walking past him while he was trying to catch up on his beauty sleep. He gave me a very dirty look, which I got the feeling I was meant to pass along to you on his behalf." He leaned a hip against the side of the counter and mirrored the set of her arms. "But the note somehow failed to explain what could possibly be so important that you had to come to work to deal with it in the middle of the night, rather than waiting until you actually have to be at work in—" He glanced at his watch. "—three more hours. Did something happen with one of the Lupines?"

"No, I just remembered the slides. I asked Ben on Sunday morning to prep some slides with samples of Rosemary's blood for me to look at. Since we couldn't seem to find the source of her infection, I thought putting them under the scope might help me figure out what was going on. Maybe I'd even be able to spot the bacteria. Though, given the power of the equipment I keep on hand, that wasn't very likely."

"So were you pleasantly surprised?"

"I was surprised, but I'm not sure how pleasant it was." She gestured at the scope. "Take a look."

"Even though I have no idea what I'm looking for?"

"Just tell me what you see."

Eli nudged her out of the way and bent his eye down to the scope. He peered inside for a minute, then shrugged. "It looks like a bunch of tomatoes, half of which recently served as ammo during a pretty vicious food fight." He straightened and looked at her. "Is that supposed to mean something?"

Frustrated, Josie ran her hands through her loose hair and tugged it absently. "Yes. It means that Rosemary's red blood cells have lysed. Basically, something has broken open the cell membrane and let the contents spill out."

"Okay. Well, that's something, then. What can cause it?"

"Usually, it's one of three things: a virus, an enzyme, or a shift in the osmotic pressure of the cell."

"So, then you were right about an infection. Unless you think it was . . . one of those other things." The confused expression he wore told Josie that Eli wasn't quite getting this.

"I don't know! That's the problem. Technically, the hemolysis—the destroyed red cells—means that I should diagnose Rosemary with hemolytic anemia."

"Hemolytic anemia?"

"A disease where red blood cells are destroyed prematurely, and the bone marrow can't replace them fast enough. It can be inherited or acquired, but if it were inherited it should have presented a long time before now. And she just doesn't present the classic signs of a chronically anemic patient."

"Which are?"

"Fatigue is one, and I think we can assume she has that, but otherwise, nothing. Her skin and gums pinked up after surgery, so they're not pale anymore. She's not showing any signs of jaundice or abdominal pain, her urine is fine, and her heart sounds strong."

"But?"

"But it's driving me crazy. I need to know what's causing the hemolysis and why she's not reacting to it the way every other living creature would."

Josie paced while she talked, her hands gesturing and her expressions shifting constantly. At least she did until Eli grabbed one of her hands in his and pulled her into his arms.

"Can you run any tests to tell you if there are problems with the enzymes and whatever else you mentioned before?"

Josie sighed and allowed herself to lean against his

broad chest. She had to admit, it felt good. Comforting. Strengthening. "I've run every test I'm equipped to do, and so far everything except for her white blood cell count is normal. Well, her white cells and now her red cells."

"So you still think this is some kind of infection?"

"That's what my gut keeps telling me. I don't know why. I mean, she doesn't have any of the classic signs of that, either. No fever, no redness at any of her wound sites. Nothing."

Eli nodded toward the microscope. "You said your equipment wasn't powerful enough for you to see any bacteria on those slides. Do you think someone else with better equipment might be able to?"

"Sure," she said dully, "and I can send samples to a microbiology lab, but it will probably take weeks for those results to come back. By then, it may be too late to help her."

"I might be able to help with that." She gave him a skeptical look and he smiled. "Not personally, but I have a few useful friends, one of whom happens to work for the military. He's a scientist, and there's a chance either he or someone he works with could do me a favor and look at something a little quicker than in a few weeks."

Hope sprang up like crabgrass in Josie's chest. "Really? That would be so amazing. He won't want my slides, though. I'll pack up some fresh samples for you to send him. I'll send copies of my case files, too. If there is evidence of an infection, he'll want to know about the antibiotics I've administered. And I'll send Bill's blood, too, as soon as I check out his slides, but I'm sure they're going to look just the same as Rosemary's. I should start that. I need to get to work."

She leaned up and kissed him enthusiastically, but her mind was already on her task. She tried to twist out of his arms and get back to the microscope.

He held firm.

"In a minute," he drawled, and his green eyes glittered at her with a newly familiar intensity. "The slides and the patients and the microscopes will still be there later. Right now, there's some work that *I* need to get started on."

Against her will, Josie felt herself softening and melting already. Her mind might be focused on other things, but her body was clearly focused only on him. With a mental shrug, she decided that he was right about the work still being there in another hour or so. Letting herself relax, she slid her hands from his chest where they had been trying futilely to push him away, and wrapped them around his neck. She pressed her body against his and raised an eyebrow in inquiry.

"I might take offense to being labeled as 'work,' you know," she purred, running her nails over the back of his scalp until he echoed the sound.

"You prefer to think of yourself as play?" His hands slid under the hem of her T-shirt and skimmed over her belly, making her muscles clench. "As in, let's play doctor?"

Josie snorted a laugh. "I don't want to think about what it would mean to play doctor with a veterinarian." Then his hands cupped her breasts and the laughter died in her throat. "Besides, I'm always a doctor. I think I'd rather play cops and robbers."

Eli chuckled against her throat and scraped the sensitive skin with his teeth. "Does that mean I should go get my handcuffs?"

She flicked open the button on his jeans and grinned up at the ceiling tiles. "No, I'll go easy on you this time. But I warn you, if you resist arrest, I might have to get rough."

With a throaty growl, Eli spun around, lifted her to sit on the edge of the counter, and tugged her yoga pants down to her ankles. After that, she didn't think about work for another *two* hours.

Eli felt mellow and limber as he strode into his office on Tuesday morning. He might not have slept all that long last night—or this morning—but what he had done had left him feeling energized. It also helped that he wouldn't be the only officer on duty all day today. Jim Cooper would be working with him early in the day, and Mike Driscoll would take over in the evening, giving Eli time to deal with the administrative details of his job. He swore the damn things bred like rabbits every time he stepped away from his desk.

Having backup also meant he'd have time to make a few phone calls. Two of those topped his list of priorities. Out of habit, Eli emptied out his uniform pockets onto his desk before he settled behind it and reached for the phone. After a check of the clock, the first call skipped over a time zone to a number on the outskirts of Denver.

"Boyle."

"I thought it was 'Colonel Dr. Stephen James Boyle, sir!' these days," Eli said with a grin.

"Only to little girly boys like you, son," the voice on the other end of the line shot back. "How's it hangin', Pace? I haven't heard from you in a while."

"Hangin' low and happy. How 'bout yourself?"

"You know I don't like to brag. You still wearing a tin star in East Bumblefuck?"

"Northeast Bumblefuck, thanks. And it beats taking orders from a lowlife like you. I don't know how those idiots stand it. But then, I guess that's why they call them idiots." With the customary exchange of insults covered, Eli moved on to the point of his call. "Listen, Steve, I was wondering if you might be able to help me out with a little problem."

"You need me to write you a scrip for some penicillin?"

Eli rolled his eyes. "Wiseass. No, I need to know if you know anyone who could look at a couple of medical specimens for me."

There was a brief silence, then Steve spoke again. "Animal, vegetable, or mineral?"

"Animal. Mostly. I have something a little weird going on around here." Briefly, he outlined the story of Rosemary and Bill and their odd symptoms. "The vet is convinced it's some kind of an infection, but she said none of the normal cultures have come up positive. She thought a microbiology lab might be able to look at a blood sample and find a germ, if there really is one hiding there. But she's afraid that if she sends it to a commercial lab, the Lupines will be dead before she gets an answer."

Another pause stretched out before Stephen replied. "I could probably do it myself. I *do* have a lab, and I *am* a microbiologist, after all."

"Is that what you are?" Eli demanded. "Well, hell, I thought you were doing a study of the total force required to make a cadet airman shit his pants."

"That's just a hobby. Bugs are my job." The scientist's

voice sobered. "Listen, though, Eli, if the vet is right and the second Lupine contracted whatever this thing is from the first one after spending just a few hours in close quarters, that would mean it's a pretty volatile little microbe. You might want to suggest that both the patients be put into quarantine until you hear back from me. Better to be safe than sorry."

Eli frowned. "I'm not sure I like the sound of that. Would the clinic staff be in danger, do you think?"

"From what you've told me, I doubt it. If it is a virus or a bacteria of some kind, I suspect it must be infectious only to Lupines. Otherwise, after all this time, they'd probably already be infected. And after you were bitten by one of them, you'd already be showing symptoms." Stephen cleared his throat. "No, I'm probably being overly cautious, but it can't hurt to take a few extra precautions until we figure out just what's going on."

"Right," Eli agreed. "I want you to know that I really appreciate this, Steve. I'm gonna owe you one. Now, how am I supposed to get these blood samples to you? The faster the better."

"Talk to your vet friend. He ought to have materials for shipping biological samples. Have him overnight them to me."

"Her," Eli corrected. "Dr. Barrett is a she. Josephine."

Steve snorted. "Oh, so it's like that, is it? Here I thought you were motivated by community service, and it turns out you're just trying to get your dick wet."

The surge of anger that spilled over Eli surprised him. "Be careful where you step here, Boyle."

"Really?" The other man sounded incredulous. "Well,

I'm impressed. I apologize, to you and the lady in question. But I'll expect an invitation to the wedding."

Eli forced himself to relax. He knew Steve hadn't meant anything by his comment, just as he knew the other man didn't mean anything now. But that didn't mean he should feel so calm and even a little bit pleased at the idea of marrying Josie Barrett.

He fiddled with the keys and loose change he'd emptied onto the desk a few minutes ago. Oddly, the thinking about Josie always gave him the urge to do something with his hands.

"You'd come to my wedding?" he shot back, trying to sound casually amused and not convinced he had succeeded. "I didn't know you owned any good dresses."

"I've got a sassy little taffeta number that would be perfect. The blue really brings out my eyes."

Eli snorted and shifted the keys to the side, exposing a small vial of clear glass. The one he'd found in the hunter's blind. He'd forgotten all about it. He'd meant to tell Josie what he'd found as soon as he saw her yesterday, but he'd been a little distracted trying to save her from a crazed Lupine. Then there had been so many other things to deal with.

To make love to.

The vial had totally slipped his mind.

"Hey, one more thing," he said, shifting the phone against his ear. "You don't happen to have any chemists around there, do you?"

"Chemists?" Steve repeated. "You think you'll need to drug her before you propose?"

"Funny. No, but there's something else I'm going to slip into that package I send you. I found something near where the Lupine was shot. It looks to me like a medicine vial—you know, the kind of thing my flu shot comes out of—but it's missing its label. It might be unrelated, but I'd still like to know if someone can tell me what was in it."

"I'll . . . see what I can do." Pause. "Go ahead and send it over."

"Thanks, buddy. Like I said, I'm going to owe you for this."

"Just give me a chance to kiss the bride, and we'll call it even."

"Like hell. You'll be lucky if I let you dance with her."

Eli hung up with images of Josie in a long white dress whirling through his mind. They ought to inspire him to panic. Instead they just inspired him to imagine peeling her out of it and making love to her until she couldn't remember her own name.

Shaking his head to clear it of the distracting image, Eli checked the clock again and placed his second call. When he disconnected a few minutes later, he'd been cursed out thoroughly for calling at what was termed "the ass-crack of dawn," but he had the information he wanted. One final call and he had everything arranged. The Portland-based witch his friend from Seattle had recommended would drive out tomorrow morning. Luckily, her shop was closed on Wednesdays, so the trip would fit into her schedule. Plus, she'd sounded curious about their problem. She said she was looking forward to meeting them.

Thinking that he'd spoken on the phone more in the last hour than he had in the entire rest of his life, Eli punched in one more number, but this time he sat back in his chair and smiled as he listened to the rings.

"Stone Creek Animal Hospital. How can I help you?"

"You answer your own phone? Don't you pay people to do things like that?"

He could practically hear her grimace. "Thank God it's you. It was a reflex. I only realized what I was doing once it was too late to turn back. I was terrified that you were going to be Mrs. Patterson calling about her damn Siamese again."

"What? You're not a cat lover?" he teased.

Now he could hear her blush. "I like cats just fine. It's Mrs. Patterson who makes me break out in hives. I swear, the American Psychiatric Association needs to back a study on her and her unique manifestation of Munchausen by proxy syndrome."

He laughed. "Well, next time let your receptionist answer."

"Deal. So what's up? I have an appointment in three and a half minutes."

"I just wanted to let you know that I called my scientist friend. He's agreed to look at the samples for us. He said to overnight them to him today and he'll make it a priority to run them through the . . . whatever."

"That's fabulous!" Josie breathed, and he could hear the rustle of papers in the background. "Okay, I've got a pen. Just give me the address, and I'll have Ben pack them up."

"Actually, I was planning to come by in a bit, so I'll give it to you then."

"Eli, I told you I can't take time in the middle of the day for lunches out. I'm sorry, but I'm just too busy."

"Calm down. I wasn't going to ask you for lunch." He lowered his voice to a tone he hoped sounded calming,

soothing, and matter-of-fact. "I'm coming to help you figure out where we might be able to quarantine Rosemary
and Bill away from any other Lupines. I doubt many wander into your clinic, but Steve thought it would be a good
idea to isolate them anyway."

"Quarantine?" Josie sounded neither calmed nor
soothed. "They need to be quarantined? Why? Did he tell
you he thinks he knows what they have? Do I need to
warn my staff? Eli, what the hell is going on?"

He grimaced. "Okay, now you really need to calm
down." He repeated Steve's reasoning and his assurances
that the illness was not transmissible to anyone other than
Lupines. "It's just a precaution, and probably an unnecessary one at that. But this thing makes me nervous, and I
don't see the harm in an excess of caution. I doubt that
Rick would, either. Not when it comes to his pack. I'll call
him and clear it, but I'm pretty sure he'd agree with me. I
don't want to take any chances."

"Me neither." He heard her sigh. "Okay. For the moment, I'll make sure everyone here understands that no
one goes near the Lupines except for myself, Ben, Andrea, and Daisy. They've all already been in contact. I'm
not really set up for quarantining anyone, but there's a
storage room that's mostly empty because I've been wanting to turn it into a physical therapy space. I suppose we
can put them in there. It's only accessible through the
back of the clinic, and no one needs to go in there for anything unless I tell them to. Will that work?"

"That sounds fine."

"Well, I have a day full of appointments here. I'll let
you have Ben when I can, but he does have other things

to do. Can you handle it yourself, or draft someone else to help you?"

"I'll figure something out."

"All right. I'll talk to you later, then."

"You'll see me later," he corrected, his mouth curving wickedly. "And then even later than that, you'll taste me."

When he hung up, he was laughing and marveling at the ability of his love to convey a beet-red blush over fiber-optic phone lines. Now, *that* was talent.

CHAPTER TWELVE

Josie loved her work. Really she did. And she told herself that many, many times on Tuesday, hoping that the reminder would prove useful. It did, she supposed, in the sense that she neither committed any felonies, nor told any of her patients that really, their pet would be fine if not for the owner's stupidity. Even the reminder couldn't stop her from wanting to say it, though. It just stopped the words from actually coming out.

When Eli stopped by at three o'clock, she barely had time to sneak a kiss in the back of the clinic before she had to race to her fifteenth appointment of the day. Thankfully, he took her brush-off with good grace, patting her on the bottom and telling her that he'd already spoken to Ben, the blood samples were already in the hands of the delivery company, and they had the quarantine setup under control. His calm demeanor help to settle her frazzled nerves, but the pat on her ass stayed with her through at least three appointments. She kept finding herself tingling and blushing at the least appropriate time. Brenda Nowicki even asked her if she was coming down with something, which had only made her blush harder.

Force of will got her through the remainder of her schedule, and even an emergency appointment with a congested guinea pig. Thankfully, she had no outcalls for large animals this week, so at least she hadn't added travel to her list of duties. Still, by the time the clinic locked its door at seven fifteen, Josie felt like she'd been running a marathon for at least nine weeks. She rubbed a hand across the back of her neck as she trudged out of the last exam room to slap a chart down on the teetering pile she still needed to catch up on.

A metallic clang drew her attention to the hallway leading to the storage room she'd told Eli he could set up as a quarantine space. Curiosity drew her down the hall to see how far the Q-Team—as Ben had dubbed them— had gotten with their project. She reached for the knob, but the door swung open before she touched it.

"Brace yourself, Doc." Ben grinned down at her, looking disheveled and disreputable and highly pleased with himself. She saw why when he stepped back and waved his hand at the newly rearranged and reequipped storage room. "The Q-Team is proud to present . . . Club Medicine!"

Josie laughed, her eyes widening as she took in the transformation. Gone were empty pallets that had once held dog food, the broken pieces of equipment, and the boxes of extra exam gloves and surgical drapes. In their place, she saw only gleaming tile floors and a floor-to-ceiling gated chain-link partition, securely bolted to opposite walls, that divided the space into an entry and work area in front and a large, enclosed kennel area on the other. Inside the kennel area, the linoleum floor had been padded with rubber mats on each end. Each mat was topped with an egg-crate dog bed.

She looked at Eli in wonder. "You guys managed all this in just a few hours?"

"It wasn't really all that complicated. The partition was the biggest challenge, but once we found the wall studs, even that wasn't so bad." He grinned. "The guy at the fence company guaranteed it would take an entire pack of wolves to take it down."

"I wasn't worried about security. It looks solid to me. Besides, our two Lupines aren't in any condition for a jailbreak at the moment."

Josie turned around slowly, taking in the front of the room. A narrow hutch had been placed to the left of the door and stocked with everything needed for the care of the Lupines, including their charts, medications, and tape and bandages for their wound dressings.

She shook her head and laughed in amazement. "It's perfect. I think putting them in the same kennel will make them both feel better once they start to become more alert. You're both hired."

"Thanks, but my contract with the town says I'm not allowed to moonlight," Eli quipped, bending down to steal a brief kiss.

When he pulled away, Josie snuck a glance over at Ben, half expecting that he'd be staring at the ceiling and whistling with a look of perfect innocence on his face. Instead, she caught him watching shamelessly and grinning. When she scowled, he only grinned wider and winked at her. She muttered something under her breath about mutiny and disrespect. Ben appeared unfazed.

"But since I'm already here," Eli continued, winking at her himself, "why don't I help Ben move Rosemary and Bill into their new digs? They're both damn heavy when they're unconscious."

Josie nodded and led the way back down the hall and across the triage area to the old kennel area, where she supervised first Rosemary's and then Bill's transfer to the quarantine space. When each of them had been settled on their own bed, she and Ben did a quick check of their injuries and made sure their IV drips remained connected and functional.

"Rosemary looks good," Josie announced when she had assured herself that the short trip had caused the Lupine no harm. She pushed back to her feet and stepped across to her tech. "How's Bill?"

Ben grumbled and fiddled with the plastic tubing of his IV. "He's fine, but his line got caught on the door of his crate back there and came loose from the needle. I think I've got it fixed, though. He should be good."

Satisfied, Josie turned and took two steps toward the front of the room. Her feet stuttered to a halt, though, when she heard an ominous rumble in the distance. She frowned at Eli through the chain-link.

"Do you know if it was supposed to rain today?"

"I don't think so. Why?"

"Because I could have sworn I just heard thunder."

And that was when Ben screamed.

Josie spun around—whether of her own volition or from the knock she took when Eli leapt past her into the kennel, she couldn't really tell. All she knew was that one minute everything had been fine, and the next minute Ben was screaming and Eli was running and Bill

Evans had his teeth sunk deep into the flesh of the vet tech's left leg.

"Out! Get out!" Eli shouted.

It took Josie a minute to realize he was talking to her. She made to step forward instead, intent on helping Ben, but the look Eli aimed at her had nearly enough force to knock her out of the room entirely. She stumbled backward and watched helplessly as the sheriff aimed a vicious kick at the Lupine's head. The blow stunned the creature and he released his grip on Ben's leg, shaking his head as if to stop it from ringing.

The moment Bill let go, Eli threw Ben over his shoulder and bolted for the gate, shoving Josie out in front of him. He slammed the chain-link panel closed behind him and leaned against it.

"Secure the lock!" he shouted, and Josie rushed to obey, flipping the pin into place and securing it with the padlock the fence company had so thoughtfully provided. As soon as the gate was secure, Eli stepped away, barely avoiding the vicious fangs of the enraged Lupine as it threw itself over and over against the fence, infuriated by its inability to reach its prey.

"That should not have happened," Josie stuttered, following Eli out to the triage room, where he placed Ben on an exam table. "He was on enough sedative to knock out a rhino."

"Yeah, well, he's not a rhino." Eli tore the soft cotton of Ben's scrubs for a better look at the wound. Eli was already calling Dr. Shad's office.

"The IV did come loose," Ben gasped, his face white with shock as he looked down at his torn and bloody limb. "It was my fault. I had a hard time getting hold of him in that cage, so when I finally grabbed him, I turned away from the door too fast. I should have been more careful."

Josie finished relaying the emergency information to Dr. Shad's nurse and hung up the phone. "It is not your fault. You heard me say it: Bill was on a massive dose of sedative. He still is. It should have been impossible for him to move that fast. Hell, even if we'd removed his IV entirely, he still shouldn't have been able to so much as open his eyes for at least a couple of hours."

Eli grunted. "Too bad it didn't actually work out that way."

When she hurried to Ben's side and reached out to examine his leg, Josie realized her hands were shaking. Embarrassed, she snatched them back and pressed them together to stop the trembling. Closing her eyes, she took a slow, deep breath, then carefully blew it out.

Opening her eyes, she reached out again and helped Eli finish tearing the left leg off the younger man's green scrub trousers. "The blood is flowing, not pulsing," she observed, using the torn cloth of the scrubs to wipe away the worst of it. "And it looks like he mainly got the outside of the leg. So that's good news. You don't have to worry he nicked your femoral artery."

Ben offered a weak hiccup of a laugh. "Oh, good. At least there's a bright side."

Josie felt constitutionally unequipped to stand around doing nothing while they waited for the doctor to arrive. Humans and animals might be different species, she reasoned, but the principles of medicine were universal. When something living had a bleeding open wound, the first thing you did was to stop the bleeding, and the second thing you did was clean the wound. She grabbed a package of sterile dressing and ripped it open.

"Has anyone else noticed that we seem to be going through even more of these wound care supplies than usual?" she asked absently.

This time, Ben's laugh sounded stronger. "Yeah, I wonder why that is . . ."

Josie smiled brightly at him, encouraging him to share the joke. "Poor practice management is my guess."

"I was going to go with insubordination and thievery in the ranks, personally."

"Well, you've always been a British naval justice kind of guy."

"Keelhauling is an underused form of punishment," he argued, grimacing when she applied direct pressure to the largest area of bleeding.

"Maybe that's because so few people these days have properly sized keels at their disposal."

Eli interrupted their banter with a light touch to her shoulder. "If you're okay here, I'm going to take a look at something. I'll be right back."

Josie looked up and nodded. She was okay, but that didn't mean she didn't hope Dr. Shad would hurry up and get here already. And it didn't mean she was really *okay*. How could she be okay when her friend was hurt, her gut told her she was responsible, and two of her patients seemed to be either going insane or dying right before her very eyes? For a woman who had succeeded at everything she'd attempted, this pill was becoming particularly hard for her to swallow.

"Young lady, I thought you and I had a deal," a voice

announced, and Josie turned to see Dr. Martin Shad standing in the doorway with a huge yellow tackle box in one hand and a cherry lollipop in the other. "When you moved back here to take over your father's practice, I assumed that we would continue with the same understanding he and I always enjoyed: You treat your patients, and I'll treat mine."

Relief flooded through her, unexpectedly intense. After all, nothing truly terrible had happened. She could see Ben's wounds weren't all that serious, and she and Eli had emerged from the kennel unscathed. But maybe she'd had to handle just a little too much over the last few days.

Just a little.

She managed to smile at the doctor, though, remembering how he'd always shared those lollipops with his young patients, of which she had once been one. "Well, that could work, provided that your patients don't turn into my patients while you're out playing with trout," she teased. "Catch any keepers this weekend?"

Martin Shad was older than her father by a decade or more, which put him well into his seventies, but he looked at least a decade younger. His white hair still grew full and thick, his eyes sparkled with no help from corrective lenses, he walked with a quick, agile step, and he carried at least twenty extra pounds on his five-foot-seven-inch frame. If he'd had a beard, the man would have been Santa Claus. It wasn't natural for anyone so round to be so healthy, but the man had never been sick a day in his life. Or at least, not in Josie's life. Not that she could remember anyway.

"One or two," the old man said in response to her question, grinning broadly. "Caught a real nice steelhead, but I had to release him. I was already at my limit." He heaved a gusty sigh. "And now I'm done for the year. Makes a man hate the winter, I tell you. Now, why don't you fill me in on what happened over the weekend? It's been some time since I heard a good tale."

While Josie outlined the situation with Rosemary and Bill for Dr. Shad, the physician frowned and nodded and turned to poke at Ben's injury, but for all his slow, gruff nonchalance, Josie had noticed that the old doctor had already removed her padding to examine the wounds, prodded the skin, and grunted his approval.

"I rescind my earlier comments about poaching patients. I think you can keep the ones you've just picked up. Sounds like you've got a better handle on their problem than me, anyway. Country doctors like me don't even do our own blood counts. We send that kind of mess out to a lab." Without opening the huge tackle box/jump kit he'd brought with him, Martin reached for the saline flush that Josie seemed to keep permanently in hand these days and began squirting it over the wounds. "I don't know if I've peered into a microscope since my internship."

Somehow, Josie had a hard time believing that, but she didn't blame Martin for wanting to stay well out of the mess she'd gotten wrapped up in. Heck, she'd have run in the other direction if she'd been in his shoes.

The doctor poked at Ben's leg and shook his head. "Young lady, it's folks like you that give physicians like me a complex. You do twice the work as me and only charge half the money. Anyone ever wises up to that fact, and I can kiss my retirement home in Tempe good-bye."

Josie ignored the doctor's scowl and bluster and took the compliment the way it was intended. "My dad always planned to take an ad out in *The New York Times*."

Martin snorted. "That wouldn't do him any good. Tell him I said go for it. No one around here reads the *Times*, except maybe some of those kids down in Portland. Now, if he'd said *The Oregonian*, then I might be worried."

"I'll let him know. With the money he'll save, he can probably buy a whole page."

Ben, watching in fascination while the doctor finished cleaning and began stitching his wounds, snorted. "Whole page? Heck, he could probably buy the whole paper."

Martin peered up at his patient through the screen of his bushy white eyebrows. "What's the matter, boy? You work here, don't you? Don't tell me you've never seen stitches go in before."

"Not into a human. What did you use for the local before you started? Was that levobupivacaine?"

"I use good old-fashioned lidocaine. What is it with you young folk, always wanting to do something different? Where I come from we believed that old saw about not fixing what isn't broken."

Ben held up a hand and shrugged. "No problem. I was just asking."

The physician set the last stitch and sighed, pulling off the gloves he'd worn during the procedure. "Done. Can I assume you know how to treat stitches, young man?"

"Keep them dry for at least forty-eight hours, use an antibacterial ointment once a day and clean gauze dressings. They can come out in one to two weeks."

Martin grunted. "That's something, then. If you come see me, I'll take them out when they're done, or you can have Dr. Barrett here do it for you. I know which one I'd vote for, if I were you."

"Me, too." Josie grinned. "I don't hand out lollipops. How do you feel about liver snaps, Ben?"

"Like I'll be going to see Dr. Shad, thanks, boss."

The old man had already grabbed his kit as he was making his way toward the door. "Call my office if you do anything stupid enough to need me again."

And with that, he slipped out the door.

Ben looked to his right. "Twenty-three stitches. How come I thought it was going to be a hell of a lot more?"

Josie hadn't noticed Eli's return from the isolation room, but she felt something inside her relax when he moved to her side and draped an arm around her shoulders.

"Probably because it hurt a hell of a lot," Eli said, giving the younger man a small smile. "And I say that as the voice of experience."

"Right. Too bad I can't pull that cool magic trick, though, and make the wounds disappear. I gotta say, that's a handy skill to have, man."

"I like it."

Josie listened to the banter, relieved to see that Ben looked mostly recovered from the incident. True, he had twenty-three stitches and his scrubs now only had one leg, but his color had returned to normal, as had his impudent attitude. Something, though, was not right with Eli. She watched him, frowning.

"Why don't I drive you home?" he offered Ben, before Josie could ask the question hovering on the tip of her tongue. "You should probably rest that leg for a few hours at least. I'm sure your boss will keep you hopping tomorrow."

"Only as far as the file room," Josie assured them. "There's plenty in there that needs to be done, and you'll be able to stay off your feet."

Ben made a face. "Geez, why don't you just have me executed? It would be less painful."

"Maybe for you, but then who would do my filing?"

Eli helped ease Ben off the table and wrapped one arm around the younger man's torso to steady him. "Think you can make it to the car this way?"

The tech nodded. "Yeah, it'll just be slow going."

"Take your time."

Josie opened her mouth to demand that Eli tell her what was bothering him, but he cut her off with a glance.

"I'll swing back around to your place after I get Ben settled. We can talk then, all right?"

No, Josie thought, it really wasn't, but it looked like the best offer she would likely get. Reluctantly she nodded and stepped ahead of the pair to open the back door.

"I'll see you in a little bit then," she managed unhappily and watched while the two men beat a slow path across the parking lot.

CHAPTER THIRTEEN

Eli found Josie curled up on her sofa wearing an ancient T-shirt that looked like it would fit three of her. She had her feet tucked up under the hem and her arms wrapped around her knees; her hair hung down around her shoulders in a dark, gleaming curtain. Beside her, Bruce lay on the sofa in a shaggy, dark-eyed lump, his chin propped on Josie's elbow. She looked about sixteen years old, which—based on where his mind went every single time he laid eyes on her—made him a damn pervert.

She had left her apartment door unlocked, and he took that as an invitation. Any other time, he'd have taken it as a cue to read her a lecture on personal safety, security, and the inadvisability of being too trusting in this day and age, but at the moment he had more important things to discuss with her. He'd get to the lecture another time.

"How was Ben?" she asked as he lifted her from her cushion and usurped her place, settling her onto his lap instead. Bruce just sighed and curled himself into a hairy, lopsided ball.

"He's fine. He was discussing where tonight would fit in his memoirs when I left him at his house. He already called one of his co-workers—Andrea, right?—and arranged to have her pick him up and drive him to work in the morning. Since he left his car downstairs."

Josie rested her head against his shoulder and nodded. "Good. I didn't think to ask him if he'd need a ride before you guys left. I guess I still wasn't thinking clearly."

They sat in silence for several more minutes, Eli stroking her silky hair while an old Cary Grant movie flickered on the television, the volume so low it was barely audible. In the end, Josie spoke first.

"I don't want you to think that I was dumb enough to go into that cage after you left," she said quietly, "but I did look into the room. I guess that was what you didn't want me to ask about before you left with Ben, huh?"

Eli sighed, feeling suddenly tired. "I just knew it would be a discussion that didn't need to keep Ben away from his own sofa. He needed to get home. And I'll admit, I did kind of hope that you wouldn't want to go back into that room after what had happened."

Josie drew back and pierced him with an incredulous look. "In the time that I've known you, have I done anything to indicate that I'm a delicate little flower of womanhood who faints at the sight of blood and loses her head in a crisis?"

"Of course not."

"Then what made you think that I wouldn't want to go back in there?"

"Because *I* barely wanted to go back in there. Seeing Bill flip out like that shook me up. At first I was afraid he was going to kill Ben, then I was afraid he was going to hurt you, and then I was afraid I was going to have to take him down with a bullet. None of those options made me a very happy man."

"And I can understand that, but I'm a vet, and at the moment, those two are my patients. I can't just leave them in there to rot. They still need food and water and medications and wound care. That doesn't change just because both of them are now acting like *actual* rabid wolves."

He swore. "Rosemary, too?"

"Yes. I thought you saw her before and that's why you didn't want me to go in there."

"No, she had started to wake up when I was there, but she still couldn't stand. I didn't want you to see what Bill did to his bedding."

"That he'd shredded his bed and marked the stuffing?" She snorted. "If you think I haven't seen worse than that on a slow night in vet school, you're out of your mind. Besides, Rosemary was in the middle of doing the same thing the last time I saw her; she was just neater about it. She had all the stuffing piled into the corner in a new bed, and Bill was guarding her from all comers. I decided to leave them to it."

"It wasn't what he did; it was what it signifies."

Josie looked confused. "What do you mean? I pretty much just assumed it signified that he was a wolf. Am I missing something?"

"That's exactly it. Bill is acting like a wolf. And apparently, so is Rosemary." When she shook her head mutely, he elaborated. "The aggression stemming from defensiveness and territoriality. The guarding of his mate and marking his territory. Those are all wolf behaviors, not things you see in Lupines."

He saw when Josie began to understand what he was getting at. "You think they're turning into actual wolves?"

"Sort of." He ran a hand over his close-cropped hair

and tried to order his thoughts. "There are rumors among all the animal shapeshifters about the dangers of spending too long in any form other than human. According to the stories, if a shifter spends too long in the between form, he or she will get stuck there and no longer be able to take on the shape of either a human or an animal. And not belonging in either world will drive the shifter into insanity."

"God, that's horrible."

"They say something similar about staying in animal form, although some people take a sort of romantic view of the idea of reverting completely to the animal form. A shifter who takes on his animal shape and refuses to turn back could be trapped in that animal form forever. He wouldn't be caught between two worlds, though. He would become fully an animal, with all an animal's instincts and emotions, but with an ability to reason much more advanced than any other in his species. And the strength to match."

"Like some kind of super wolf?"

"Something like that, yes."

Josie sat up straight and turned to face him, her expression reflecting both horror at the idea and a sense of guilt at not being able to stop it. She seemed determined to take the entire world's troubles on her shoulders.

"We can't let that happen," she declared firmly. "We have to find a way to fix this."

"I agree. And that's why we've sent the blood samples to Steve, and it's why the witch is going to come out to evaluate Rosemary and Bill tomorrow."

"Right. I just hope she can evaluate from a distance,

because there's no way I'm letting anyone into that kennel until I can figure out a way to get them sedated again."

Eli blinked. "You think you can do that?"

"Clearly, sedatives have worked up until now. If we're lucky, their bodies are just learning to cope with the chemicals they've been exposed to in the past, building up a resistance. If I can find a new chemical, one they haven't been exposed to before, it might buy us some time to either treat them or keep them from hurting anyone else."

"And you think that could work?"

"Theoretically, but I won't know for sure until I try."

The image of Josie walking into the kennel with a syringe in one hand and a dog biscuit in the other made him blanch. "You're not going to try just giving them shots until you find the right drug."

She looked at him like he'd lost his mind, which strangely made him feel better.

"Do I look suicidal to you? I don't think so. Since we're the only vet in a bit of a drive, we're licensed to provide emergency care to wildlife, some of which don't take well to being handled by strangers. We have an air gun that shoots tranquilizer darts. I can use that and shoot through the chain link. If I hit one of them, I just wait to see if they go down. If not, I try another drug, and if so, I shoot the other one."

That really only offered him a minimal amount of comfort. "I still don't like the idea of you getting too close to them."

"I can't treat them if I can't touch them."

"And you can't touch them if they rip your arms off," he shot back. "I want you to promise me that you won't go in that cage on your own even if you think they've got them both sedated."

"If they're unconscious, I don't see what they could do to hurt me."

"Promise."

"Eli—"

"*Promise.*"

She gave in with very little grace. "Fine. I won't go in the cage unless I have someone else around."

"Unless *I'm* around."

Josie rolled her eyes. "Eli, I can't put my practice on hold and wait around for you to get off duty before I perform a medical procedure."

"I'm not asking you to let me know when you have to put a splint on the leg of a cocker spaniel," he argued, cupping her jaw in his hand. "This is a special circumstance, and this is the only time I'm going to insist. But I *am* going to insist. Understand?"

"Fine."

Her grace seemed to be slipping away like the tide. He discovered he liked that. He didn't want to think of Josie being cautious or polite with him. He wanted her to be comfortable and honest and completely herself. He wanted her to argue with him. Anything less would bore him silly.

His mouth curved and he leaned forward to kiss her forehead. "Thank you."

"You're welcome," she muttered, reaching up to drag him back down to her. "But just so you know, your aim stinks."

Then she planted her mouth on his and proceeded to drive him crazy.

Absently, Eli heard Bruce heave a disgusted sigh and

felt the sofa cushions shift. The dog jumped to the floor and padded his way into the bedroom. Absently, because Eli had much more important things to think about than Josie's dog. Like Josie herself.

His hand moved from her jaw to the back of her head so he could hold her still while he turned the tables on her. He went from an ordinary male with bad aim to a pillaging conqueror in the space of a breath, and then he decided to steal her breath as well.

If it were possible, he wanted her to feel his hunger, actually experience it alongside him, not just respond to the evidence of it. He wanted her to know how warm and soft and feminine she felt in his arms, not just wriggle and strain in his grip. He wanted to share with her how it felt to slide inside her and feel that amazing, mind-blowing sensation of coming home.

And if he couldn't do all of that, he at least wanted to imprint himself on her soul, so that she would never forget how he felt, how he smelled, how he tasted. Gods knew he could never forget her.

The hunger he had sated that morning stirred awake like the kraken rising from the sea. It welled up inside him until he wanted to swallow her whole just so he could carry her always inside of him. The crazy part was that he knew he was being ridiculous, but it didn't matter. He couldn't stop himself.

He slid his hands under the hem of her oversize shirt and found nothing but warm, silky skin, and that by itself made his head spin faster than a mouthful of straight whiskey. He stroked her hip, her back, the curve of her waist and wondered who enjoyed the caresses more, the touched or the toucher? At the moment he felt like he could stay this way forever, just holding her closer, tasting her, breathing her in, and feeling the living velvet of her flesh beneath his hands.

She became impatient well before him. With a frustrated groan, she yanked the shirt off over her head and tossed it to the floor, leaving Eli to experience the epiphany of finding her more beautiful tonight than she had been last night, the first time he'd seen her nudity, or this morning under the bright lights of her clinic. He'd expected that the magic of looking on a lover for the first time could never be recaptured. It lived in that instant, in the revelation of something previously unknown. But he'd had it all wrong.

This was magic, this knowing that the sandy pink of her erect nipple would flush the most beguiling shade of rose when he circled it with his tongue, then deepen further still from the pressure of his suckling mouth. Magic lived in the way he knew that the tiny little cluster of moles on her left hip formed a shape like a compass rose. The magic nearly flattened him when she leaned forward and he felt the familiar weight of her breasts against his chest, the perfectly remembered fit of their bodies aligned.

Magic, he realized, had nothing to do with novelty.

Thirsty, he bent again to her mouth and drank of her sweetness. His hands stroked up her sides, cuddling her breasts in his palms, thumbs strumming against her nipples until she mewled like a hungry kitten. The sound echoed inside his head and left him dazed and aching. Her smallest sounds, her lightest touches, affected him like nothing else ever had. Her restless movements, however, warned him that for Josie, small and light was not nearly enough.

Suddenly urgent, her fingers fumbled with the fastening of his jeans. Eli reached down to help her. Between them, they managed to rid him of the confining fabric and that, too, fell unheeded to the floor.

Her hand closed around him and wrenched a sound from deep inside his chest. His head dropped back to the cushions behind him and his lips arched into her touch. Her graceful, elegant fingers tightened with surprising strength around the base of his erection and milked upward until he had to grit his teeth against the urge to beg. He felt no shame at the idea of leaving himself vulnerable to her, but he didn't know whether to beg her to stop or to move faster, and he feared that if he opened his mouth, the wrong answer would spring forth.

He suffered the glory of half a dozen slow, taunting strokes and opened his mouth to beg for mercy, but thankfully, Josie showed him none. Gripping him with one hand, she swung her leg over both of his and slowly, slowly— cruelly slow—sank down and enveloped him.

And what had been magical became miraculous.

Her name poured from his throat in a tight, hoarse, rasping shadow of sound. He felt her inner muscles tighten around him, felt her body weeping in welcome, and thought that this was what it must mean to be blessed.

His control broke with a resounding snap, leaving his inner beast free to spring to the kill. His hands closed like a steel vise on her hips, wrenching the reins of their mating from her grasp. Ruthlessly, relentlessly, he held her down as his body pounded up into hers. Her breathing turned into a shuttering, gasping series of breathless pants, and he felt her thighs begin to quiver alongside his, but he ignored her and pushed them both farther toward oblivion.

Again and again their bodies slapped together in a

primitive rhythm. Again and again Eli thought the next stroke would be his last, and again and again his beast would roar its displeasure and demand one more. One more. One more.

But there would always be one more, because Eli knew in the deepest recesses of his self that he would never have enough of this woman. Never have enough of his mate.

Never have enough.

But his body was as weak as hers, and they could take only so much. He rose up, slamming deep within her and touching off a shuddering series of internal contractions that dragged him over the edge with her.

Head back, jaw clenched, he screamed his pleasure and dominance to the night, and at the same time surrendered himself utterly to the woman he would never let go.

CHAPTER FOURTEEN

Wednesday, Josie decided, was a gift from God. Not only had the day started with an amazing bout of lazy, sleepy sex, but by ten o'clock the sun beamed down, the sky and attained the color of a Tiffany's box, and a late-season surge of warmth brought the temperature up to a glorious sixty-five.

If it hadn't been for the two wild Lupines locked in her storage room, Josie might have assumed her epidemic of bad luck had run its course. Still, she had definitely had worse days.

To top it all off, on Wednesdays the clinic opened late as a trade-off for their Saturday-morning hours, and on this particular morning, her last appointment before lunch called to cancel, giving her an unheard-of extra twenty minutes all to herself.

Well, all to herself and the stack of paperwork she needed to catch up on.

And the large, hairy, drooling mass at her feet.

She nibbled a sandwich while she worked, so she had her mouth full when Leah, her receptionist, paged her from the front of the clinic.

"Dr. Barrett?"

Josie grabbed the receiver. She hated talking into a speaker. "What's up, Leah?"

"There's someone here to see you. She doesn't have an appointment, but she says you're expecting her? Her name is Mary Applewhite."

For a minute Josie stared blankly into space. She didn't know anyone by that name, did she?

Through the intercom, she heard a rustling and some muffled voices, then Leah spoke again. "She said to remind you that Sheriff Pace asked her to come to the clinic to consult with you on some patients."

Another vet? Josie thought briefly, then the lightbulb clicked on and she almost smacked herself in the head. Not a vet, a witch.

"Right," she said, dropping her sandwich and dusting her hands off on her lab coat. "I'm sorry, Leah, I should have told you she was coming. I'll be right there."

Mary Applewhite, Josie decided as they shook hands in the clinic's bright and sparsely furnished waiting room, looked a little like a witch and a little like a coffeehouse barista. Her face had that sort of ageless look that said she could have been anywhere between twenty-seven and forty-seven. She wore her strawberry-blond hair very short, in a spiky modern pixie cut, and a series of six earrings decorated her left ear. In the right, she wore only two—one dangling from the lobe, the other a ring around the cartilage at the very top of the auricle. Those things made her look like a barista. The warm smile, silver pentacle necklace, and glint of ageless wisdom in her slate-blue eyes made her look like a witch.

Josie liked her immediately.

Especially since she wore her pentacle and earrings

with a pair of faded blue jeans, a snug T-shirt the color of rhododendron leaves, and purple high-top sneakers.

"Come on back," Josie invited, turning to lead the way. "I'm so glad you were willing to drive all the way out here from Portland."

"It's a pretty drive," Mary said. Her voice sounded more barista than witch, rough and quick, as if she might be a smoker, or had grown up with them. "And it gave me the chance to do a last little bit of wildcrafting before the frost sets in."

Josie looked her question.

"Collecting wild-growing plants and herbs," Mary explained. "Always responsibly and always in authorized areas."

"Don't worry," Josie said, grinning. "I grew up here in Oregon, but I'm not a member of the environment police. I swear." She gave Mary the stool from the desk and grabbed another for herself from the other side of the room. Bruce ignored them completely. "So, um, I'm not entirely sure what Eli told you—"

"Sheriff Pace? He said that there was a concern that two people from your town might have been cursed somehow, or maybe enchanted, and he asked if I would be able to tell if that were true if I met them." Mary watched Josie calmly, her gaze steady and gentle. "I told him I would. And I will. If there's some sort of unnatural magic around, I can find it."

"I apologize, but we don't have that many witches here in Stone Creek, so I'm not sure how you do what you do . . ."

"Don't worry. It's not complicated. Usually, I just have to be in the same room with the person or thing that's been affected by magic. I can give you a yes or a no based on the energy the thing gives off. Then I can try to tell you what kind of magic was used, and sometimes I can try to trace it back to its source, but I can't make guarantees about that. That's a lot more complicated, and it usually requires that I touch whatever has been cursed."

Josie held up her hands and shook her head. "No, we'll have to do without that because touching isn't going to be possible in this case."

"Fair enough." Mary nodded and tilted her head to the side as if trying to figure something out. "Why don't you tell me a little more about what's going on? Or we can get right to the scrying, if that makes you more comfortable."

"No. Well—" Josie paused and pursed her lips. "Well, I can't let you go in blind, but I kind of assumed that Eli had told you a little more about our situation. The problem that we're having has to do with two Lupines, both members of the local pack." She raised an eyebrow. "You don't have a problem with shifters, do you?"

The witch grinned. "I might be human, but I'm not exactly Ms. Average American. Don't worry. I don't get all het up over the idea of people getting furry occasionally."

"Good. Um, these two Lupines both seem to have the same problem, and we're trying to figure out the source. Each of them shifted from human into wolf form at some point this past weekend, and between then and today, neither of them has been able to shift back. They're stuck. Now, my theory is that they have some kind of disease— not one that's transmissible to humans, so don't worry— but that there's some sort of bug infecting their systems and making them too sick to shift. Unfortunately, other than one abnormal test result, we're having trouble finding any evidence about what that bug might be. The leader of the local pack said that the only other thing he thought could be preventing these Lupines from shifting for so long was a curse. And that's where you come in. We don't have any experts on that kind of magic in Stone Creek, so we had to look somewhere else for help, and you were recommended to us."

Josie watched Mary's face as she spoke. The witch's sympathetic demeanor never changed, but her expression grew more and more solemn as the story went on. When Josie finally fell silent, the other woman shook her head.

"This is unfortunate. I'll definitely take a look at the Lupines and let you know if I can sense a curse around them, but it's not a good sign that they've gone so long without changing. Remaining in a nonhuman form for many days can have serious consequences."

"I know. Eli told me, which is why I really want to do whatever we can to help Rosemary and Bill before it's too late."

Mary stood and brushed her hands on her jeans. "I'm ready if you are. Should we go and have a look?"

Josie led the way down the short hall and into the isolation room. The minute the outer door opened, two enormous heads turned and four feral amber eyes glared at the intruders. The larger, lighter wolf—Bill—lunged immediately toward the front of the partition, as if he could throw himself through the metal barrier and take the humans down like deer. Behind him, Rosemary's salt-and-pepper fur stood up straight between her shoulder blades. She remained near the center of the enclosure, her legs spread and braced, her head down as she snarled low in her throat, her feelings about the other women plain.

The witch stood directly in front of the kennel gate and stared intently at the wolves for all of thirty seconds. Then she blinked, turned around, and headed back the way she'd come. "I've seen enough."

Wondering what exactly Mary had seen, Josie followed her back to the triage room and waited anxiously.

The other woman stood in the center of the room, breathing as if she'd just sprinted the length of a football field. Her head was down until her chin rested nearly on her chest, and she had planted her fisted hands on her hips while she struggled to catch her breath. Josie couldn't pretend to understand it, but she stayed back and watched until the witch exhaled deeply and resumed her seat on the stool.

Josie joined her, perching on the very edge of her seat and leaning forward.

"It's not a curse," Mary said without prompting. "I'm sure of that. There's no magic in that room, aside from what is naturally part of the makeup of a shapeshifter. Their being is a kind of magic, after all."

"Oh, but that's good, right? I mean, we don't actually want them to be cursed."

Mary laughed in a way that indicated absolutely no amusement. "Believe me, there are worse things than curses out there. Much worse."

A strange flush of dizziness made Josie blanch. She could actually feel herself going pale. "What do you mean?"

"I am a practicing witch, and I do have a fairly extensive knowledge of curses, but that isn't my only talent," Mary admitted. "I'm psychic."

"Psychic?"

"Clairvoyant. I can look at people and see things, things that happened in the past, situations they've been in, people connected to them. And sometimes things that might happen in the future."

Josie felt like she might be having a premonition of her own. She knew that Mary had seen something bad when she'd looked at the Lupines. And Josie knew that she had to ask what it had been.

When she did, the words emerged as a whisper.

"There's no black magic associated with the Lupines," the witch reiterated, "but there is something very wrong attached to them anyway. Something negative and . . . malevolent. I can't see exactly what it is, because—"

"Because why?"

"Because there isn't much human left inside them."

"You mean—"

"They don't have a lot of time before they'll be trapped. They're already three-quarters of the way there. Maybe more. You said they first changed this weekend."

Josie nodded.

"What time? Specifically."

"Uh . . ." Josie racked her memory. "Bill said Rosemary left after they had a fight in the middle of the afternoon, and that she usually shifted and went to the woods to work off her mad, so maybe . . . between two and four on Saturday? And I was there when Bill shifted. I think it was a little before ten on Sunday night."

The answer made Mary frown. "I'm surprised, because the male is farther gone than the female. I would have guessed that he'd shifted first."

"No, it was definitely Rosemary. But . . . she was unconscious longer. For the first day, from Saturday evening right through until yesterday, Rosemary was completely out. Could not being awake have made a difference?"

"Maybe. I wish I could say for certain, but I just don't know. This doesn't happen all that often, so I'm hardly an expert."

Josie tried to conceal her disappointment. She swallowed a sigh. "Well, I do appreciate what you were able to tell me. At least now we know it's not a curse. Which leads us back to my pet theory. It's got to be some kind of infection."

She could see a flicker of hesitation in the witch's expression. And she jumped on it.

"Are you saying it's *not* an infection?" Josie demanded. "Can you see things like that? Can you tell if they're sick?"

"Of course they're sick. Even if they don't have some exotic virus, it's obvious that something that compromised the wellness of their minds, at least." Mary sidestepped. "It's just—"

"Just what?" Josie had sensed that the other woman was holding something back, and she went after it with the determination of a terrier.

"It's just that there's something very deliberate about it. About that malevolence," the witch finally admitted. "Something about the negative energy that surrounds them doesn't feel like it came upon them by chance. When I looked at them, I got the impression that this was something that had been done to them. The impression seemed especially strong for the female. To me, that doesn't jive with an illness. Illness is random; a creature randomly encounters a germ, the germ causes the illness. That's just not the feeling I get from the Lupines."

Frustration nearly made Josie howl like one of the Lupines in question. "Can you be any more specific?"

Mary shook her head and looked sincerely regretful. "I'm sorry. I've told you everything. They are hard to read because so much of them is animal now, and the impressions I did get seemed lightly removed from them. Distant. It's probably because they can no longer think in the same way that you and I do."

And she would have to content herself with that, Josie told herself as she escorted her guest out of the clinic a few minutes later. The witch couldn't tell her what she didn't know.

Unfortunately, no one else seemed to know, either.

Exp. 10-1017.03
Log 03-00137

Stage 4 product goes into the field to-night. The one brief in vivo laboratory trial demonstrated rapid uptake, success-ful loading, and desired end point. Will consider a complete success.

NOTE: Laboratory test subject did demon-strate violent tendencies and unpredict-able behavior with infliction of both internal and external damage. In a

sustainable population this might be
seen as a weakness and an undesirable
trait in the product, but I believe that
this will only enhance the end goal of
the experiment—a final solution to the
single greatest problem currently facing
mankind.

CHAPTER FIFTEEN

The meeting with Mary Applewhite continued to nag at Josie all through the afternoon and into the next few days. She had shared everything she could remember with Eli that very night as soon as he'd gotten off his shift. He had listened intently, asked a few deliberate questions, then expressed his own frustration. The problem was that while Josie stayed frustrated well into the weekend, Eli put the emotion behind him after approximately fifteen seconds and demonstrated that he thought the best way to put the problem out of their minds was for them to screw each other senseless.

And while that plan worked very well in the short term, as soon as her breathing returned to normal, Josie's mind went right back to the problem at hand.

She stayed busy on Thursday and Friday with a full schedule of appointments, but she found it hard to concentrate. Her mind kept wandering back to what Mary had said, turning it over and over as if the words represented the colored blocks on a Rubik's Cube, and if she just kept moving them around, eventually they would fall into place and show her the solution to the puzzle.

Saturday turned out to be the worst. The hours until the

clinic closed seemed to drag by, and no matter how many problems she diagnosed, cures she dispensed, or ears she scratched, Josie felt helpless every time she so much as thought about the Lupines. Worse, she felt useless. After all, Mary had said she didn't think they had much time left, and Josie couldn't even figure out what the heck was wrong with them.

She tried to assuage her feelings of impotence by experimenting with different sedatives in the hope of rendering Bill and Rosemary unconscious again. Unfortunately, so far none of them had proved effective. But that didn't keep her from thinking that maybe her theory about Rosemary's progress being slower because she'd been unconscious longer had some merit. If that was the case, then finding a way to tranquilize the pair again might help to slow their deterioration and give them more time to find a cure.

Of course, first it would help to know what it was that they were trying to cure.

When she locked the clinic doors on Saturday afternoon, she rounded on Eli with a muffled scream of frustration. "I thought you said your friend Steve was going to take a look at our samples as soon as he got them."

Eli blinked at the sudden attack. "He did."

"And we sent the samples by overnight express on Tuesday, right?"

"Yes . . ." He drew the word out like he thought it might be a trick question.

Josie ignored him. "So that means they were delivered to him on Wednesday morning, correct?" When he opened his mouth, she held up a hand to silence him. "That was a rhetorical question; I already know the answer. And do you know how I know? Because the delivery company offers this handy little service that allows customers to go online to track the status of their packages. So I know for a *fact* that our package was delivered at nine fifty-two on Wednesday morning. And do you know what else? That same handy little service tells me that the package was signed for by Mr. Stephen himself. So there's no need to wonder whether or not someone accepted the package for him and then forgot to hand it to him. Or set it on his desk where it got buried under an avalanche of paper. Or whether it fell off the back of the truck and was consumed by a wandering Gila monster. He *has* the samples, Eli! *When the hell is he going to take a look at them?*"

She finished her rant on a near screech and stood panting up at him, her eyes blazing, her hands fisted, and every muscle in her body tensed for a fight. Eli just crossed his arms over his chest, quirked a dark eyebrow, and waited.

And waited.

After several tense seconds of silence, he finally asked, "Am I supposed to answer that question? Because you seemed to be handling both sides of that conversation just fine on your own. I thought you might like to finish up the same way."

Damn it, the man couldn't even have the decency to fight with her when clearly she was spoiling for one. How was she supposed to deal with something like that, huh? Didn't she already have enough on her plate?

Deflated, Josie slumped against the clinic's front door and wondered if maybe she should just try one of those sedatives she'd been experimenting with on herself.

"I'm sorry," she muttered and grimaced. "I'm acting

like this is somehow your fault when I know perfectly well that it isn't, but sitting around waiting like this is driving me crazy. I'm a doctor. My job is to solve problems, not wait around for other people to solve them for me. I'm not equipped to deal with this."

Eli crossed the floor and pulled her into his arms, cradling her against his chest. "You're equipped just fine," he murmured against her hair. "You're just frustrated. Believe me when I tell you, so am I. But Steve is doing this as a favor to me and on his own time. I can't ask him to prioritize that over his work. That wouldn't be fair or realistic."

"I know."

"We'll get the answer when we get the answer, sweetheart."

"I know."

"And in the meantime, you are not doing nothing, so don't let me catch you saying that again. You work harder than anyone I've ever met. You put ridiculous hours into your practice, and when you're not working you're running a series of experiments that would put your average university research lab to shame. How many different drugs have you tried on Bill and Rosemary now?"

"Seven."

"Seven. In the last three and a half days. In between running your practice, tending to your patients, and pretending to have a social life."

"I haven't been pretending," she muttered against his shirt. "It's been real every single time."

Eli chuckled. "I appreciate you telling me that, but I'm being serious, Josie. You're too hard on yourself. You push yourself too hard. You need to cut yourself some slack."

"You know, you might find this surprising, but I've heard this speech once or twice before during my life."

"I imagine you had it memorized by the time you graduated from college."

"High school." She tilted her head back and smiled wryly up at him. "But that doesn't mean I didn't need to hear it again. Thanks."

He kissed her. "You're welcome."

They stood in the silence of the waiting room for several minutes, wrapped in each other's arms and perfectly content to be there. Finally, Josie pulled away and sighed. "I had another idea for a sedative. I suppose I could give that a try now. It's either that or twiddle my thumbs while I wait for the phone to ring. For your phone to ring, I mean."

Eli shook his head. "No way. You're going to drive yourself crazy. What you need is a break. A real break. You need to get away from the clinic, away from your apartment, away from Stone Creek. What do you say that you and I run away together?"

"Run away." Josie snickered. "And do what? Join the circus?"

He smacked her behind and guided her toward the back room. "No, smart-ass. Run away and do something fun. Just the two of us. We could go into Portland for dinner. Or maybe drive out to the shore and walk on the beach. The clinic is closed tomorrow, and I'm off duty. We could even drive up to Seattle and spend the night."

"You're trying to distract me with sex."

"Is it working?"

She laughed.

"Sex was actually only part of the plan. I'm serious about getting out of town. I think it would do both of us some good."

"But we can't leave Bill and Rosemary all alone."

"You have a whole staff here who are almost as well equipped as you are to keep an eye on those two. At this point, we can't do much for them except keep them fed and in that pen, right?"

Josie frowned. She supposed that was true, but she didn't exactly relish hearing him give voice to the powerlessness she kept fighting not to feel.

"Maybe, but . . ."

"But what? You think if you don't stay within fifteen feet of them for the rest of your life, you'll miss the song-and-dance number where they reveal the secret to curing them?"

She made a face. "Very funny."

"Come on," he urged. "You need to take a break before you run yourself completely ragged."

"I don't know . . ."

Eli tugged her back into his arms and pursed his lips. "Well, I did have one other idea . . ."

"Which is?"

"We could go back to my place and have sex."

He grinned at her and wriggled his eyebrows like a silent-film villain.

Josie laughed, then tilted her head to the side and frowned. "Actually, do you know that I have no idea where you live?"

"That's because you lured me to your web of seduction and kept me a prisoner in your wicked lair."

She thumped him on the shoulder. "I'm serious. I

don't know where you live. I've let you see me naked, and I couldn't even tell you your address."

"As I recall, when you got naked, you let me do a whole lot more than look."

"I know. I'm such a slut."

"And I thank my lucky stars every day and night."

"Yes, but now that it's been brought to my attention, I don't know if I'll be able to bring myself to sleep with you again unless I've at least seen your . . . house? Apartment? Cave? What?"

He chuckled. "Would you believe cabin? I like having privacy. When I took the job as sheriff, I bought a cabin out in the woods behind Douglas Park."

Josie eyed him for several seconds. "Now, when you say 'cabin,' do you mean as in 'a little cabin in Aspen we keep for the ski season'? Or do you mean 'that old miner's cabin where the outhouse overflowed back in '67'?"

"Strictly indoor plumbing. I promise."

She decided to trust him. "Okay, let's do that then. But we're stopping at the grocery store on the way. If you're whisking me off into the woods to have your wicked way with me, you're going to have to feed me, too."

"Deal."

They did stop at the grocery store—the only one in Stone Creek—to pick up provisions of French bread, Brie cheese, thin-sliced prosciutto, and crisp local pears before setting off in Eli's big black SUV. Bruce's initial reluctance to abandon his spot on Josie's sofa was quickly overcome by a slice of prosciutto, and he grudgingly consented to ride in the backseat, provided that Eli rolled his window down until he could hang his entire floppy head out and let his flews flap in the breeze.

Josie, having never had the opportunity to ride in a "cop car" before, spent most of the short trip enthralled by the police scanner, official computer, lights, sirens, and other bells and whistles that set the vehicle apart from others in its class. She literally had to sit on her hands to keep from pushing any of the fascinating buttons.

When the Jeep slowed, she did manage to look up just in time to see Eli guide it to a halt in front of a small but snug-looking clapboard cabin with a wide, welcoming porch and a front door painted a welcoming shade of blue.

"Relieved?" Eli teased, turning off the ignition and pocketing the keys.

"I'm reserving judgment until I see the inside. And the plumbing."

He was laughing when he rounded the trunk and opened both passenger-side doors, having grabbed the single grocery bag from the cargo area on his way past. "I'll give you the grand tour. Before I rip your clothes off, even."

Unlocking the door, he pushed it open and stepped back, inviting her to precede him. Josie did so eagerly, pleased but not entirely surprised to find the front room spare, but neat. He might be a bachelor, but Eli had never struck her as the kind of man who would be content to live like a pig. Still, she couldn't resist teasing him.

"Did you clean up in the hope of luring me into your clutches?"

"Why? My clutches seemed to work just fine at your apartment."

She humphed and ran her fingers over the timber mantel above a snug fieldstone fireplace. The wood was old, smooth as silk, and stained a dark cocoa brown. "Looks like whoever built this place did a pretty good job."

"I like it."

He left her to admire the decor, which consisted mainly of a deep, inviting leather sofa—on which Bruce immediately made himself at home—and a club chair in a shade that matched the mantel almost perfectly. A low cocktail table in weathered gray wood squatted in front of the sofa, and when Josie bent for a closer look, she saw that it wasn't a table but an old carpenter's truck, obviously antique, with traces of green paint still clinging to the corners. At each end, heavy metal D-rings had served as handles. She fell instantly in lust with the piece and wondered if she could seduce Eli into letting her have it.

The room boasted little else, except for a couple of lamps, a tall one in the corner between the sofa and the chair and a short table lamp on a tiny magazine table at the other end of the sofa, near the fireplace. She noticed sheets of newspaper stuffed into the bottom where the magazines would go and guessed he used them to get his fires going.

Turning away from the fireplace, Josie moved to the doorway on the right where Eli had disappeared and found herself looking into a surprisingly spacious kitchen with old-fashioned checkerboard tiling on the floor in blue and white. The cabinets had been painted white, the appliances chosen to match, and the counters, instead of the laminate she'd been expecting, were topped with wooden butcher's block.

Eli stood at the counter, emptying the groceries into the refrigerator, which contained a lot more than beer and leftover Chinese food containers, she noticed— sheesh, it looked like the man usually ate healthier than she did! At the front end of the kitchen, a snug round table for four sat beneath the curtained window.

"This is really nice," Josie commented, giving in to the urge to touch him, even if it was just a hand on his broad back. As she approached the counter, she noticed a low hum and a faint flicker of static in the background. She tilted her head. "What's that noise?"

Eli reached up and tapped a rectangular black box mounted to the underside of the upper cabinet. "Scanner. Sheriff is always on call, especially since our force is so small. I need to be reachable in case of an emergency."

Josie made a face and pulled her pager out of her pocket. "The local vet is always on call, too. But for me, it's just this and my cell phone. I don't get the fancy super-secret cop toys. Admit it, you just like seeing all this manly equipment scattered here and there, don't you?"

He bumped the refrigerator door closed with a hip, spun around, and hauled her against him. "Wanna see my nightstick, baby?"

"You mean that wasn't what you showed me this morning?" She laughed up at the mock scowl on his face.

He growled and kissed her ferociously and thoroughly. She emerged several seconds later feeling flushed, rumpled, and aroused. She figured she probably looked that way, too.

"Come on," he said, taking her hand and tugging her back toward the living room. "There are still one and a half rooms left in this grand tour, and one of them is my favorite. I'll let you guess which one it is."

The lascivious wriggle of his eyebrows kind of gave that one away.

Eli stepped into the living room and turned immediately through a doorway at the rear of the cabin. His free left hand flicked a switch on the wall, and the mellow light of a slender iron lamp illuminated the bedroom. For furniture, it boasted a five-drawer dresser, a single nightstand, and a bed the size of a small Central American nation, covered with a satiny chocolate-colored spread. Josie could see two doors in the right-hand wall separated by a narrow wooden desk. She assumed at least one of the door opened into a closet.

"I hope one of these leads to that indoor plumbing you promised?"

He grinned and gestured toward the far door. Josie strolled through, froze, and let out a gasp of astonishment.

She'd been expecting a bathroom to match the rest of the cabin—neat, spare, and just a little old-fashioned. She'd been prepared to be charmed by a claw-foot tub, maybe an antique wood-framed mirror, a porcelain pedestal sink. Instead she got a lesson in modern decadence cloaked in the mask of tradition. The pedestal sink was there, as was the wood-framed mirror, but the tub was built into the wall abutting the kitchen, huge, round, and gleaming white. Jetted. Deep. Big enough for two. If it weren't for the inevitable pruny skin, Josie would have wanted to live in it.

"Sandbagger!" She turned on him with narrowed eyes, saw him laughing.

"Does that mean you like it?"

"The tub and I will be sending out engagement announcements shortly."

"You should eat something first. I hear all that pre-wedding planning can take a lot out of a girl."

She followed him back into the kitchen and collapsed into one of the seats at the table. "Was that here when you moved in, or did you do that yourself?"

"I'd like to take the credit, but it was here. The couple

I bought the place from used it as a vacation getaway. They had planned to renovate the kitchen, too, but then their work transferred them to the East Coast, and they decided this would just be too far for quick weekends away anymore."

Josie shook her head. "For a bathroom like that, I'd rack up the frequent flier miles."

"Yes, but you're special."

Something intense lurked under that teasing comment, something that made Josie's heart pound and her belly do somersaults and her adrenaline gland launch into panic mode. Unable to find a reasonable answer, she just smiled and felt like an idiot.

Thankfully, Eli took pity on her.

"Are you ready for dinner yet, or would you like to go for a walk first?"

"Walk. It's still early. Now watch this." She grinned, turning to lean over into the living room. "Hey Bruce! Wanna go for a walk?"

The normally lethargic mutt threw his head back on a throaty howl of joy and leapt immediately for the cabin's front door.

Eli and Josie were still laughing minutes later as left the cabin hand in hand and walked a short distance down the quiet, single-lane road to the top of a path that angled off into the woods. It looked broad and fairly well used, and they stepped onto it readily and followed it away from the cabin. Bruce roamed in front of them, zigzagging back and forth across the trail, nose to the ground and tail waving high in the air.

"It's moments like these when I think I should have a dog," Eli said, mocking himself as he watched the mutt's antics. "A Labrador gamboling on ahead of me, chasing a stick, then bringing it back so I could throw it for him to chase again."

"And again. And again." Josie grinned. "It's a nice image, though. Why don't you get one? I'm sure a dog would love it out here."

"Dogs don't love me. I think it might be the fangs. Or maybe I just smell like their mortal enemy."

"Really? I'm surprised, because Bruce has no problem with you." Josie frowned. Eli seemed so incredibly normal most of the time that it was easy for her to forget he was a shifter. "Then again, you did bring him meat loaf, and he is cheap. Haven't you ever had a pet?"

"I also smell like you a lot of the time." He smiled, looking almost as wolfish as a Lupine. Then he sobered and shook his head. "No, I never had a pet. But on the other hand, my family was never bothered by unwanted strays showing up on the doorstep, either."

"Don't joke. That's sad." She tugged his hand to scold him. "I can't imagine growing up without pets. My sister and I both got kittens as soon as we were old enough to take care of them, and my dad always kept at least one dog. Usually a hunting dog, like a retriever or a hound. And of course, we always played with whatever animals came into the clinic, as long as they were well enough. And now I have Bruce."

"I think you develop a different perspective on animal ownership when you spend some time as an animal."

She scowled up at him. "You're not going to go all PETA on me and say that humans shouldn't be allowed to domesticate or own any animals from cows down to ferrets, are you? Trust me, left to his own devices, Bruce would be miserable. He's lost without meat loaf takeout and a nice, cushy sofa to sleep on."

He laughed. "No. I'm convinced that cows are too damn dumb to be allowed out of a pasture on their own. They need us to save them from themselves. I've got nothing against humans taking care of an animal, but there is something about confining one inside all the time that give me a few skin crawls."

"I could give you my vet speech about how dogs and cats kept as indoor pets live longer, healthier lives than not only outdoor pets, but also those who are allowed to move back and forth between outdoors and in."

"You could."

"But then I'd be a big old hypocrite, because clearly I don't keep Bruce inside twenty-four seven."

The dog gave a ferocious flurry of barks and made a mad dash after a squirrel, who evaded neatly and then proceeded to perch on a high branch and taunt the frustrated canine.

"And also I'd picture how I'd feel if someone locked me in a house twenty-four hours a day and asked me to use a litter box, and all your impassioned pleas would go unheard." He grinned down at her. "Or do you think I might be anthropomorphizing?"

"Well, if anyone has an excuse to do it, it's you."

"Maybe. But I also grew up in an area with lots of wildlife and fewer pets, so that might be a factor, too."

"Where are you from? The gossip tells it that you moved here all the way from big, bad Seattle."

"For once the gossips have it right, but I grew up in Colorado. I moved to Seattle later on. It's a great city, though. For a city."

"Just a country boy at heart?"

Eli shrugged. "I like going to a city from time to time, having access to good restaurants and shows and all that, but I think I'm done living in them. After I while, it just starts to get hard to move around in one. And I definitely wouldn't want to try to have a family or raise kids in one."

Josie felt her stomach give that nervous little flip. "You'd like to have kids one day?"

"Sure. And before I get too old to chase after them." He grinned.

"More than one?"

"Definitely. Being an only child sucks."

She laughed it off. "Sometimes, so does having a sibling."

They continued to walk along the path through the trees, crunching leaves and twigs underfoot as they went. Or rather, Josie and Bruce crunched. Eli seemed to move in a kind of unconscious silence, as if he weren't even trying but didn't know of any other way to move. It was a little disconcerting, actually. At least partially because it made her feel about as graceful as a herd of elephants in comparison.

They crested a small rise in the trail, and the view as they continued down the other side made Josie's breath catch in her throat. The trees opened up onto a gentle slope down to a fast-moving stream. The water frothed and gurgled over submerged rocks, and aspen and birch trees clung to the banks, their bright leaves rustling in the wind high above the dark, shiny surface. Bruce headed right for it, gave a cautious sniff, then leaned down to lap delicately, careful not to splash any water on himself as he drank.

"This is gorgeous," Josie breathed. "Is this your land?"

Eli nodded. "Up to the bank and for about another five

or six yards that way." He pointed away from the cabin. "This is the far edge of mine, and the stream continues across my property, but this is the prettiest place to come look at it."

She continued to drink in the loveliness of the sight. "Wow. Take my advice: Don't show this to Dr. Shad. He'd take one look at it, plant his butt on that downed log, cast his line in there, and that would be that. You'd never get rid of him."

"Hm, I wonder if he'd still come out after he heard that there's a big old cranky lion around here who likes to sun himself over by that log?"

His eyes twinkled down at her, and Josie found herself laughing at the image of the two men coming face-to-face in that . . . er . . . situation. Or maybe that would be face-to-whisker. "I think that depends entirely on how good the fishing is."

"Let's take a closer look and you can tell me what you think."

She let him tug her down toward the rocky bank. Josie peered into the clear, dark water for ten seconds and saw a flash of something silver. She shook her head.

"It's perfect. You're doomed."

When Eli didn't answer, she looked up and found him staring intently at the ground about six feet upstream in the direction of his cabin.

"Eli? What is it?"

He squeezed her hand, then released it. "I just want to check that out."

She followed behind him, puzzled when he moved to the place he'd been staring at, hunkered down, and studied the rocky forest floor as if expecting it to sit up and do

tricks. She tried briefly to figure out what had him so fascinated, but was forced to give up. All she saw was rocks,
dirt, tree roots, and pine needles.

"Okay, I just need to know. What in the world are you
staring at?"

He pointed to the ground. "Tracks. Fairly fresh ones."

Josie squinted down, but the view didn't change. She
saw nothing unusual. "Tracks from what?"

"People. Two, it looks like. And I'm guessing they
came through here within the last few hours."

"Really?" She stared at him, disbelieving. "How on
earth can you tell that? I don't see a thing."

He pointed to what looked to her like a smudge in the
dirt, an area of around three inches by four inches where
some pine needles had been swept away and formed tiny
walls on either side of a valley of crumbly soil.

"That's a partial footprint. The guy who made it bal-
ances on his toes instead of his whole foot. And he was
moving pretty fast. And his friend"—he pointed to another spot about a foot and a half away—"toes in. The
print is deeper on one side than the other."

Josie was astounded. "You can tell that from those
little . . . bald spots? That's amazing!"

He shot her a dry look. "It's pretty average for a good
tracker, halfway decent for a predatory Other. There are
Lupines and Felines with advanced military training who
can follow a trail more than a week old on desert footing.
Just miles of sand and bare rock and they can practically
have conversations with each individual grain of sand. I
can't even tell you if these guys were traveling light or
heavy. I suspect light, but that's just because I'm not seeing
enough to make me think different."

"I'm still amazed. I didn't even realize those were footprints until you showed me, and I still think I'd lose them if I looked away for a minute. I only see them because you pointed them out."

Eli grunted and rose, taking a few long strides forward. She followed quickly.

"They're headed farther onto my property." His voice sounded grim.

"That worries you?"

"It makes me curious, which is worse. There are no strange cars in the area, and my neighbor and I have an understanding about trespassing. The only reason anyone would need to get onto my property would be for hunting or fishing. Fishing season just ended, and I'm posted for no hunting. Plus, hunters and fishermen both use cars to get to their spots. Where's the car these guys drove in with?"

"Could it be farther down the road we came off?"

Eli shook his head. "Only a few yards past where we turned off, the road curves into my neighbor's drive. There's no place to park down there. At least, not on the side of the drive."

"So maybe they parked in the woods."

"Only reason to do that would be if they didn't want anyone to know they were here."

Josie thought about that and frowned. "Poachers?" She looked around warily for Bruce, who had thrown himself down in a patch of sun for an impromptu snooze.

"Maybe."

"What else could it be?"

"Last summer when we had that trouble with the protestors and all, some of those skinheads—the young, stupid ones, mostly—decided they shouldn't have to pay a fee to camp. It's a free country, right? So I had to . . . discourage a few of them from helping themselves to a couple of clearings on my land." He grimaced. "A few of them seemed to take a dislike to me."

As diplomatically as Eli put it, Josie could envision the scene in her head. With reasonable people—like most of the citizens of Stone Creek—the sheriff maintained an easygoing, mellow, and friendly demeanor, but she'd seen what happened when he got mad. She'd also encountered a few skinheads in her time, since the breed seemed to like the Northwest quite a bit and not to feel any need to hide their beliefs from a mainly white population. She didn't imagine the two immovable forces would deal well together.

In fact, she was pretty sure that when the two groups mixed, the combination could prove explosive.

"But why would they come back now? Things have been pretty calm on the whole Others-versus-humans front lately, right? I haven't heard about any upcoming protests."

"Neither have I." He scanned the tree line and the opposite bank of the stream like a soldier looking for an ambush. "Things *have* been quiet for quite a while now. That might be part of what's making me nervous. Plus, something about this smells funny to me. There's no reason for strangers to be sneaking around on my land."

"Like I said, maybe it's poachers."

"If it is, they're not from around here. Locals and local hunters know to stay away from here, because they can't be sure they won't be shooting someone's relative. We have Deerskin in the community, so folks who know Stone Creek don't like the idea of accidentally shooting the high school English teacher because they mistook her for an actual western mule deer. And even those who aren't from Stone Creek have usually heard of us by reputation. They stay away out of fear of running into a Lupine who's pissed off they took down one of *his* prey items."

She nodded. "Okay . . ."

"So the only people who would be out here sneaking around would be folks who haven't got honest intentions. Or ones who don't really care what they shoot."

Josie winced. "Oh. What are you going to do then?"

He sighed. "If I were alone, I'd follow the trail, find the people who left it—or their camp—and have a little come-to-Jesus talk with them. But since that can't happen at the moment, I'm going to take you back to the cabin, call the station, and let my staff know they need to be on alert for strangers wandering around in or outside town."

"Why do you have to take me back to the cabin? I'll go with you to look for these guys. I don't mind a hike."

Eli shook his head and reached for her elbow, guiding her inexorably back the way they'd come. "No, we'll go back now."

"Eli—"

"There are some things that I don't believe in leaving to chance, Dr. Barrett," he said firmly, "and the possibility of putting you in danger is one of those things. It's not up for negotiation."

"Um, excuse me?" Josie dig her heels into the ground and refused to move any farther. "I believe that if the descriptor *my* or *mine* precedes a noun, that means that *I* am the only one who gets to make decisions about that noun. As in safety. The operative term there is that it's *my* safety. You don't get to decide what to do with it. It's *my* safety, so if I want to toss it to the wind, light it on fire, or run it through a blender, that's my decision, and you don't get a say in it."

"That's not how this is going to work, Doctor."

"Not how *what* is going to work, Sheriff?"

"This relationship."

Oh please, dear God, Josie prayed, don't tell me he's really this stupid. Please.

She opened her eyes very wide and blinked at him. "I'm sorry, are you referring to *my* relationship with you? Which is all of about five days old at this point?"

He stepped forward until they were poised toe-to-toe and he could glare down at her from his vastly superior height. Why did big men always try to use it against a woman? she wondered idly. And why did she keep falling for them anyway?

"No, I was discussing *our* relationship. With each other. And who the hell cares how old it is? The operative word *there* is the *is*. It exists; you'll have to adjust. End of story."

"Right, clearly I missed the point in this conversation when we stepped into the time warp and were transported back to the Neolithic era. Because that kind of sentiment is not only out of place and outdated, it exists in the realm of time before written speech. It frickin' carries a club and is afraid of fire!"

"Well, you can adjust to that, too."

He started forward again, practically dragging Josie along behind him. Infuriated, she jerked her elbow from his grasp and bellowed for Bruce. The dog leapt to his feet in obvious surprise, but took one look at his owner's face and immediately trotted after her.

Josie stomped ahead of Eli, all but jogging back up the path. The faster she got to his cabin and called someone to come drive her back to town, the happier she'd be. In fact, she might not even wait for a ride. At this point, walking back into town would be preferable.

Eli stalked along behind her like an angry bear. Or a pissed-off tomcat.

"So now you're going to give me the silent treatment because I'm trying to protect you?"

Her eyes narrowed, but Josie didn't bother looking back toward him. Maybe if she could have turned him to stone like Medusa, it would have been worth the effort. "First, I'm not giving you the silent treatment. And second, if I were, it wouldn't be because you're trying to protect me. I have no problem with being protected. In fact, I prefer it to the alternative of being maimed, tortured, or killed. The reason I have every right to be quite justifiably displeased with you is that in the process of trying to protect me, you stopped treating me like an intelligent and capable woman with enough common sense to protect herself when such behavior is warranted, and instead began to act as if I were either six years old, brain-damaged, or both."

"I didn't—"

Finally, Josie paused just at the point where the path curved around to offer a glimpse of the opening to the road beyond. "You did. And you should probably know right now, Eli Pace, that I do not appreciate being treated like an imbecile, nor do I appreciate being ordered around like some kind of subservient human being. If you want me to do something because you're concerned for my safety, *tell* me you're concerned and then *ask* me to do what you believe is necessary for me to preserve that safety. Don't turn into a raving barbarian, because all that's going to do is piss me the hell off."

There was a moment of silence as the two of them stared at each other in the dappled light of the woods, struggling to come to terms with the stark reality of suddenly having someone both to worry about and who worried about them right back. For Josie, it was a revelation. Judging from the look of exasperation, concern, tenderness, and manly determination of Eli's face, she guessed he might be feeling something similar.

"Piss you off, huh?" he finally said, his tone softening to something close to musing. "I think I might have noticed something like that."

Josie crossed her arms over her chest. She felt the unraveling of tension as the worst of the storm clouds between them passed, but she didn't want him to think she was some kind of pushover.

"Well, that's just because you're unusually perceptive for a man, Sheriff Pace," she quipped.

He grinned and reached out to grab her by both elbows and tug her not forward, but close against him. A much wiser use of his strength overall, she decided.

"Thank you for noticing, Dr. Barrett," he murmured, his eyes dropping to her lips. "But I have one question for you."

She cocked an eyebrow.

"If I'm not allowed to act like a barbarian, can I still kiss you like one?"

He really didn't give her time to answer, but that didn't matter. She figured he must have read her response in her eyes. Or maybe in the way her lips parted, her arms opened, and she stood on the tips of her toes to meet the fierce descent of his mouth.

She loved the way this man kissed. If the darn things had any real nutritive value, she would have happily lived on them. The taste of him made her tingle; the scent of his skin sent her stomach into a roller-coaster ride of spins and flips, and the thrust and stroke of his tongue made a complete mess of her panties.

All he had to do was look at her, and she wanted him. When he touched her, she lost all connection with reality.

She reminded herself of that when she felt him walk her backward several steps into the tree line and push her back against the trunk of a wide old pine. He managed it without lifting his lips from hers, and Josie marveled at his sense of direction. Especially since she could no longer tell which end was up.

She figured it out only when she felt the world tilt on its axis, followed by the cool, uneven surface of the forest floor. He laid her on the ground and settled his body above her, all the while continuing to consume her mouth as if she were his world's only source of nourishment.

In the past, the idea of outdoor sex had always seemed to Josie to be completely implausible. She figured no one in her right mind—her, specifically, since guys never noticed things like this so long as they were getting some—would agree to take off her clothes where there were bugs and cold breezes or hot sunlight and bits of sand or leaves or dirt or who knew what else that could get stuck in places where God had never intended such things to be. She had always thought that there was a reason why people had invented beds and other pieces of furniture, and it wasn't just because they needed something to prop their pillows on. Beds made things more comfortable, as did sofas and lounge chairs and tabletops and even the occasional piece of carpet. So what kind of idiot would let herself be seduced right there in the euphemistically "great" outdoors.

Her kind, apparently.

The kind who stretched out beneath an amorous and insistent Feline who kissed like a dream, possessed magically gifted hands, and fit against her body like the other half of herself.

Instead of lodging a firm protest, she lifted her hips to help him remove her jeans, and she was the one who tugged her own T-shirt up over her head. She knew it was worth it, though, when his mouth latched on to her breast and proceeded to suck her soul out through her right nipple.

She moaned and squirmed when his fingers slid between her bare thighs, teasing the curls over her mound before parting her soft folds and doing their best to drive her completely crazy.

Fair was fair, she told herself, releasing her grip on his hair and reaching for his shirt to strip it off. Unexpectedly, he growled a protest and caught her hand pulling it up over her head. Abandoning her center for a moment, he dragged the other up alongside it and pinned both of her wrists to the ground in one of his large, powerful hands. Then he returned to his previous task with a purr of satisfaction.

Josie swore and squirmed, but his grip remained unbreakable. Not only did he outweigh her by a good seventy-five pounds, but he had the strength of any three men his size. Easily. She'd have had an easier time bench-pressing his SUV than breaking free and moving when he wanted her to stay still.

But that didn't mean she didn't try.

She drew a leg up untl she could press a knee to her own chest, which allowed her to press her foot against his shoulder and use her powerful thigh muscles to push him away. She didn't really want him to stop touching her, but something inside her demanded that he at least have to work for it.

Eli didn't budge. He kept her hands pinned to the forest floor and made a low curious sound in the back of his throat. Before Josie had time to speculate about what it might mean, he swapped his grip on her wrists to his other hand so that he could grab the leg she still had extended and position it to mirror her other—bent totally in half, her foot on his shoulder and her knee pressed up near her ear. Then he pressed a brief, affectionate kiss to her belly, shimmied south, and opened his mouth against her weeping core.

She screamed. She didn't mean to. In fact, the sound of her own voice nearly scared her witless. She hadn't realized she could even make that sound. It was barely human, but then, Josie barely felt human as Eli ran his tongue through her swollen folds, tasting her and purring with pleasure. She felt like flame, weightless and burning, dancing up from the wreckage of something else. Her past self, maybe, or the part of herself that had thought she could control this thing that had grown between the two of them.

She had been fooling herself, obviously. Who could control something this intense? This unexpected?

This perfect.

The knowledge exploded in Josie's consciousness along with the sensation of his wicked, talented tongue flicking over the tiny button buried between her folds.

She needed to give in. There was no other option. She had to surrender, not just to Eli or to this moment, but to the inevitability of their togetherness. The back of her mind acknowledged the fear that came along with such a momentous shift in her reality, but that little voice was completely overwhelmed by the sense of certainty that created it. The decision, she realized, had never really been hers to make. It had been made somewhere else, by some force she didn't even understand and could never hope to control; because she belonged with him.

He belonged with her.

They belonged together.

The knowledge flashed white-hot and overwhelming as his mouth began to draw on her, pushing her over into the abyss. She felt herself hanging there, floating, suspended between the now and the infinite for what felt like days, yet raced by in seconds. From a distance, she heard her own voice calling his name. And then just calling, a high, rich, exultant sound that echoed in the woods around her.

She collapsed, utterly spent, utterly boneless. Her hands ceased their determined struggle to be free, and her legs slid like water off his shoulders and onto the ground. She could feel bits of leaves and dirt clinging to her sweat-dampened skin. She couldn't have cared less. What she cared about was the man hovering over her.

He watched her face with an intensity she could sense even through her heavy eyelids. His entire being focused on her. It made her feel as if the fate of the world hung on her next move, her next word. Only she couldn't think of any words to say. Nothing seemed appropriate. What were her options? *Wow*? Talk about an understatement. *I love you*? Inappropriate. They hadn't reached that point yet, had they? They couldn't have. They had known each other less than a week. Love didn't happen like that, even if it felt almost like it already had.

But she couldn't hide behind this deliberate blindness forever. He deserved more than that, some piece of herself, besides the ones he'd already stolen. And besides that, she wanted him to know, even if it was too early for love, what she felt for him. The strength of it, if not the name.

Her eyes flickered open, and she found him exactly as she'd pictured him in her still-reeling mind, intent, hungry, and expectant. So she gave him what she could. She let him see the smile that had built inside her, the one that spoke of peace and profundity and a well of unspoken emotion.

With a supreme effort of will, she coerced her hand to move languidly from the position in which he had held it pinned and cupped his stubble-roughened cheek in her palm. Her thumb tracked the sharp blade of his cheekbone, and her fingertips hinted at all the things she couldn't quite say. And then she whispered.

"Thank you."

CHAPTER SIXTEEN

It took close to half an hour before Eli could trust her to stand on her own two feet. Before then, every time he tried to prop her up, her knees would buckle, or she would stumble over thin air, or she would just kind of melt against him in a way he appreciated, but felt constrained from taking advantage of. He couldn't quite put his finger on why, because Josie gave no indication that she felt they required more privacy or more comfortable surroundings to finish what they had started. He was the one who decided that the rest of their business should be concluded in bed.

In his bed.

In the bed where he'd been imagining her ever since he'd walked through her back door and seen her snap in an instant from a weary, wrinkled, and grumpy stranger to the professional, efficient, and dedicated woman he knew her to be.

Quickly, he collected Bruce, who had occupied himself quite nicely digging for woodchucks, and wrangled all three of them back to the cabin, where he shut his bedroom door in the dog's impassive face.

When Eli finally had Josie where he wanted her, he took his time.

He made love to her slowly and thoroughly, and then after a restorative break for sustenance, he allowed her to do the same to him. Or maybe he should have said, she insisted on doing the same to him and he could find no reason to argue. Nor any motivation. Afterward, they fell asleep in a purely contented tangle of hair and limbs and heartbeats and slept like kittens after unraveling a ball of yarn.

He woke a few hours later, shifting from sleep to wakefulness as he always did—in a silent dizzying rush, dreaming one moment and capable of calculating complex combat strategies entirely in his head the next. He'd always been that way, his Feline antecedents notwithstanding, and he'd come to view it over the years as quite a useful skill to have. Nothing ever caught him unawares while he slept, and that had saved his skin more than once.

Tonight, it saved Josie's.

Even before he opened his eyes, his senses alerted him to the fact that something wasn't right. Josie slept on undisturbed, sprawled half atop him, boneless and breathing deeply. She was exactly where she belonged. The problem was that something had changed in their environment. All was not as it had been when sleep had claimed him, and his senses clicked instantly to the problem.

A crisp autumn breeze wafted lightly over his bare skin where Josie's body did not cover him. Only when they had fallen asleep, all the windows and doors in the cabin had been closed.

Eli felt rather than saw a movement, felt it as a shift in the atmosphere, and he clamped his arms around Josie's back to pin her in place as he threw himself into a roll that spun them across the sheets and onto the floor while their attacker's hand still had not reached the apex of its preparatory backswing.

They landed with a thud on the floor between the bed and the rear wall of the cabin. The impact jerked Josie out of a sound sleep and she cried out reflexively, bewildered by the abrupt change in elevation. On the other side of the closed door, Bruce barked like a hellhound and threw himself at the wooden panel until it shook on its hinges. Eli simply rolled again, pinning Josie to the floor before leaping to his feet to face the intruder.

Unlike the characters in poorly scripted action films, he didn't bother to ask who the person was or what he wanted with Eli and Josie. Eli had always held the belief that in situations like this, it was better to maim first and ask questions later.

He dove at the man in a blur of motion and bare skin. The reflection of the moonlight through the window allowed his black-clad assailant to see him better than if he'd been dressed, but nature evened the odds with Eli's acute Feline night vision. He could see that the figure standing across the bed was definitely male, probably fairly young, and dressed surprisingly well for a breaking, entering, and attempted murder plot, when one discounted the idiocy of targeting a sheriff—and an Other sheriff at that—with such a scheme. The youth wore a black sweater and trousers made from a light-absorbing material that covered him from high on his neck down to the backs of his hands. He had covered those hands with dark gloves, and used black greasepaint to darken the skin of his face and throat. But he had left off the requisite balaclava, allowing Eli to note that his dark hair had been shaven close to his scalp. He definitely qualified as Caucasian, and behind his left ear, he sported a dark brown mole that hadn't received quite enough dark paint to cover it.

It took Eli all of three seconds to develop a complete description of the subject that he would be happy to share with his deputies and every law enforcement agent from San Francisco to the Canadian border. Just as soon as he made the idiot pay for putting Josie in danger.

One spring of his powerful legs closed the distance between them from approximately four feet to less than as many inches. The man's left hand came up and something in his hand glinted in the darkness. Eli's right forearm rose to block the downward thrust while he simultaneously drove his left fist into the attacker's unprotected gut. The black-clad figure grunted and jackknifed forward with a gagging sound. Surprisingly, this stirred little to no sympathy in Eli's soul.

"Josie! Out! Now!" he snapped, and was gratified to see her hand come up to drag the sheet off the bed. Two seconds later, she had the fabric wrapped around her like a toga and was flying across the room toward the cabin's exit, calling her dog to her as she went.

He'd really thought he was going to have to argue that one.

As soon as Josie disappeared into the living room, Eli twisted his arm and captured the intruder's wrist in his hand. He slammed it against the bedside table and listened to the clatter of an object dropping to the floor from the man's nerveless fingers. Then he finally gave root to his frustration, picked the intruder up in both hands, and flung him across the room like a pile of dirty laundry. He landed with a particularly satisfying *thunk* but failed to fall unconscious. Fortunately, Eli would be happy to rectify that oversight.

He prowled around the bed, each step deliberate and malevolent. He intended to first beat this asshole a little harder; then he would find out who the stranger was and what he was doing in Eli's cabin, threatening Eli's mate with some sort of weapon while the couple slept. Because that was just rude.

When Eli rounded the first corner of the bed, the black lump on the floor stirred, eyes widening until the white sclera seemed to glow in the otherwise darkened room. Tensing, Eli braced himself for a renewed attack or an onslaught of frenzied pleading. He got neither. Before he could take another step, the figure rushed to its feet and poured every ounce of its remaining strength into an upward leap, throwing itself out the open window and into the darkness of the nighttime forest.

Roaring in fury, Eli gave chase, determined to catch the assailant and question him, but just as his hands closed on the windowsill in preparation for a relentless pursuit, Josie's voice from calling to him from the front of the cabin froze him in place.

"Oh my God! Eli!"

Cursing viciously, Eli spun on his heel and raced through the door to face the new threat. Instead, he found Josie standing on the front porch in the center of a virtually unrecognizable space.

The pale pine and reed rocking chair that had always sat beside the bright blue door had been smashed into little more than kindling and scattered across the floorboards and onto the neat front lawn. A pot containing a huge sunflower that had been given to him by the PTA when he'd first moved to Stone Creek had also been broken, the tall plant now upended on the front steps. But worst of all were the vile words scrawled in red across the bright blue door.

FREAK FUCKER RACE TRAITOR ANIMALS ARE MEANT FOR SHOOTING

"It's not terribly eloquent, but I think the author got his point across," Josie quipped, her voice thin but steady. When she turned to face him, though, her eyes were clouded with fear and concern. "Are you okay? I heard some banging but not much else, so I figured you were doing okay. He didn't have a gun, did he?"

Eli grabbed her hand and tugged her against him, wrapping her up in his arms like a frightened child. "I didn't see one. He had something, but I'm thinking knife. The bastard was stupid, but he wasn't dumb, and guns attract a lot of attention."

Josie ran her hands over his arms and back and pressed herself closer. "He didn't cut you, did he?"

"I'm fine," he assured her. "Not even bruised." He pulled back until he could look into her eyes and press a kiss against her forehead. "You did exactly the right thing by running. Thank you for doing what I asked."

She rolled her eyes at him. "You ordered again, but despite what you may think, I'm not an idiot. I know that in matters of self-defense and hand-to-hand combat, I'm not the expert in our relationship. If we're in a truly dangerous situation where you have things under control and I'd only get in your way, of course I'm going to leave when you tell me to. I just want you to be aware that when it's not a directly life-threatening situation, I reserve the right to tell you to go screw yourself if you try to order me around."

"So noted."

"Good. Now, what happens next? I know you *are* the police, but after a person's house has been broken into and they've been assaulted with a deadly weapon, isn't it customary to call the cops? Maybe the other cops?"

He nodded. "I'll radio the deputy on duty and ask him to bring a crime scene kit. He can go over it with me, and we'll see what we find."

"Any chance you'll find my clothes, or are those part of the crime scene evidence now?" When he looked sideways at her, mouth twitching, she shrugged. "I like a good forensic science documentary. So sue me."

"I'll get you something to wear. Come on, let's go inside. We'll get dressed, I'll call Cooper, and we can wait for him in the kitchen."

"Let's make coffee. That may I might be able to stay awake until he gets here. Seeing as how it's about two fifteen in the morning."

Eli steered her back into the cabin and away from the intruder's nasty words, but Josie clearly hadn't forgotten them. Ten minutes later when she sat at the kitchen table wearing one of his buttondown shirts over a pair of his cotton boxers, she rested her chin on her fist and watched him put together the coffee. Her free hand ruffled absently through the shaggy fur on Bruce's head.

"Do you think I was his target?" she asked.

Eli paused for a moment, then continued measuring grounds into the filter. "I'm not sure. You may have been, but we were so close together it's impossible to tell. He could have been going for either one of us."

"Clearly, he dislikes me, though. Or at the very least, he dislikes the idea of me having a sexual relationship with a shapeshifter. Actually, I'm assuming he dislikes the idea of any human ever having any kind of relationship with any Other. His wording sounded a bit . . . sweeping."

Eli slammed the filter drawer shut and pushed the button on the coffeemaker. Then he turned to glare at Josie. "We are not having a sexual relationship."

"Could have fooled me."

"We're having a relationship. Period."

Josie watched him, her expression very neutral. "What's the difference?"

"What do you mean what's the difference?" He leaned back against the counter and crossed his arms over his chest and his feet at the ankles. The better to glare at her. "One implies that our only interest in each other is how many times the other one can make us come. The other means states that we're more to each other than a warm body on a cold night."

"Are we?"

Fury washed over him. He darted forward and slammed his hands flat on the table across from her. Then he leaned in until their noses almost touched. "What the hell is that supposed to mean?" he demanded.

Josie shrugged, and her gaze skittered away from his. "I just mean that we've only been seeing each other a few days. Heck, we've only known each other that long. I wouldn't want to assume anything about the way you feel about me based on the fact that we've spent every night together since the third one of our acquaintance."

He grabbed her chin in his hand and forced her gaze back to his. "Now is not the time to ask how I feel about you, Josephine, because right at this very moment, you happen to be *pissing me the hell off.*"

"I'm so sorry," she snapped, sarcasm dripping from her tongue. "Please forgive me for not knowing how exactly I'm supposed to be reacting to a situation I've never found myself in before. Clearly, I should have read the damn manual on human–Other social interactions before I agreed to let you and the Stone Creek Alpha eat pizza at my apartment!"

Finally—and belatedly—the note of mingled anxiety and confusion wormed its way through Eli's instinctive anger at being dismissed as less than Josie's predestined lifemate. He grabbed a sharp hold on his temper and sank down into the chair opposite her.

"Okay, sweetie, I think it's time we talked about what's really going on here. What's making you so upset right now? You tell me yours, and then I'll tell you mine."

Josie made a frustrated sound in her throat and bowed her head. "That sounds about as appealing right now as a root canal." She fisted her hands in her hair and tugged sharply. "How about we just forget the whole thing and drink our coffee until Jim gets here?"

"No. Now spill."

She closed her eyes and let her arms flop to the table. Bruce made a disgruntled sound and took refuge underneath. "I just . . . feel like I'm playing without a rule book here. I don't understand how this thing is supposed to work, and whenever I feel like I'm starting to get a handle on things, it's like the rules have changed and I've said exactly the wrong thing."

"Wait, what do you mean by 'how this thing is supposed to work'? Do you mean our relationship?"

"See, I don't even know if that's what I'm supposed to call it! I've never done this before. Every other relationship I've ever had has been an ordinary experience with an ordinary guy. And now suddenly there's you, and the last thing you are is ordinary, and I don't get how it's supposed to work now."

Eli wondered briefly if she was actually speaking English, because he felt as if he were listening to a foreign language he'd studied in high school and not heard since—he understood about one in every ten words, and even then he couldn't seem to make any guesses about the context in which she used them.

"Are you all twisted up because you've never dated an Other before? Is *that* what this is about?"

"Don't say it like that," she snapped, glaring at him. "Don't dismiss it as if I'm being ridiculous. Don't act like it doesn't mean anything that I'm human and you're not. We're different species. I mean, even more than most men and women feel like different species from each other, *we* actually *are*. We think differently, see differently, sense differently. Even our bodies don't work exactly the same way. Our cultures are different. This is not a ridiculous thing to be concerned about."

He growled. "Yes. It is. It's ridiculous, because you're making it sound as if the things that differentiate us from each other are somehow larger and more important than the things that make us alike. We both live in the same world, we both know the same people and frequent the same places. We even laugh at the same jokes and like the same movies. How are any of those things less important than that we don't have exactly the same chromosomal makeup? Where did you get these ridiculous ideas about humans and Others not being able to mix? I would have thought that growing up in Stone Creek would have made you understand that we're a hell of a lot more alike than we are different."

She leaned away from him and looked hurt. He hated that. He was trying to make things better, not make her feel worse. "You make me sound as if I'm a worse bigot than the idiot who wrote those things on the front door, but that's not what I mean. I don't think that you're any less of a person than I am; I don't even think you're any less 'human' than I am. Whatever that means. I just think that whenever we start to talk about *us,* we seem to be using different languages where the words sound the same, but the meanings are just a tiny bit different. Like I'm speaking Italian and you're speaking Spanish, and we sort of understand what the other one is talking about, but we're actually missing half of every conversation we try to have."

"So then let's trade definitions," he offered. "We don't need to make this harder on ourselves. If what we need is an Eli-to-Josie dictionary, let's write one. This is too important to let it fall apart over a little thing like varying definitions."

Josie pointed at him and made a sound of triumph. "See, that's exactly what I mean! You say this is 'too important,' but what do you mean by *important*? Because I'm a cautious girl by nature, and I don't want to assume that when you say it's important you mean that it's something you expect to be part of your life for the foreseeable future, when what you really mean is that it's a lot of fun at the moment and you don't want to screw it up while the sex is still so good."

Eli blinked against the glare of the light suddenly dawning directly in front of him. "That's what this is about," he breathed, and felt as if Atlas's globe had just been lifted from his shoulders. "You don't understand how I feel about you, do you?"

She blinked. "Am I supposed to? Because if you told me, I completely missed it. Was I drunk? Did I hit my head? What happened?"

He shook his head. "You didn't miss anything, sweetie. I think we've just had so much going on that neither of us realized it might be important to make a few things clear to each other. Let me go first."

He took her hand and clasped it between two of his. Instantly he felt better. Calmer. More whole. Everything always improved when he was touching her. If she couldn't see that, she must be blind.

"I've been trying to be all considerate and understanding about the fact that you seem to go into this state of panic every time the subject of our relationship comes up. I kept thinking it was because you thought things were moving too fast. I thought you needed more time, and I should just play it cool and let things progress naturally until you realized what was happening between us. I thought that by going slow I was going the right thing, but if I was wrong, I am more than happy to correct that mistake right here and right now."

He caught her gaze and held it, needing to be connected to her in every way possible while he made this clear.

"I am utterly and completely enthralled by you. I don't know why I didn't see it before, or how I wasted three years living in the same town with you without ever so much as really seeing you. The only way I can explain it is to say that I was a complete idiot. For some reason, I didn't realize you existed as more than a name and a profession. And it kills me to think about how much time I wasted because of it. I could kick myself. Except that I've come to understand that it doesn't matter. All that matters is that now that I've met you and spoken to you and felt you and tasted you, I'm done. That's it. You're the end for me. I am not going anywhere, so I'm going to suggest that you don't even try to get rid of me."

Josie's eye widened and her mouth opened, but he leaned forward to kiss her into silence.

"No, let me finish. I don't really care what you decide to call what's between us. The fact of the matter is that it exists, and that's enough for me. The only thing I care about is that it makes you happy. What I don't want is for it to make you confused. So I'm going to lay this out: I don't want you to tell me how you feel about me tonight or tomorrow or the next day. I want you to wait. I want you to really figure it out and get comfortable with it. It needs to stop confusing you and making you crazy, and frankly, I don't think sanity is in the cards for us until we figure out what's going on with Rosemary and Bill."

Her eyes closed, and she sighed at the reminder of the mess waiting for them back in town. He squeezed her hands and waited until her lashes drifted back up.

"So here's the new rule. No declarations, at least not until the issue with the Lupines is resolved. Then, we can talk again about how you feel and how I feel and how we're going to deal with all of it. Now is a crappy time to be making decisions about anything, especially the rest of our lives."

He kissed her once, briefly, and smiled at her gently.

"Just remember—the way I feel about you is not going to change. I've waited my whole life for you, for this, and I intend to spend the rest of my life savoring every last minute to come."

She frowned and tried to speak, but he shushed her and squeezed her hands.

"Nope. Not until this is done. Besides, I just heard Cooper's car pull up, so we have other things to do right now. We'll talk again when this is behind us."

With that, Eli rose and went to meet Jim, leaving Josie behind at the kitchen table. She would need a minute or two, he decided, before she had to deal with making a statement. She could thank him for being so insightful and understanding another time.

CHAPTER SEVENTEEN

Dear God! Clearly the man had been dropped on his head as a child. More than once. And from a considerable height. It was the only explanation for how he could possibly had gotten to be so mind-bogglingly, jaw-droppingly, awe-inspiringly stupid.

So *she* needed time to think, did she? No way could she possibly know her own mind about the man she was having a relationship with! A feeble-minded and opinionless woman like herself couldn't ever be trusted to make anything as complicated as her own decision, and even if she had, she would *obviously* need time to mull it over and over in her vacuous little head until the two brain cells she barely had to rub together had worked out all the complexities of such a thing as her own bloody emotions.

Of all the arrogant assumptions! The man was lucky she didn't march out onto the porch, carafe in hand, and dump the entire pot of scalding-hot coffee onto his head! In front of his damn deputy!

If she had brought her own car out here this afternoon, she would have changed into her own clothes, grabbed her keys, and been halfway back to Stone Creek before the moron managed to pry even half of his size twelve boot

out of his condescending throat. To hell with the responsibilities of citizenship and looking out for a neighbor. He
could fill out his own police report. It would serve him
right if she developed a sudden and debilitating case of
amnesia every time the subject of the break-in was even
mentioned.

Of course, after that little lecture inside, if she did pretend to have forgotten the evening's incidents, he would
just chalk it up to her overwrought female nerves and add
it to his list of asinine reasons why she couldn't possibly
know yet how she felt about the miserable jerk.

As if she wasn't perfectly capable of acknowledging
that she loved the miserable son of a bitch!

Men!

Her temper was frayed, to say the least, as she yanked
open cabinet doors until she found a shelf of coffee mugs.
She grabbed one for herself, filled it, dumped in the requisite flood of cream—Trust a Feline bachelor to keep
half a gallon of real heavy cream in his refrigerator. Josie
hadn't even known the stuff came in half gallons!—and
returned to her seat at the table. When they wanted to
hear what she had to say about earlier events, they could
damn well come and get her. She wouldn't be going out
of her way for them anytime soon.

She sat alone for almost fifteen minutes, nursing both
her coffee and her rage. Unfortunately, the coffee was
the only thing that cooled in the time before the two men
filed into the kitchen and helped themselves to the still-
brimming pot.

"Well, that was a nasty bit of work he did outside there.
I'll give him that." Jim Cooper sighed as he eased himself
into a straight-backed chair. "I'm happy to say we don't

see much of that kind of sentiment around here, Dr. Barrett, and I'm real sorry that you had to see it tonight."

What the hell? The man spoke as if she hadn't spent twenty-two of her thirty-two years living in the frickin' town and becoming aware of what people saw around it and what they didn't. Was Eli's stupidity contagious? Was it an epidemic among the male population of Stone Creek? Would she go into work on Monday morning and discover that Ben had forgotten how to take a patient statement or use the CBC machine?

"I believe I'll survive the trauma, Deputy, but it's . . . kind of you to be concerned."

Jim nodded, perfectly content to believe in her sincerity.

Dear Lord, what was the world coming to?

"I agree with the sheriff about it, though," the man continued in his slow, steady tone. "I don't think it was done by anyone local. Based on the wording of the graffiti and the description Eli gave of the attacker, I'd say it's likely we've got another skinhead incident on our hands."

Oh my goodness. They had managed to figure that out for themselves, had they?

"You may be right," she acknowledged steadily. "But last time, the incident was a bit different, wasn't it? Less personal and more disseminated. Protests and riots instead of a personal attack. Why do you suppose they changed their tactics? Assuming it's the same group, I mean. And why wait a year after the protests that summer?"

Eli shook his head. "I'm not sure we can assume it's the same group, but we probably shouldn't rule out the possibility at this point, either. Oregon, Washington, and Idaho unfortunately have more than their share of white and human supremacist groups. But since they usually leave Stone Creek alone, I wouldn't be surprised if there was a link to last year's events. We'll need to look into it, definitely. As for the time lapse . . . we made it fairly clear last year that their kind weren't welcome in town. Maybe it took this long to reorganize, or to come up with a new strategy."

"A whole year should make for more of a strategy than one random attack."

"I think they changed tactics because the things they tried last year didn't work," Jim concluded. "All they got for their pains was a night in jail, a court summons, a couple of fistfights, and a lot of bad press. Maybe they figured since they couldn't change the whole town's mind about Others, they'd just take care of things themselves, one sympathizer at a time."

Josie blinked at that. "You still think he was after me?"

"We won't be able to really say until we've taken a look at the bedroom and seen what his attack angle was and things like that. But the graffiti on the door does make me a mite suspicious."

She drained her coffee and stood, crossing to the counter and depositing her mug in the top rack of the dishwasher. "Then I say we go on and take a look."

Jim retrieved a large, thick, briefcase-style bag from his truck and accompanied Eli into the cabin's bedroom. Both men insisted that Josie remain in the doorway so that she wouldn't "compromise any evidence." As if she wasn't already part of the damn evidence. Still, since that wasn't the fight she was in the mood to start at that particular moment, she held her peace and remained where she was, mimicking Eli's favorite position by leaning one shoulder against the doorjamb and crossing her arms over her chest.

Eli insisted that they start the search for clues by the window, which he dubbed the point of entrance. "He didn't have to break the window. It wasn't locked. There aren't usually any people out here to worry about keeping out, and I'd had it open this morning for some fresh air. It was closed when we went to bed, but not locked."

Josie noticed that Jim didn't even blink at Eli's use of the plural in the context of bedtime. Apparently, the entire town either knew they were sleeping together or assumed it, which didn't do all that much to improve Josie's temper. Oh, she knew better than to think that Eli had been bragging about her to people as a conquest, but at the moment she was in the mood to hold the deputy's attitude against the sheriff anyway. Mostly just for spite.

"When we're done in here, I'll head around back and check for footprints and debris and whatnot," Eli mentioned.

"Wouldn't it make more sense to wait until morning? When there's light?" Josie asked.

"I'll check then, too, but I want to get a sense tonight of where he came from and where he ran off to."

She fell silent again and watched as they worked to process the scene. Eli appeared interested mainly in logistics, while Jim performed the basic tasks of dusting the window for fingerprints—even though Eli had said the assailant wore gloves, it was procedure to check, apparently—and scouring the room for trace evidence. She had to admit that the deputy performed his job with thorough determination. He pored over every inch of the room, collecting anything the attacker might have touched, shed, or left behind. He used a couple of different flashlights to search for latent evidence, even checking in the bedsheets and under the furniture.

After the first hour, though, neither he nor Eli had yet located a weapon.

Finally, Jim worked his way around the bed toward the door and knelt in front of the nightstand with his cheek to the floor and his high-powered flashlight aimed underneath. He passed the beam from left to right and jerked to a halt. He made a noise that Josie interpreted to be a combination of surprise and excitement, with maybe a tinge of concern thrown in.

"Hey, boss, come here and check out what I just found."

"Did you find the weapon? Is it a knife? I never got a good look at it." The sheriff had the words out even before he rounded the end of the bed.

"I suppose you might consider it a weapon," Jim drawled, "but it sure as heck isn't a knife."

Reaching out with latex-gloved fingers, the deputy carefully stuck his hand under the small table and emerged holding the plunger end of a full, unused medical syringe.

Josie stared in astonishment. "What? He attacked us with that? What's in it? Some kind of poison? Or was he just going to drug one of us? Or was it supposed to be some kind of a kidnapping?" She frowned. "I don't get it."

"I don't know if I do, either." Eli had his gaze fixed on the needle, and something in his expression made Josie take notice.

"Eli? What is it?"

He shrugged, but the look on his face was far from unconcerned. "It might not even be related," he said slowly, "but when I went to look at the site where Rosemary was shot, I found a hunter's blind that I think was used by her shooter. In the underbrush there, I found an empty vial—the kind that doctors draw medications out of. Using a syringe."

A wave of cold swept over Josie. She couldn't decide if it came from a premonition of something sinister, or from a sense of hurt that Eli hadn't shared something so significant with her. "And you didn't tell me? Why didn't you show me the vial? Maybe I could have identified what was in it."

"I told you, there was nothing in it. It was empty."

"But I'm familiar with all kind of drugs, and even if I didn't recognize the name, I could easily have—"

"There was no name on it," Eli explained. "The vial had no label. It was just plain glass. And it's not as if I deliberately didn't tell you. I found it just before I heard the call about Bill going berserk in the clinic. Frankly, at that point I forgot all about it because I was scared to death that you were hurt."

"But why didn't you tell me later?"

"Because things kept getting in the way. Every time I thought of it, something would happen to distract me. Like more wolf attacks. But I did realize it would be good to know what it contained, so I sent it to Steve along with the samples from Bill and Rosemary."

"Oh, great, so that's one more clue that we can't interpret because it's being held hostage by your friend in Colorado." Josie threw up her hands and spun around to stalk back toward the kitchen. She could feel Eli trailing along behind her even though she couldn't hear his footsteps. He moved more silently than a ghost.

"Stephen isn't holding anything hostage." His voice

sounded strained, as if he had to struggle for patience. Poor thing. "I already told you, he's doing this as a favor to me because he owes me, but he's doing it on his own time. He does have a job to do, and I can't ask him to make us a higher priority than that."

Josie didn't care how sane and logical his argument was. She was sick and tired of waiting around for answers while her world sailed merrily down to hell in a handbasket. "Maybe your favor isn't a high priority with him, but the lives of Bill and Rosemary Evans *are* a high priority with me. In fact, at the moment, they're almost my only priority, and every day we have to wait for answers is another day when they get worse instead of better. Someone has to do something, and if that means me flying to Colorado and standing over your friend's shoulder while he runs his tests, then by God that is exactly what I will do."

How much farther the argument would have gone, Josie didn't know. Before Eli could form a response, Jim stuck his head in from the living room, looking almost as if he feared someone might snap it off.

"What?" Eli barked, his scowl ferocious.

"Sorry to interrupt, boss, but I kept hearing this weird noise in the other room, and I couldn't figure out what it was until I realized it was coming from the doc's . . . uh . . . from her clothes. I think it must have been a cell phone or a pager. You want me to bring them to you, Dr. Barrett?"

She shook her head. "No, don't bother. At this hour, it must be the clinic." She looked at Eli. "Mind if I just use your phone to check in?"

"Be my guest."

Josie picked up the receiver and dialed the number of the clinic. Given the time, someone must have reached the night service with an emergency. Mentally bracing herself for a rush back to town and into her surgery suite, she waited until the line picked up before saying, "This is Dr. Barrett. Is there an emergency?"

Instead of the voice of an anonymous call screener, Josie heard her secondary vet tech Andrea, and the woman's voice was shaking.

"Dr. J, I got a call from the alarm company because something tripped the system at the clinic and they couldn't reach you on your cell."

"I'm sorry, I didn't hear it ring. Did you have to tromp all the way out there for another falling IV stand?"

"No." Andrea made a choking noise that sent Josie's heart into overdrive. "Dr. J, it wasn't a false alarm."

Impatience melted into concern. "Someone broke in? Was anything taken? Did anyone get hurt?"

"No. Yes. I mean . . . No one broke in. The alarm went off when something broke out."

And just like that, Josie knew it was bad. Very bad.

"The wolves somehow managed to get through the gate, Dr. J. Bill is gone. He's missing. It looks like he went out the window in the file room."

Her grip on the receiver tightened until her knuckles turned white with the strain. "And Rosemary?"

"God, Dr. J. She's dead. And it looks like Bill killed her."

Exp. 10-1017.03
Log 03-00141

It is nearly time to move into the final
phase. It becomes difficult to conceal my

enthusiasm and to maintain the proper
distance of a trained scientist. I
have worked so long toward this goal
that to come so close to its final
realization . . .

Words fail me.

Soon it will be past time to collect data
and record observations. Anticipation is
my constant companion. Anticipation and
elation.

The end is near.

CHAPTER EIGHTEEN

Josie white-knuckled it all the way back into town, and she wasn't even the one driving. She sat beside Eli in the front of the Jeep and stared through the windshield at the eerie flashing red and blue of the emergency lights unaccompanied by the shrillness of the sirens; it was almost four in the morning, after all. The silence didn't matter, though, because she still thought she could hear a high-pitched wailing noise without them. Too bad she knew that sound came from inside her own head, not out of it.

Behind the wheel, Eli's features were set in a grim cast, the telltale muscle of his jaw twitching from the clenching of his teeth. He had said barely a word since the call, just switched into his super-efficient-sheriff mode, barked an order at Jim, hustled Josie into the car, and peeled out of the drive as if it weren't already too late for speed to do Rosemary the slightest bit of good.

"Jim will be right behind us," he said, breaking the silence with the gruff attempt at reassurance. "And he put out an all-hands call from my radio. I will have every man on the department working on this, Josie. I promise. We'll find Bill."

She said nothing, just clenched the hands on her lap

together in one big fist and squeezed until she could feel her fingers growing cold from lack of circulation.

"I never should have stayed away last night," she murmured. "None of the sedatives was working and Bill was getting more and more violent and aggressive by the hour. I should have stayed. I should have realized this was a possibility."

"Don't be stupid." He shot her a hard look, softened a bit by the expression of compassionate concern in his green eyes. "No one saw this as a possibility, and there was no reason we should have. Bill and Rosemary were married for ten years. And more than that, they were mates. I've never even heard of one mated Lupine killing another, and I doubt Rick has, either. This kind of thing doesn't happen, Josie, and you can't beat yourself up for not predicting the unpredictable."

"Don't say it 'doesn't' happen." She meant to snap it out, but it sounded more like a plea. "You can't say that. Because it just did."

He made no response to that, just fixed his attention on the road and drove in tense silence.

When they pulled up in back of the clinic, one police cruiser had already beaten them to the scene. Eli parked beside it, but he'd barely finished applying the brake before Josie had the door flung wide and was sprinting for the entrance, past a very surprised Deputy Able.

Eli shouted at her to wait, but she ignored him. She heard him slam his door and curse, knew he would be following hot on her heels, but she didn't slow down. Something inside compelled her to hurry—faster!—as if by getting to the scene a second or two sooner she could force the news not to be true. If she reached Rosemary before anyone else, maybe she could save her. Maybe she could make it all go away and both wolves would be locked inside the makeshift kennel, glaring and growling and pacing like ticking time bombs. She could live with time bombs, so long as she could turn back the clock and be here before one of them went off.

But of course, she couldn't.

She bolted past Andrea, huddled on a stool in the triage area, looking white and shaken and miserable, and slammed into the wall of the hallway because she had taken the corner too fast. She blocked out the pain of the impact and kept running, reaching the isolation room breathless and desperate.

And it made not the slightest bit of difference.

She skidded to a halt just inside the doorway of the small windowless chamber and felt her stomach heave at the sight that greeted her. It looked as if some kind of monster had torn through the chain-link enclosure with the sheer force of his hate. And maybe that was exactly what had happened. A sharp and twisted mass of thick wire framed a hole the size of a hula hoop in the center of the gate. Blood and bits of fur clung to the ends of some of the wire, which looked not as if they had been cut neatly with a man-made tool, but as if they'd been simply snapped in some places and in others stretched until they gave out against an enormous force. The slightly bloody evidence of Bill's passing, though, failed utterly at preparing her for the sight of what lay just beyond the fence.

Part of Josie wanted to laugh at the sheer amount of gore in the compact space, just because it seemed so impossible for something this horrendous to be real. It was logical to think that a Hollywood film crew had broken into her clinic and used the isolation room to stage an elaborate and ostentatious shot of the aftermath of a mad slasher's latest murder spree. Surely that had to be it. Those couldn't be pieces of Rosemary Evans lying like chunks of bloody meat on the perfectly polished linoleum floor.

They couldn't be.

Eli threw himself into the room behind her, nearly knocking into her before he saw exactly where she was standing. He took one look at her chalk-white face and followed her gaze to the evidence of the Lupine massacre. He uttered a brief, filthy, Anglo-Saxon epithet and grabbed Josie, attempting too late to shield her from the sight. If only he could erase it from her memory.

That, of course, was impossible. As was her fantasy of saving Rosemary. The wolf wasn't just dead, but torn apart. Clumps of fur and flesh lay everywhere, and more blood than it seemed possible to contain in one body pooled and dripped and dotted every surface. Josie would never be able to look at this room again without seeing the thick, dark liquid and the gruesome evidence of her failure. She had wanted so badly to save these creatures, and she wondered if what she had done had been worse than if she'd never involved herself with them at all.

"You don't need to look at this," Eli rasped, his voice harsh and strained against her hair. Despite his words, his hands remained exquisitely gentle where he cradled her to him. "Come back out of here and sit with Andrea. She's still shaking. You guys can be together and help each other through this. My men and I will deal with what happened in here."

She shook her head and pulled carefully away from his comforting strength. She knew he was trying to help her, trying to make things easier for her by shielding her from the even more horrific task to come—that of sifting through what remained of the female Lupine in order to piece together what had actually gone on in this room. That would be the first step in figuring out where Bill had gone, and no matter how it turned her stomach, Josie intended to be there for every minute of it.

She took a deep breath, let it out slowly, and pulled carefully away from him. "I'm fine. I mean, I'm not fine, but I'm not going to fall to pieces. I can cope. And I want to be part of this. I have to be. I need to help sort this out, and I need to help make it right."

For several long heartbeats, Eli said not a word. His bright eyes studied her face, noting the pallor of her skin, the bruised look beneath her eyes, and the determined set of her jaw. "You're already tired. You haven't gotten enough sleep tonight."

"It's already morning. And neither have you." The steadiness of her voice surprised even Josie, and she drew strength from the sound of it.

But she still didn't have it in her to argue. She didn't want to argue; she'd had enough of fighting. More than enough. She just wanted to help.

"Please."

He watched her a moment longer, his gaze searching. Then he nodded. "All right, but anytime you need to take a break, you do it. No heroics and no need to make a fuss about it. You leave and you take exactly as long as you need before you come back. Understood?"

"Understood."

Josie did leave to talk to Andrea, but only long enough to ensure that the woman's boyfriend had already been called and was on his way to pick her up. Since the clinic was closed on Sundays, there was no reason for the tech to linger after the police had finished taking her statement, but she shouldn't be alone, either.

Once she had that taken care of, Josie dug a spare pair of scrubs out of a cabinet and went into the file room to change. When she stepped out again, she felt steadier in the familiar green uniform. The soft cotton cloth comforted her, and with her hair pulled up and back with a black clip, she felt almost ready to face the isolation room again. She grabbed a box of latex gloves and a pair of long tweezers on the way.

By now, the triage room was crowded with the entirety of the Stone Creek sheriff's office, with the exception of only the secretary and part-time dispatcher, Cindy Lautenberg. Jim Cooper and the other full-time officer, Mike Driscoll, were carrying crime scene cases through to the isolation room, while part-timer Tim McGann quietly interviewed Andrea, her boyfriend Stu now standing with her, his hand on her trembling shoulder. Eli was near the door giving orders to Greg Able and Will Chkalov.

He turned when he saw her and immediately dismissed his men to start their search for the missing Lupine, covering the ground between them in four long strides. When he looked down at her, his expression held a wealth of concern and more than a hint of tenderness.

"You're sure you want to do this?"

She nodded, once. "Positive."

He waited only a second before he took her at her word. "Okay. Then let's get started."

The isolation room felt crowded with four adults packed

inside, but somehow all the living bodies working side by side helped to minimize the devastating effect of seeing someone they all knew lying in pieces at their feet. Eli led her to the now fully opened gate of the kennel enclosure and stepped back so that she could get an unobstructed view of the carnage.

"If you really want to do this, you can help me most by telling me about Rosemary. If I know exactly what he did to her, it might help me figure out not just what happened here, but what could happen next."

Josie took a breath—through her mouth so that she wouldn't have to smell the sickly sweet odor of death—and tried to separate what lay in front of her from the living person she had treated throughout the last week. She wasn't completely successful, but she did manage well enough to start.

Adopting an attitude of academic professionalism, she moved closer to Rosemary's remains, being careful to step in the smallest amount of blood possible.

"Her lower body seems mainly intact," she began, relieved at the sound of her doctor voice. She'd been afraid she would sound more like a terrified and devastated little girl. But she managed to keep that voice locked inside for now. "She had cuts and bite wounds on her flanks, including the left, where she sustained her previous injury, and on her legs, as well as blood on her paws, which indicates that although she was injured fairly seriously, she continued to struggle for at least a time before she was overcome."

Josie moved her gaze along the mangled body and had to work to suppress a shudder. "Her abdomen and chest appear to have sustained the worst damage. She's been eviscerated, and her large and small intestine, liver, stomach, and one kidney are clearly visible outside the abdominal cavity. The organs also look as if they've sustained severe trauma, and I suspect that pieces of one or more of them have been removed and possibly lie scattered in another part of the room."

She could feel Eli watching her closely, but she intended to give him nothing more than the mildest sign of the turmoil inside her. She refused to be taken away from her scene, her patient, her clinic. She'd stick this out if it killed her, until Bill was caught and the source of his violent rage was found.

"Two of her lower left ribs have been displaced and broken, and these look like teeth marks here." She pointed to the stark surface of a bone exposed beneath a missing chunk of muscle tissue. "Whether they got here because of an attempt to feed or merely an attempt to inflict further damage, I'm not sure. I'm suspecting, though, that it's the latter. While there are pieces of . . . the victim . . . not attached to the carcass, there appears to be sufficient matter in the room to account for what isn't right here. Plus, I'd expect to see more exposed and displaced bone if an attempt to feed had been made, and it would be likely that the liver and at least part of the stomach would be completely gone. The liver being the most prized piece of meat in a wolf's kill."

Eli nodded. "Anything else?"

"Well, I see plenty of defensive wounds, so she clearly didn't go down without a fight. There's blood and fur in her mouth, so she bit her attacker, and the fur on the nails of her front feet indicates more than just walking in shed fur and blood. She put up a pretty fierce struggle. For all the good it did her."

He nodded grimly. "She didn't stand much of a chance. He outweighed her by a good fifty pounds, for all their overall size was similar. Plus, she stayed unconscious longer and took longer to recover from that than he did. Chances are, she still had some lingering weakness that made her an easy target."

"That's the point I don't get," Josie admitted. "Why in the world would he target her? They were mates, and wolf pairs are notoriously loyal to each other. A male wolf is a hell of a lot more likely to kill *for* his mate than to kill her. What could have motivated him?"

"Is insanity a motive?"

She looked surprised. "You think Bill was insane? I didn't notice anything odd in his behavior until after he shifted and all this other stuff started."

"I don't think Bill was insane, but I think there's a chance that whatever he's been turning into since his failure to shift back to human form could be. I imagine that sort of situation, being trapped and not really understanding why or what's going on . . . that's the kind of thing that could play games with a person's mind. Don't you think?"

"But this isn't just, 'Oh, woe is me! I'm so confused!' This is *Jack the Ripper, Texas Chain Saw Massacre, Freddy Krueger's got nothing on me* violence for the sake of sadistic pleasure and the release of rage. Could just a few days have pushed him that far?"

"I don't know, but I think it's possible."

"Then why did Rosemary not do this yesterday? She shifted first, a whole day before Bill. If it's about the length of being stuck in the wolf form, why didn't she snap first? Why is Bill not the one lying here in pieces?"

"Maybe it also has to do with the person's state of mind before they become trapped. Maybe Bill had some underlying psychiatric issues we're not familiar with. Who knows?" He raked a hand impatiently through his hair and looked harried and angry and frustrated. As frustrated as she was. "Or maybe since we've been working on the assumption that he caught an infection from Rosemary that prevented his change, the virus has mutated somehow. It could be anything, but I'm not a scientist so how much my opinion matters here, I can't tell you."

"I am a scientist, and I don't know that I can explain what's been happening, either," she admitted, feeling frustration boiling up inside her. She *hated* feeling helpless. Hated it. "But I know that I want it stopped, and I want it as soon as possible."

"We're on the same page there." He reached for his cell phone, glanced grimly at the time, and flipped it open. "I'm calling Steve, though. There's a difference between not pressuring someone who's trying to do you a favor and standing back while people start to die."

Josie refrained for breaking into a chorus of hallelujahs, but just barely. She watched him dial, then step out into the hallway and pace while he waited for an answer. She didn't feel even the least bit bad about following him and openly preparing to eavesdrop. She needed this information as badly as he did.

It seemed as if they waited forever, but in reality only a few seconds passed before she saw Eli's body tense and his expression sharpen.

"Steve. I've been hoping to hear from you for a few days now."

He listened for a second, then made an impatient noise. "Save it. I didn't call to lay on a guilt trip, but things have changed since I sent you that package, and it's just become a lot more important that we get those results yesterday."

Another pause.

"Man, hold on. I can't understand a damn word you're saying. Except for the occasional *but, and,* or *the.* You'd better talk to the girl who speaks your language."

He thrust the phone at Josie, and she didn't hesitate for a second before snatching it up and pressing it to her ear.

"Let me hear what you have."

She heard a surprised silence. After several tense seconds, a voice spoke. "I'm afraid that I don't quite know who I'm speaking to."

"My name is Josie, but at the moment that's about the least important thing about me. I'm a veterinarian. I went to UC Davis, took microbiology from Stanley Kulcharsky, and I know my way around a damn serum scan, so tell me what the hell you've found."

The voice responded in a tone noticeably harder than the last. "There's a slight problem with me doing that, Josie. You see, some of what we've found is a matter of concern to more than a small-town veterinarian from North Podunk, and I'm not at liberty to divulge all of it to random strangers."

"Don't jerk me around," she snapped and saw Eli wince. When he reached out to snatch back the phone, she danced out of his reach and stomped out to the now almost deserted triage area with the device still pressed to her ear.

"I don't know who the hell you think you are, or even who the hell you really are, but I've been willing to trust you because Eli said you could help. Well, I've yet to see proof of that. But if you want talk about being at liberty, how about you chew on the fact that right now, what's at liberty is the second Lupine we suspect has contracted this infection you will neither confirm nor deny the existence of."

"Where's patient zero?" the stranger demanded in a near bellow.

The use of that term made the hair on the back of Josie's neck stand up. Used mainly in medical circles and specifically in the field of infectious disease, *patient zero* referred to the patient suspected of being the source of a specific disease outbreak.

In other words, the cause of an epidemic.

That term sealed the deal for Josie. Not only did she now know that they were dealing with an infection, she now knew several very important and frankly terrifying facts about it: (1) It appeared to be of great concern to a microbiologist connected with the US military; (2) Said microbiologist appeared to be acting under either an assumption or a direct order that information about this disease ought to be kept extremely confidential, if not outright classified as top secret; (3) the scientist and/or the military suspected that this disease was highly contagious, potentially capable of launching a full-scale epidemic; and (4) an infected patient with symptoms more severe than those of patient zero had escaped from quarantine and was now roaming the Oregon woods with a bad attitude and a potential for extreme violence.

All of that added up to make the alarm on Josie's bullshit-o-meter squeal like a baby pig.

"You want to know where patient zero is, Doctor? Why don't I let you see for yourself. Talk to Eli for a minute while I scrape enough of her off the floor to mail to you."

Disgusted, she moved to hand the phone back, but a shout from the other end of the line stopped her. "Wait! Wait! Dr. Barrett."

Against her will, she found her hand returning the receiver to his ear, but she didn't speak.

"Dr. Josephine Barrett. That's you, right? You're the one Eli told me about. You've had both Lupines at your clinic for the past week, right?"

"I did. Up until sometime last night."

"Tell me what happened." Steve paused. "Please."

"While we waited to hear from you," she began pointedly, "we noticed that the subjects began to display different symptoms than we originally saw. The sedatives we had been giving them seemed to lose their efficacy, and when they regained consciousness, they displayed markedly more wolf-like and more aggressive behaviors. We kept them isolated from the town and from visitors and patients, but we left them together as it seemed to keep both of them slightly calmer. Then this." She briefly outlined what they knew of the night before, which mostly consisted of Rosemary's condition and Bill's disappearance. "So now we'd very much appreciate knowing what we're dealing with and how the heck we're supposed to stop it."

She heard a sound somewhere between a horrified chuckle and a moan of fear.

"First, you need to find that second Lupine. The only chance we have to contain this thing is to keep him from infecting any more Lupines."

She felt a tingle of triumph sneak up on her anger and irritation. "So the danger is confined to Lupines?"

"It is," Steve acknowledged. "Only Lupine shifters can be infected, either by bodily fluid contact or by direct exposure."

Josie thought of Bill tenderly licking his mate's wounds and winced. He must have ingested her blood, but the amount had been so minute, she never would have expected transmission of a disease. She'd really thought the mode of spread would be airborne. "Exposure to what?"

He sighed. "A genetically engineered virus. One that was still in the experimental stages and was about to be deemed too dangerous to proceed with when it disappeared. Twelve hours before it was slated to be destroyed completely."

Christ, it was the kind of nightmare scenario that kept espionage thrillers in business. A military-engineered virus unintentionally set loose on an unsuspecting public. All they needed was for a wildfire to be headed straight for town and they could film a bloody movie of the week!

"Is there an anti-virus? A drug? A vaccine? Anything?"

"No, which was on the list of reasons for its destruction."

Josie gave a muffled shriek. "You guys are morons, you know that?"

"To paraphrase great words of wisdom: In our own defense, we do know that. Believe me, Dr. Barrett, an investigation into how this happened is already under way. We don't know yet how the virus got out of the lab, but we think we know how patient zero contracted the infection."

"Tell me."

"The drug vial that Eli included with the blood samples. It contained three doses of the virus when it was last seen at a facility in southwestern Idaho. When I received the package from you, it was empty, and Eli says that's how he found it."

"I never saw the vial," she said. "I didn't even know about it until last night, but if that's what Eli says, that's what happened."

Her own words jiggled the back of Josie's mind until something broke free and tumbled straight into her conscious thoughts. Her stomach clenched.

"Oh, shit. The syringe," she whispered to herself.

Steve, though, apparently had a perfectly healthy set of ears. "What? What syringe?"

"Last night, this night, the night that's just barely over. Before we found out about Rosemary, Eli and I were at his cabin and we were attacked by someone we thought was trying to kill us. But when the guy got away and Eli and one of his deputies started to search the room for the weapon, all they found was a filled syringe. We had no idea what was in it, and we forgot about it as soon as we got the call about the incident here at the clinic."

The scientist cursed roundly. "I need to see that syringe, and I'm not waiting for the mail. I'll get a chopper and fly up myself. I can be there in less than four hours."

"Only if you bring me images of that virus. I want to see the evil little bastard that's caused us so much trouble this last week."

"I can't do that, Dr. Barrett, but I'm afraid the images wouldn't prove very illuminating in any case. You likely wouldn't be able to distinguish the LV-7 virus from one with which you're already quite familiar. The people who worked on this project chose the prototype for their creation very well—it was engineered from the common rabies virus."

Well, fuck a duck.

Josie groaned and shook her head. "I changed my mind, Steve old buddy. You people aren't morons, you're frickin' insane. All of science has been working for more than a century in a futile attempt to cure, contain, and control the rabies virus, and your people decide to see if they can make it an even bigger threat to the world? Nice going. Someone deserves a medal for that, you know?"

"I can assure you, Josie my dear, that these were *not* 'my' people. I wasn't even aware of the project's existence until I started looking at your samples, and the reason I never contacted you is that I'm still waiting for the clearance that will authorize me to find out what I've already told you. I could be court-martialed for this conversation, and to be frank, I likely will be at some point before this is over. But I think the safety of the Northwest—the entire United States—actually takes precedence over my own career concerns, so I want to see this stopped at least as much as you do."

"Noble. But there's one more thing I want to ask before you go commandeer yourself a helicopter."

"What?"

"You said this LV-7 virus is only transmissible to Lupines."

"Right."

"Then I don't think it can be the same as what was in the syringe our attacker had last night. What would be the point of injecting either me or Eli? I'm human, and

Eli certainly isn't Lupine. We should both be immune to the virus that left your lab."

Steve swore again. "Three hours," he barked.

The phone went dead in Josie's ear. Flipping the headset closed, she handed it back to Eli.

"It looks like we'll at least have some company while we try to get this all sorted out," she informed him. "Your friend Steve is on his way here to lend us a hand."

The sheriff blinked. "Steve? Is coming here?"

"You're surprised?"

"I didn't think the man knew how to find the door out of his lab. That, or that he wasn't authorized to leave. I haven't seen him in person in at least five years."

"Okay, then you go ahead and think today's your lucky day," she offered. "At least until you hear the rest of the story."

Then she proceeded to tell it to him. By the time she had finished, no one felt very lucky. Except maybe Bill. And everyone else involved in the whole mess intended to make sure that feeling didn't last for very much longer at all.

CHAPTER NINETEEN

By seven thirty that morning, they had developed a new plan. Eli had called Rick immediately and left an impatient voice mail when he'd gotten no answer. Ben, having heard all about last night from a still-shaken Andrea, had showed up at the clinic just before seven and demanded to be told how to help. Josie immediately planted him in front of the phone with a list of area zoos, wildlife rehabilitation centers, veterinarians, and veterinary supply companies. Air guns, she informed him. They would need lots and lots of air guns. And, she added after checking her depleted stock of sedatives, more succinylcholine and any other strong paralytics the groups could spare. No one, she had determined, was going to continue hunting for Bill until they were suitably armed with massive doses of tranquilizers and a safe way to administer them.

While she organized that and helped Jim and Mike to complete the task of processing Rosemary's remains, Eli began organizing the rest of his men and planning a systematic search of anyplace that Bill Evans was known to frequent in either of his forms. Greg and Will had already been to the man's home and searched the immediate vicinity, but since the Evanses had lived on a quiet street with plenty of other houses around, they hadn't expected the search to yield anything beyond what it did. Which was nothing.

Josie was just prepping her only set of tranquilizer darts with three-milliliter doses of the high-potency sux when the clinic's back door flew open and Rick Cobb crashed inside.

"Pace!" he shouted, sharp and breathless. "Where the hell are you?"

Eli broke away from his deputies and took a step forward. "Where the hell am I? Where the hell have you been? Did you get my message?"

"Message? Unlike our local police force, every single member of which appears to be sitting in the back of a vet's office at the moment, I haven't had the time to catch up with my phone tree. I need you or at least one of your men to come with me. Now."

Eli's entire frame went taut. "Why? What happened?"

The Alpha's expression hardened. "There's been an attack. One of my men has been injured."

Josie felt the attention in the room suddenly shift to the Lupine. It was as if he'd turned into a giant magnet and they were all obedient pieces of metal. She might not be a mind-reader, but she could make a damn good guess as to what each of them was thinking, too. It started with a *Bill* and ended with an *Evans*.

"Where?" Eli demanded, but he didn't wait for an answer before he gestured to his men and grabbed the air gun Josie had dug out of the storage room just a few minutes earlier. She had leapt into motion as well and was grabbing up her darts and heading for the door.

"He's at Dr. Shad's office right now getting emergency

treatment," Rick answered, "but he was attacked out near your place. By that little stream that runs along the back of your property."

Eli stopped and turned to stare at the Lupine in confusion. "What the hell was he doing out there?"

"I didn't ask. I was too busy trying to keep him from bleeding to death to worry about that."

Josie stepped forward. "Has he shifted recently? Is he in human form?"

"Of course Jackson is human, otherwise Dr. Shad wouldn't be treating him. He doesn't treat shifters in animal form. The anatomy is too different."

Rick looked surprised and annoyed by the question, but Josie didn't care how stupid he thought it was.

"Good. You need to make sure your Jackson stays that way while we go try to find Bill, or there's a good chance he'll end up like Rosemary. Or worse, like Bill himself."

"What the hell are you talking about?" the Alpha demanded in a rough bark. "What do Bill and Rosemary have to do with this? They've been here for a week now, and even if they've left, unless their condition greatly improved without you telling me, neither one of them had a reason to shoot Jackson, let alone the ability to hold a gun. That's a lot easier to do with opposable thumbs, from what I hear."

Now it was Josie's turn to look confused and Eli along with her. "Shot? You mean it wasn't a wolf attack? Bill wasn't the one who attacked your friend?"

"What the—? Of course not! Are you kidding me? Bill is locked up in here, isn't he? Trapped in wolf form. Or am I missing something significant here?"

"I think we all are," Eli said with a sigh. "And I think

that right now, you ought to sit down while I get you caught upon our side."

He summarized for the other man what had occurred between Rosemary and Bill last night, as well as what they had learned about Bill's condition. Rick's expression shifted farther toward confusion with every word until that became too mild a word for it. By the time Eli finished, the Lupine appeared absolutely dumbstruck.

"I had no idea," he muttered, finally sinking onto the seat Eli had suggested he take several minutes ago. "People are talking about why the whole sheriff's department appears to be parked behind the vet clinic this morning, but no one thought it could be anything serious. Since when does serious shit happen in Stone Creek, for the moon's sake?" He looked at Josie. "Rosie is really dead?"

She nodded, feeling a renewed wave of grief at seeing him react to the loss. "I'm afraid so."

"And now you know why we jumped to the conclusion that Bill had to be responsible for the attack on Jackson," Eli said, "so now why don't you explain what you've been talking about when you say Jackson's been attacked or shot or whatever."

"No whatever," Rick said. "He's definitely been shot. Dr. Shad confirmed it just before he started digging the bullet out of his shoulder. His guess is a .50-caliber hunting rifle, but he'll know for sure when he gets a look at it. I came here looking for you so you could help me track down the fucking bastard who did it. Do you think it could be the same one who shot Rosemary?"

"The same ammunition is too big a coincidence to overlook, but we shouldn't jump to conclusions. That's one of the most popular ammo choices for deer rifles, after all.

And shooting a human-looking Lupine is a bit different from shooting what looked clearly like a wolf." He shook his head. "It's too early to make the call. Especially when you add in the fact that the attack happened on my property, near where I was attacked by someone with the intent to possibly inject me with the same virus that made Rosemary and Bill sick."

"Which still doesn't make sense to me," Josie grumbled as she struggled to put together puzzle pieces that didn't seem to want to fit. "If this virus is Lupine-specific, it would be worse than useless to attack you with it, since it wouldn't infect you and the idiot who tried it risked being caught. In fact, he almost was."

Eli shrugged. "Maybe Steve can tell us more once he gets here. In the meantime, I do think it's worth it if Rick and I go see if we can track down who took the shot at Jackson. Do you want to wait here for Steve, or go consult with Dr. Shad about whether or not Jackson got hit with a needle?"

Josie felt her eyebrows fly toward her hairline. "Truthfully? Neither. I'm pretty sure Jackson would have mentioned if someone had stuck a damn big hypodermic in him somewhere, and Steve won't be here for another couple of hours. Can I help you and Rick?"

"Not a chance in hell, darlin'," Eli said firmly, his jaw clenching.

She sighed, unsurprised by that answer. "I'm going to go crazy if I have to stay here while you and Rick go off and play the Great White Hunters. At least I'm as immune to the damn virus as you are. Are you sure Rick should be going with you? Why not take a deputy instead?"

"He might not be immune, but he's an Other and a

Lupine and one of the better trackers in the area. Frankly, I need him along."

"And I intend to go along," Rick agreed. "This is happening to my pack. I'm not going to stand aside and let someone else take care of my responsibilities, no matter what I might catch along the way."

"Fine," she growled, the frustration of impending inactivity weighing heavily on her. "I'll stay here and keep the bloody home fires burning."

Rick snorted, but Eli just yanked her to him and kissed her, hard.

"I'll call the minute we find out something important. I promise. I'm not cutting you out, just trying to have each of us stick with what we're best at."

"Diplomat." She shoved him out the door before her impatience got the better of her. "Go. Hopefully your friend Steve will break some aviation laws about speed and helicopters, and I won't be sitting around like a useless idiot for long."

They left without another word, which was far too eagerly for Josie. She took to pacing around the room until the deputies scattered like sparrows from a house cat. Ben had more fortitude. He outlasted them by a good thirty seconds.

"Would you stop that?" he finally demanded, slamming the phone down in its cradle. "You're reminding me of the way the wolves would never keep still. If you're going to rip my liver out, I'd rather you just have done with it now and save me the sense of anticipation."

She glared at him. "Don't tempt me."

"Whatever. Since you're in such a cheery mood, I'll leave you here to wait for the paint to peel," he griped.

"I'm going to go pick up a box of stuff the Near Shore Wildlife Center is going to let us use. I'll be back before I know it."

She ignored him. Other than flicking an obscene gesture at his back as he limped out to his car.

Of course, she instantly felt guilty and childish. None of what was going on was Ben's fault. In fact, none of it had all that much to do with him, but it had turned her life completely upside down, and she was taking out her unhappiness on whoever happened to get in her way at any given time. That was unfair.

And really not as satisfying as she had hoped.

With any luck, Eli and Rick would be able to actually find out something useful. She crossed her fingers and turned to start another lap.

The tracks at the site of Jackson's shooting turned out to be even easier to follow than the ones by the stream had been. This time, Eli located a single set of tracks by searching for and finding another carefully constructed hunter's blind.

"Okay, forget what I said back at the clinic," he told Rick. "It's definitely the same shooter. It's the exact same MO—treat it like a deer hunt, only shoot at the Lupine, not the mule deer. This guy's a real bastard."

"No argument."

He didn't have to point out the tracks leading away from the blind to Rick; the Lupine's eyesight was as keen as his, and his nose arguably better. Certainly the other shifter was more attuned to following a particular scent like a pointy-eared bloodhound. They moved swiftly and silently through the woods, occasionally side by side along the path of the shooter's footprints, and occasionally with Rick roaming outward to follow the airborne scent that drifted slightly downwind from the actual path.

They hiked a good forty minutes in the wake of those footprints, and Eli could see the Lupine's tension wind higher and higher as the strength of the scent trail increased. Finally the footprints veered toward the stream and halted. If Rick had possessed whiskers at that moment, they would have been quivering.

"New scents," he murmured almost soundlessly. "Two—no, three more. Not far now."

Eli nodded. He'd caught a whiff of something new as well, the smell of more men, something distinctive and out of place in the dense heart of the forest. A quick series of hand signals passed between them. In perfect accord, they went in low, though not as low as they might have otherwise. They had acknowledged the risk of approaching this particular individual in animal form—specifically for Rick—and decided to remain human; but human didn't have to mean conspicuous. As they neared a thinning of the vegetation, another signal had them splitting apart, one heading north, the other west, coming up on a small clearing from two sides.

From two sides of the bare spot near the stream came loud, hissing curses.

"Fuckers couldn't have left more than an hour ago," Rick swore, kicking the toe of his scuffed boot through the ashes of a dampened campfire. Near the bottom, he could feel that the coals were still warm.

"If that," Eli agreed, noting the matted areas of pine needles where two small tents had pressed down. "They sure didn't stay long after they found out Jackson had gotten away without being infected."

"And they didn't even bother to pack out their trash." Rick sneered and picked up an empty beer can, one of many, crushing it in his fist. "Filthy humans."

"I'm hardly going to side with them on this one, although I hope you won't use that term around *my* human."

Rick snorted. "As if I hadn't seen that coming. You two circle around each other like cats in heat."

"Thanks for that descriptor." Eli glanced around the remains of the camp and spotted a piece of paper several inches away from the fire ring, partially singed but with some print still visible. He scooped it up and looked more closely. "This looks like some kind of newsletter. Part of the masthead is right here. You recognize this?"

The Lupine took the paper and studied it for a few seconds, his eyes narrowing. "Hell, yeah, I recognize it, and you should, too, buddy. We saw enough of this trash floating around Stone Creek last summer. I'm guessing most of it ended up lining birdcages and litter boxes." He looked at Eli and saw the connection hadn't yet been made. "See the letter *T* right here? Or part of it anyway. That's how they print it—so it's looks like a swastika. This is *The Loyalist,* instruction manual and Holy Bible to all your finest members of the Nation of Aryan Humans. Human power skinheads."

Rick spat the words, which Eli realized was about what they deserved.

Human power had become the rallying cry of those skinhead groups who had so zealously embraced the addition of anti-Other sentiments to their menu of violent hatred. Not content with shouting about white power and

Zionist conspiracies and lone wolf actions for the "liberation" of the white race, these groups had decided that their requirements for continued life weren't narrow enough—you couldn't just be Protestant and white, you had to be 100 percent human, too. No Others or changelings or Other hybrids need apply.

As if any would want to.

As soon as Rick named the group, Eli remembered them and the "newsletter" they had forced on anyone who walked by their protests in the middle of Stone Creek. They had showered the townsfolk with hate speech and obscenities and then decried the lack of welcome they received from a populace they had alienated to the tune of almost 70 percent.

No one could call them the brightest group in the world, either.

Still, they had gotten mixed up in a very complicated plot, which meant that someone connected to them at the very least had to have a brain.

"Nation of Aryan Humans," Eli mused. "Who would have thought they had this in them?"

"Not me." Rick shook his head. "I'd have credited them with the smarts—just barely—for an Oklahoma City–type bombing. Maybe. But if the virus thing you and Josie mentioned is really the case, that seems way beyond the capabilities of the idiots I saw at last year's riots. Those punks were all propaganda and sucker punches, not genetic engineering and genocide."

"Remember, though, we likely only saw the rank-and-file working bodies of the organization last year. Who knows who they might have heading it up? Have you heard any names?"

The Lupine paused to think. "You know, I don't think I have, and that makes me curious. Usually that kind of bastard likes getting his name out there. Likes to be 'respected' by fools who think like he does. I wonder why the head of the NAH would want to keep quiet about having all that power?"

"I don't know, but I think it bears looking into. They're headquartered out here somewhere, aren't they?"

"They started up in Idaho, I think, but it's getting crowded for racist shitheads out there these days. I think I heard they relocated to either here or Washington. I can ask around. A few of the boys took last year's brouhaha pretty seriously. I think one of them may have kept tabs on the group."

Eli reached for his cell phone. "Find out for me, will you? I'm going to let Josie know what we found."

Rick smirked even as he dug his own cell from his pocket. "Aren't you a good boy, keeping your promises like that?"

Eli snarled and punched in the clinic's number. "Fuck you, Fang," he snapped and turned away to wait for the sound of her voice.

CHAPTER TWENTY

Steve turned out to be nothing like Josie expected. First, although she had known he was in the military, obviously, she hadn't known that he would actually turn out to be Colonel Dr. Stephen James Boyle of the United States Air Force. Especially when she realized he was, at best, a year or three older than her own thirty-two.

She also hadn't expected to like him, but it was hard not to when he sat with her at an exam table in the back of her clinic, drinking an enormous insulated glass of—she didn't believe him at first and made him let her taste it to be sure—chocolate-malt-flavored Ovaltine and answering her questions with an unanticipated level of candor.

"Officially, this intel is too classified for me to know about, so you, clearly, don't even exist," he told her with a grimace. "Unofficially, now that patient zero is dead and patient one is MIA, standing back and doing nothing is not an option. And since I haven't received an official order to keep my big nose out of it, my CYA factor could be worse. The shit's already hit the fan. What we're looking at now are the cast-off patterns, and this one is a doozy."

Josie thought about the more than three dozen evidence

bags full of Rosemary that currently rested in her morgue cooler. She couldn't have agreed more.

"They must have known that what they were playing with was taking an incredible risk. What were they thinking? Or were they thinking at all?" she wondered.

"Oh, they were thinking. Just about all the wrong things. They were looking for a weapon, of course. Something that could be used against enemy soldiers who are otherwise invulnerable to most of the currently available biological weaponry."

It felt good to hear him say it like that, Josie realized, flat-out and honest. She had guessed as much, but it meant something to hear the truth from someone who should know.

"This is also something that's not talked about," he continued, "but a couple of years ago there was another program, this one run by the army, that was looking for a way to transfer Lupine traits to otherwise non-Lupine soldiers. Specifically, they wanted a strong, fast soldier with rapid healing capabilities and a nearly indestructible immune system. I mean, who wouldn't, right? But things with that went belly-up when it turned out that the general in charge had a few too many bats in his own belfry, if you know what I mean."

Josie could certainly guess.

Steve swallowed more Ovaltine. "After things went south for that program, the government in general and the military in particular got a lot more cautious about how they were going to play around with experiments affecting Others. It had been hard enough to hush up what happened in New York, and the army lost an elite team of soldiers familiar with the Others and their facility in warfare because of the way they handled things. To give them a little credit, they at least realized that they didn't want to make the same mistake twice."

"So they settled on making a brand-new one, one with the possibility of causing a cascade of death and destruction that would trickle down all the way to the human population? Good call."

"I know." Steve winced. "I'm not saying they went about it the right way. Believe me. But the truth is that the world of warfare is changing these days in a way it hasn't since World War Two and the introduction of the tank to battlefields. Now that it's been a few years since the Unveiling and the world has had a little time to adjust to knowing about the Others among us, there are some nations out there that are actively and forcefully recruiting shapeshifters into their ranks. To the extent that they're virtually conscripting some of them the way the British navy did in the bad old days—just plucking them off the street, forcing them into a uniform, and marching them off to war. And when an army of humans comes face-to-face with an army of Lupines and Felines and all the other massively powerful creatures out there, who do you think are going to be the ones to walk away after the dust settles?"

"I get that. Really, I do. I just don't get how no one could have anticipated what might go wrong with genetically engineering a virus that is still incurable in humans who've carried the bug for more than a couple of weeks?" She shook her head. "It just defies my brand of logic."

"They did anticipate the effect on humans, actually," Steve said. "They just anticipated the wrong one. The first thing they did when they began working with the virus was to render it harmless to humans by inserting a genetic sequence designed to initiate a self-destruct action in the presence of human immunoglobulin."

"Which is great for everyone who isn't carrying AIDS or on chemotherapy or vitamin-D-deficient. Gee, thanks!"

He sighed and leaned his forearms on the shiny steel tabletop. "Yeah, every time I find myself saying that, I know it's going to sound stupider than the time before. You're right about that measure not being good enough, but it was enough of an advance to get them approved to continue working, which was really what they were after. It bought them another six months."

"And that's when they discovered how to drive a Lupine crazy in six easy days?"

"They never got that far. They knew the virus showed promise in limiting the ability of a Lupine body to shift, but they didn't know if the effect would last more than a couple of hours, so they certainly had no idea of what might happen after a week, or even after a day. All they were after was something that could be deployed in a combat situation to give our guys time to either win or get the hell out of Dodge. It wasn't supposed to spawn the next Holy Roman Crusade."

Josie pursed her lips. "When is it ever *supposed* to turn to shit?"

"True. It's not. And this wasn't, either. And when one of the directors of the facility overseeing the development realized what could potentially happen if the virus was released on a force of Others who still kicked the crap out of our boys, he pulled the plug on the whole thing. He ordered research to cease immediately and that any samples already generated be destroyed according to standard protocols for biologically hazardous materials."

"And yet," Josie pointed out, "here we are."

"Right. Here we are." Steve drained his mug and set it aside. "The problem is that when doing the background checks on the biological engineers called up to perform this research, no one anticipated that it might present a problem if one of the staff members had an apparently loose affiliation with a human supremacist organization. It didn't look like it amounted to much more than an occasional donation at a whacked-out fund-raiser or two, and it wasn't as if he belonged to a group of Others supporters who might try to undermine a project aimed at potentially harming them. He slipped through the cracks."

"That's not a crack, it's the Marianas Trench."

"Again, not arguing. But shit happens, and as I've learned in the military, shit happens a lot more often when the goal is to do something not-so-bright in the first place."

"Then instead of destroying the samples of virus as ordered, this engineer stole them and ran off to put them in the hands of some radical hatemonger with a hard-on for new-style furries? Have you been able to locate him?"

"Yes and no."

Josie just waited. She almost thought she might be becoming inured to bad news.

"Yes in that I was able to find out his name and what facility he went to when the LV-7 project was discontinued. No, because I just found out yesterday at noon, and by the time I went to talk to him, he'd heard about my asking questions and already headed for the hills."

"So he could be anywhere. Is that what you're saying?"

"I have a few friends unofficially working to track him

down, but like I said, his connection to the human supremacist group was a tenuous one, and the group has a presence all over the country. We're digging deeper, but these things take time."

Every time she heard a phrase like that, Josie wanted to scream. "The problem, Steve, is that our time has already run out. Of the two Lupines we know have contracted this virus, one is already dead, and the other, who is responsible for the death of the first, is on the loose God know where, disemboweling God knows whom, all for shits and giggles. I don't want to see anyone else die."

He met her gaze levelly and nodded. "And I don't want to see anyone die at all. Now, why don't I take a look at the syringe you told me was meant for you or Eli? I want to know what exactly is in it and if it's one of the missing doses from Idaho before we do any more speculating."

It took a few minutes for Steve to set up the portable yet extremely powerful microscope he'd brought with him from his lab but only a second for Josie to retrieve the hypodermic from where she had it stored in her medical fridge. She watched as the scientist prepared a sample of the clear liquid and placed it under the magnifying lens. He stared intently through the oculus for several minutes, changing the focus, the lighting, and the orientation before he finished. When he sat back and turned to Josie, she found that she'd been holding her breath in anticipation.

He waved her toward the scope. "Take a look."

She peered through the lens. "It looks like the images I've seen of the rabies virus in textbooks and journal articles," she confirmed. "But how does that tell us anything new?"

"It doesn't." He took a small vial out of his breast

pocket and added a minute amount of a vaguely yellow-ish liquid to the sample they'd been examining. "But this will."

He gestured back to the scope, and Josie took another look.

She frowned. "Was something supposed to happen?"

"You mean it didn't?" He looked truly taken aback.

"No, it looks exactly the same." She double-checked, shook her head. "Nope, no changes."

Steve began to pale. "I have a feeling that's a very bad sign."

"What did you add?"

"Concentrated canine serum cells." The man grabbed a fresh sample mount and a sterile needle and pricked the tip of his finger. When a bead of blood welled to the surface, he created a mount of his own blood, added a drop of the liquid from the syringe, and examined the new sample.

After only a few seconds, Josie saw his shoulders sag in relief.

"Thank God," he muttered. "For a second I thought this might be a modified form of the virus designed to activate with human cells. I can't tell you what a disaster that would have been."

He didn't need to, because a scenario even more disastrous had just occurred to Josie. Disastrous on a more personal level.

"Hold on a minute."

She crossed to the fridge and reached in with trembling hands, withdrawing a slim vial from a collection of similar tubes. She checked the label and handed it to Steve.

"Make another slide. Only use that this time."

Steve read the label on the vial, raised an eyebrow, and did as she requested. He withdrew a small quantity of blood from the vial and prepared a new sample with the addition of the virus. When he looked through the scope this time, Josie saw him frown and felt her heart drop into her surgical clogs.

"Who exactly is 'Patterson, Clovis'?" he asked, reading off the label on the new vial of blood.

"Not who," Josie managed, reaching out to lean on the counter for support. "What."

"Excuse me?"

"Clovis Patterson isn't a who," she repeated, forcing each word carefully and quietly from between frozen lips. She was afraid if she spoke too loud or too fast or too anything, the words would come out on a scream instead of a whisper. "Clovis is a what, and he belongs to Mrs. Helen Patterson. He's her purebred seal-point Siamese . . ."

"Siamese . . . cat," Steve finished with an expression of dawning horror. "The virus hasn't been modified for humans. It's been modified for other . . . Others."

"For Eli," she bit out, anger beginning to join in with her panic. "It makes sense. If this is really about a human supremacist thing, they wouldn't want to modify the virus to attack humans. Humans are the master race. They'd want to destroy just the races they don't like. Or the species, anyway."

"And that explains where Garrett England ran off to. The engineer who went missing," Steve explained. "I've never heard of anyone in the skinhead community with the kind of skills it would take to modify the virus beyond even where the original facility took it, but someone has managed it with this. The only way that makes sense is if Garrett had secretly continued to work on the virus after he sent the original stolen samples to his friends. He couldn't have made these changes in one day, and no one else I know of—beside his co-workers, all of whom are accounted for—could have made them at all."

"So not only did he send the original virus off, he included version two-point-oh before he realized anyone was on to him."

Their eyes met and Steve nodded grimly. "We need to let Eli know. He's hunting these people down with the idea that the virus can't hurt him, only his Lupine friend. He needs to be aware that he's in as much danger as the wolves."

"I'll try his cell, but if he's on to something, he might not answer."

The clinic phone rang before she even touched it. She grabbed up the receiver and put it to her ear.

"Hello?"

"Hey. We found something out here," Eli told her, his voice a welcome sound in her ear. "Picking up the shooter's trail turned out to be the easy part. It led us straight back to what looks like a base camp. It looks like it's been used for a good space of time, too. Maybe since before Rosemary was shot. And we found some evidence pointing us toward who we think might be behind this whole mess."

"So did—"

"I'll tell you all about it when we get back, but right now Rick is checking out a few things for me. It was a good call to come out here, though. This stuff is going to be helpful."

"Yeah," Josie managed to add when he finally wound down. "We found something back here, too."

"'We'? Is Steve there already?"

"Yes, and we've already made a lot of connections that you need to know about," she told him, trying to keep her urgency from coming out in her voice. "When are you and Rick coming back here?"

"Soon," he assured her, then paused. "Is everything okay?"

"Fine, but we really need to let you know that we've figured out what was in the syringe that skinhead at your cabin had the other night. It was definitely the virus that Rosemary was infected with, only—"

Josie heard the sound of a scream, a shout, and then silence. She froze in place, not believing her ears until the landline in her hand began to beep, letting her know that her call had been disconnected several seconds ago.

Right when she'd heard the unmistakable sounds of someone very close to Eli being viciously attacked.

Exp. 10-1017.03
Log 03-00142

Stage 4 product has shown evidence of spontaneous mutation.

This is beyond even my highest expecta-
tions. Techs report that one of the last
test subjects has demonstrated that the
product is indeed causing more rapid

progression of effects with each generation.

Going immediately back to work in the lab. If able to harness this mutation, could create a product able to produce end-stage effect within minutes of administration. Final solution could be reached within days instead of weeks.

CHAPTER TWENTY-ONE

Whatever Josie had meant to say, Eli missed it. He simply couldn't hear it over a shrill yeowl of feline rage, combined with Rick's blasphemous curse, blended in an ear-splitting cacophony of confusion and pain.

He whirled around and saw his friend staggering under the weight of the good-size western bobcat that had launched itself at Rick's head from just beyond the tree line. It took a second for his eyes to convince his brain that they weren't playing a trick on him. Bobcats were usually small, shy things that stayed away from people at all costs. While a lion might attack a person if it felt threatened, had cubs to protect, or even if it got hungry enough, a bobcat faced with a human would just turn tail and run.

Then a puff of air brought Eli the scent of the animal and things became horribly clear. That might look like a bobcat, but it smelled more like a Bob in cat's clothing. Somehow the virus that they'd all assumed affected only Lupines had found a way to spread to Felines.

This was all kinds of bad.

Instinct kicked in while Eli's mind continued to work through the problem, and he jumped to Rick's aid, grabbing the bobcat by the back of the neck and wrenching it from the Lupine's back. The animal snarled in fury and turned on him so quickly, Eli had three long scratches on his left cheek even before he managed to release his grip on the creature's scruff.

The bobcat hit the ground hissing and spitting, but it didn't stay on the ground for long. Ignoring Eli, it turned again on Rick, but this time the Lupine was ready. He blocked the animal's second attack with a swift kick that knocked it back several feet until it landed at the base of a false cedar.

"The damn thing just doesn't know when to stay down," Rick shouted when the bobcat twisted immediately to its feet, shook off the fall, and crouched in preparation for another leap.

Eli shook his head, the Feline's ferocity sending a chill down his spine. It was like watching one of those horror movies where the villain turned out to be a child-size doll possessed by the soul of a serial killer. On the one hand, the idea of being attacked and killed by something less than half the size of a grown man made any sane person want to laugh; but on the other, when the thing just kept coming and coming and coming, ignoring every setback, every injury, just relentlessly attacking again and again, each time with a renewed sense of fury and agression . . . Well, it was hard not to feel a little sense of anxiety. Determination and a sharp set of teeth had won smaller victories in the history of man versus nature.

What truly disturbed Eli, though, wasn't the animal's viciousness or its unwavering focus on Rick; it was the bright, avid gleam of madness behind the narrowed yellow eyes. Somewhere inside that body was the mind of a man who was probably perfectly nice. Before he'd turned into a frenzied monster, Bob the bobcat had probably paid his taxes, mowed his lawn, held doors for little old ladies, and loved his wife and kids. Someone, somewhere, would probably cry if they could see how that man had been changed by one single prick of a needle, or one bite from a strange, frenzied wolfish-looking creature with eyes that had once been human.

In the end, the eyes told Eli what to do. He saw in those eyes the same thing he'd seen in Bill's, right before the end—rage, bloodlust, and a complete absence of any sense of humanity. The men they had once been had died at the hands of the beast, and there would be no coming back from that brink. There was no tomorrow for a creature who had lost its place in the world.

Reluctantly, grimly, but efficiently, Eli drew his service revolver from the holster at his waist, took aim, and shot the bobcat once in the back of its head as it sailed through the air toward Rick one last time.

It fell to the ground with a sick thud, a limp, thick-furred casualty in a war it probably didn't even know had been waged. The need for it left a bitter taste in Eli's mouth, and he shoved the gun back into its leather holder with a grimace of distaste.

"What the fuck just happened here, compadre?" Rick asked, in a voice of utter astonishment. "Please tell me that I have not seen what I think I've seen."

"The rules have changed." Eli glared at the bobcat's corpse, then picked it up and tossed it over his shoulder. "It looks like your pack members are no longer the only ones under attack, my friend. And I, for one, think it's time we revised the game plan."

With that, he turned and began to stalk through the

woods to the west, in the direction of his cabin. They had parked there and hiked to the spot where Jackson had reported being shot. At the moment, Eli just wanted to get to the Jeep and get back to Josie as quickly as possible. He had to let her know what was going on.

"Oh, shit!" he snarled. *Josie.* He had cut off their phone call when the bobcat had attacked. The last thing she'd heard on her end of the line had probably been Rick's scream, the Feline's cry, and his curse. She'd be half crazy by now.

At least, she would be if she felt about him the way he hoped she did.

"Here. Take this. I think we've both been exposed to whatever we're going to be exposed to by now." He thrust the cat into Rick's hands and dug out his cell phone again. "I need to call Josie back."

"Wait!" Rick grunted and shifted his grip on the limp carcass. "Why the hell are we bringing this thing out with us? As far as I'm concerned, it can stay in the woods and rot."

"Because Josie and Steve might be able to get something useful out of it," he snapped, dialing with his thumb. "At least it will back us up when they hear about it attacking."

The phone picked up before the first ring.

"Eli?" Josie demanded, sounding fantic. "Are you all right? What happened? Are you hurt?"

"I'm fine," he rushed to assure her. He hated having worried her, but he couldn't help the little thrill that ran through him when he heard the terror in her voice. "We had a little incident, but it's not a big deal. Rick and I are both okay."

"Then what was that horrible noise I heard before the phone went dead?"

He hesitated, but there was no way to avoid telling her. She would know soon enough, and better that she be prepared.

"Rick was attacked," he said carefully. "By a bobcat. Actually, it was a bobcat shifter. And, Josie, I'm pretty sure it was infected."

"The bobcat? I'd say that's a sure bet. Otherwise what would it be doing attacking a full-grown man."

"You don't sound surprised," Eli said, knowing he did. "Did you hear me? I just told you that the virus has spread to Felines. It's not only contagious to Lupine shifters anymore."

"I know," she answered impatiently. "That's what I was trying to tell you when the phone went dead. Steve and I identified the drug in the syringe our attacker carried the other night. It was the LV-7 virus, but a new strain. Maybe we should call it LV-8 now? Anyway, it's a long story, but basically we think that one of the scientists who originally developed the virus to attack Lupines secretly modified a strain of it to infect Felines as well, and he passed both of them on to whoever gave it to Rosemary."

"Shit."

"Precisely. Steve has ideas about who's behind all this, too, but we can talk about that when you get back. You are on your way back here, aren't you?"

Eli stalked up to his Jeep and popped open the rear hatch, slamming it back down as soon as Rick had the bobcat stored safely inside.

"We're leaving now," he told her, "and I'm putting on the lights. We'll see you in ten minutes."

The two men slid into the car, and Eli flipped on the sirens as well as the emergency lights. He could tell Josie and Steve that they had already discovered who was behind this fiasco when they got back to the clinic. Right now, the important thing was getting there before anything more could go wrong.

Josie took one look at Eli's face and turned the color of hotel linens.

"Oh, my God," she breathed, lifting a hand to touch the scratches. "Were you bit? Please tell me you weren't bit, Eli."

He pulled her to him and kissed her fiercely. "I wasn't bit. I promise. There was absolutely no exchange of bodily fluids. I'm not infected."

Josie shook her head, her lips pressed together in a thin line. "You can't know that for sure. We barely know anything about this virus. We don't know that the skin cells cats shed every time they scratch something don't contain copies of the virus that are at this very moment already coursing through your bloodstream!"

"Come on, Colonel, tell her." Eli turned to Steve with a pleading look. "The virus can only be transmitted through the exchange of bodily fluids or through direct administration with a needle. Isn't that what you told us? I can't get it from a couple of little scratches."

"It's highly unlikely," the other man agreed, but Josie could see the shadow of uncertainty in his eyes. "The cells that shed off a cat's nails are from dead tissue. Even if the infected animal left copies of the virus in the scratch wounds, chances are they're dead as well. Still, you should probably clean those right away. Just to be safe."

Her heart in her throat, Josie stomped off to get yet more saline and gauze as well as Betadine solution and plain strong soap. By the time she got done with those scratches, there wouldn't be a germ within three counties hardy enough to survive in them. She'd make sure of it.

Because she didn't know what she would do if anything happened to Eli.

"Do you want to check the bobcat's claws and see?" Josie heard Rick ask the scientist. "Eli decided we should bring it back with us in case you or Dr. J needed to take a look at it."

"Absolutely!" Steve replied with an enthusiasm that Josie found slightly distasteful. "It's an amazing opportunity to get to see exactly what happens to the body as the virus runs its course. From what Josie tells me of patient zero, there really wasn't enough left of her to do that kind of study."

Slamming the bottle of wound cleanser down on the exam table, Josie gnashed her teeth and tore open a package of gauze with excessive force.

"Her name isn't 'patient zero,' Colonel," she bit out. "It's Rosemary, and she's more than a biology class fetal pig, you know. So is that bobcat out there. They deserve not to be talked about like pieces of meat or lab room slides."

Eli flinched under her hand. Instantly, Josie eased the pressure with which she was scrubbing out his wounds.

"I'm sorry," she muttered, though the apology made her feel no better. At this point, she wasn't sure if anything could make her feel better.

"Sweetheart, I'm okay." Grabbing her free hand, Eli raised it to his lips, pressing them gently against the center of her palm. "Really."

Josie curled her fingers against the warmth of his kiss and let out a long, shaky breath. "Right. I'm sorry. Again."

"No, I'm the one who should apologize," Steve said. "You're right. We should all be respectful of the dead, even the doctors and researchers who learn from their misfortunes."

She waved away his apology and felt color rush to her cheeks. "True, but I'm acting like an idiot. You haven't said or done anything wrong. Taking a look at the bobcat will certainly give us some incredibly useful information about how the virus changes the host, and personally I think the brain deserves a good, close look. But at the moment, I'm less worried about understanding the actions of the infection than I am about stopping it from spreading, and that means we need to find the people responsible for infecting shifters and stop them."

"Eli and I think we know the answer to that," Rick said, pulling out the scrap from *The Loyalist* and handing it to her. "We found this at the shooter's campsite. It's from a newsletter published by an organization called the Nation of Aryan Humans. It's a group of yahoos who advocate the cause of—"

"Human supremacy," Josie finished. She glanced down at the paper with distaste. "Steve and I already discussed the possibility, or rather the likelihood, that a human power group might be behind this. It turns out that one of the developers of the original LV-7 virus had ties to one of these organizations."

"This exact one, as it happens," Steve cut in, his eyes narrowing. "How's that for a coincidence?"

"I highly doubt that it's anything of the kind." Eli nodded to the Lupine Alpha. "I think that the combination of what Steve has been able to tell us and what Rick and I uncovered clinches it. The NAH are behind this. The question now is: Who's behind the NAH, and where can we find him?"

"I was about to make a call and ask one of my pack-mates if he knows who's currently running the group when the bobcat attacked," Rick said. "Ever since some of our males volunteered to help with crowd control and law enforcement during the anti-Other riots last year, a couple of them have turned into real experts on the subject of the human supremacy movement. My beta in particular makes it a priority of his to keep track of these bastards. He says that it's a matter of 'keeping his enemy closer.' They know who we are, so we need to know who they are."

"Your beta is right," Steve agreed. "Every intelligence agent in this country knows that the only way to prevent a terrorist attack is to take down the cell leaders. You can go after the soldiers from now until eternity and not make an ounce of difference because for every one you catch, three more are ready to take his place. But very few people in this world have what it takes to mastermind a real terror plot. Thank God."

"So is that what we're going to do?" Josie asked. "We find out who the leader of the NAH is and . . . and what? Take him down? Take him out? Kill him? What?"

"Josephine Barrett, I am shocked at you!" Rick teased. "Don't you know that murder is both immoral and illegal?"

"But arresting a suspected biological terrorist isn't." Steve looked over at Eli. "Do you know of anyone with the powers of arrest, by any chance?"

Josie frowned. "Wouldn't that depend on where the

leader was when we found him? I mean, if he's in Nebraska or someplace like that, there would be jurisdictional issues, right?"

"Possibly, but I'm pretty sure that I've heard the NAH was forced to relocate its headquarters from Idaho to somewhere in our vicinity within the last couple of years," Rick said. "Either northwest Oregon or southwest Washington."

Eli's jaw tightened, his eyes fixed on Josie. "Let's all hope it turns out to be the former. Rick, I think you should go ahead and try making that call again. Steve, if you'll excuse us for a minute, there's something I'd like to talk to Josie about."

He took her by the elbow, and she could tell just from the feel of his grip what he wanted to discuss, so she dug her heels into the floor and flatly refused to budge.

"If you mean that you want to drag me away and yell at me for thinking that I should be a part of this plan to catch the bad guys, don't waste your breath," she told him. "I've been in the middle of this mess from the beginning, and I intend to stay in the middle of it until it stops being so messy. A lecture from you is not going to change that. These are my patients. I can't just step aside and not do everything in my power to help them."

His eyes narrowed to slits of glittering green, and his lips nearly disappeared altogether. In her peripheral vision, she could see Steve watching them in rapt fascination.

"I don't give lectures," Eli snarled, "but if I did, I can't think of anyone in the world who deserves one more than you. Have we not already discussed the fact that I am not willing to see you put yourself in danger?"

"You know we have. Which is why I see no reason to repeat the experience."

"This is not a joke, Josephine. This is serious, and this is not the time to argue with me. What we are planning to do not only is dangerous, but might be foolhardy. You can't expect me to stand by while you place yourself in a situation where you might very well be injured or killed. I won't do it."

"And I won't stand by while you put yourself in that same situation. Don't be such a bloody hypocrite!"

"This isn't being hypocritical; it's being logical. There's a very big difference between me going into a situation where people on both sides will be armed, suspicious, and more than willing to shoot anything that moves. I've been *trained* to do that, it's my *job* to do that, and I've *been* doing it for fifteen years."

She immediately saw his point, and deliberately paused to draw in a deep breath. "Okay, I understand that. I understand why you're worried about the idea of me putting myself in danger. I'm worried about you doing the same thing. But I'm not trying to horn in on your manly fun just for shits and giggles. I think it's important for me to be there when you find the people responsible for this fiasco. Especially if one of them is a scientist. I know you care about me, but you care about your friends, too, and you're not objecting to Rick and Steve going along."

"First, Rick is Lupine, which means he's at least four times stronger than the average homicidal skinhead and about ten times stronger than you," Eli bit out. "And second, Steve is a colonel in the US Air Force. He didn't earn that rank by crocheting doilies. He got it through combat training, firearms training, and training in strategy and tactics. He's seen real combat and lived to tell about it. And third—"

"What's third?"

She could almost hear Eli's teeth grinding together. "Third is . . . third."

"I'm glad to have it cleared up," Steve muttered.

Rick looked around, his cell phone still pressed to his ear, and rolled his eyes, mouthing, "Thank God," to the room at large.

Josie ignored them both, and luckily Eli didn't seem to notice them. Otherwise, she'd have been breaking up a fight before she managed to pry another word from her man's tight-lipped mouth.

"Third," he finally gritted out between clenched teeth, "is that if you think my feelings for *you* and my feelings for *them* have even the slightest thing in common, we're going to have a very long and very athletic conversation just as soon as this whole thing is over with."

Josie fought valiantly against the urge to roll her eyes. "We've already talked about the fact that I can no more stand by while you put yourself in deliberate danger than you can do it with me. We love each other. That's how that's supposed to work, and since neither one of us seems likely to change our minds about that, we need to just move on to the real problem instead of continuing with a never-ending argument."

"See, that's the difference between you and me," Eli said, glowering at her, "because I'd be happy to keep arguing if it meant that your life would last for more than the next twenty-four hours. I want to keep you around for as long as possible, even if I have to listen to you spouting nonsense the whole time!"

Through the rushing hiss of fury pounding in her ears, Josie heard the sharp intake of Steve's breath. She also saw him take a reflexive step backward as his eyes darted to the exits.

"And I think that's my cue to leave," Steve said. "I, uh, I need to . . . go . . . somewhere else. Right now."

He suited actions to words, Rick following hot on his heels.

Josie took a very deep breath and counted to ten. "Eli, I know that you don't want to see me in danger. Trust me, I don't want to see myself in danger, but I'm not insisting that I go along because I'm looking for a cheap thrill. These people developed a virus that's killed or killing my patients. I took an oath to try to save them. I *need* to save them. And the best chance for me to do that is to go with you and collect whatever notes and samples and dust rags I can find that might have a bearing on these cases. You and Rick might be trained fighters, but you're not doctors. I am."

"So is Steve. He can gather whatever you think you'll need and bring it back here with him."

She raised an eyebrow. "Oh, so you're not going to need Steve to do anything more suited to his other military skills? Like fighting or shooting or sneaking around without being detected?"

Eli's jaw flexed, but he didn't answer.

"Look, I might not be Other and I might not have gone through basic training, but I grew up in this town and I learned how to shoot a rifle when I was ten years old. I learned to shoot a pistol when I was twelve. Am I a sniper? No, but I can defend myself if I need to. And when it comes to having a strong stomach, I've probably seen more blood and had my hands in more gore than you and your friends put together. I can handle myself in a crisis, because that is what I've been trained to do. I can promise you that I will not be a liability."

He opened his mouth, and she held up a hand to stop him. At the moment, she had no interest in hearing from him.

"You can worry about me all you please, because I can guarantee that I will be worrying about you just as hard. You can forbid me from going with you. You can even tie me up and lock me in a room if you feel you have to do that, but I can guarantee you that I will find a way out, and when I do, I will come after you, because I couldn't live with myself if I stayed behind and that cost my patients or my friends or my neighbors their lives."

Her expression serious, she reached out and took one of his big hands in both of hers, feeling the tension coiled in the fine muscles there. "I know that there's no way you're going to be happy about me tagging along, and I'm sorry that I'm going to be causing you worry, but if it helps, I'll make you some very sincere promises right now."

Her brown eyes met his green ones and held steady. "I promise that from the moment we step out of this clinic, I will follow any order you give me, because I'm smart enough to know that the strategy devised by a trained law enforcement professional and a military colonel is probably better than what I could come up with on my own. I promise that if you say run, I will run, and if you say hide, I will hide. I promise that I won't take any chances that I don't feel are absolutely necessary, and I promise that I'll think with my head and not my heart."

She saw the muscles in his throat work as he swallowed,

then she saw his expression soften as he leaned down to press his forehead to hers. "Do you promise me that you absolutely will not get hurt?"

Lips curving, Josie reached up and pressed her mouth to his. "I promise. Do you?"

"Anything you want, Josie. Forever."

CHAPTER TWENTY-TWO

The current leader of the Nation of Aryan Humans went by the name George A. Huddlesford. Among Eli, Steve's connections in the government, and the information Rick gleaned from his beta's extensive research, they even managed to learn a little more about the man than just that one mundane fact. To tell the truth, within two hours of reconvening at the clinic, they had moved the base of operations up to Josie's apartment at the top of the house, and what they *had* learned absolutely boggled her mind.

First of all, the man's name turned out not to be George A. Huddlesford at all; it was Frances Joseph Foryski. He'd been born in Scranton, Pennsylvania, and he had a rap sheet that made for very interesting reading. He'd also changed his name at least three times. So far.

Shortly after his eighteenth birthday, he'd gone to court to legally switch his name from the one bestowed on him at birth to Frank Allen Josephs. Three years after that, he went to prison, and when he emerged, he'd begun calling himself Joseph Allen Huddlesford, allegedly after a character in a book about a young skinhead who rose to power by brutally and anonymously assassinating the nonwhite president, vice president, and Speaker of the House of

Representatives, thus sparking a race war in America. In the book, of course, the Aryans won and ushered in a paradisiacal future in which America had been freed from the oppressive influence of minorities.

Joe had lasted more than twenty-five years, but about a decade ago, he had run afoul of some rather dangerous types while living in Chicago. He'd dropped off the map for almost two years, and when he'd reemerged, his waistline had expanded, his hair had gone white, he'd grown a mustache, and careful surgery had altered his nose and chin just enough to throw his old enemies off his trail. Curiously, he'd chosen to keep most of his old name, now introducing himself as George Allen Huddlesford of Athens, Georgia. As far as Steve's sources could tell, he'd never actually been south of the Mason-Dixon Line.

For George aka Joe aka Frank, life as a career criminal had started with his days as a juvenile delinquent, when he delighted in such constructive pastimes as graffiti writing, truancy, vandalism, petty theft, and the occasional breaking and entering of such establishments as his school, his friends' schools, and a local youth center. From there, he had graduated to advanced breaking and entering, burglary, robbery, assault, battery, drunk and disorderly, numerous traffic violations, grand theft auto, and ultimately the trifecta of grand larceny, resisting arrest, and assaulting an officer that resulted in six years served at a Pennsylvania state prison facility. There he fell in with the community of white supremacist skinheads that altered the course of his criminal activity forever.

The Huddlesford years showed a distinct disinclination to remain a rank-and-file member of the white power and later the human power movements. Joe/George had plans,

grander plans than almost all of his fellow young skinheads, and grander even than many of his elder superiors.
In his mind, it wasn't enough to subjugate those who were
different—and therefore inferior; such beings should be
eradicated in order to ensure that no further pollution of
the white human gene pool would even be possible. And,
he eagerly demonstrated, that process had already been
too long delayed.

Within a month of his release from prison in Pennsylvania, Huddlesford was suspected of planting a bomb in
a Philadelphia community center in a poor black section
of town. No one had died in that incident, but more than
seventeen had been injured, many of them children, and
failure had only provided a potent incentive for the man
to work harder to achieve his goals.

Josie sat and listened to the entire story, marveling at
the infinite capacity of people to hate other people. It boggled her mind. She herself had taken to disliking a number
of people during her life—including Helen Patterson—but
she could not honestly name a single soul on the face of
the earth whom she really hated. In her mind, hate required that the object of it be entirely without redeeming
value. If even the smallest aspect of that person engendered
sympathy or empathy or pity—or even simple logical
comprehension—how could she bring herself to hate them?

For Huddlesford, though, she believed she might be able
to make an exception. Although his background in an abu-
sive, alcoholic family stirred a slight wave of sympathy
within her, his actions throughout his life had demonstrated
a kind of steadily increasing maliciousness that had no basis in logic or experience. As Steve and Eli continued with
their list of his crimes since joining the human power

movement, Josie saw no motivation for his actions other than sadistic enjoyment of the suffering of others and a baseless hatred of anything not exactly like him.

If Eli had thought she might still change her mind about joining in the hunt for this monster, he should have tied her up and locked her in another room before he began reciting this information. Now that she'd heard the full story, she didn't just want to see this bastard stopped, she wanted to shoot him herself.

The sheriff, though, had said very little since their last talk at the clinic. After she had stalked off and left him, she had made her way outside—where Rick and Steve had been hiding from the crossfire—and upstairs to take a much-needed shower and put on some real clothes. She'd also received a clear message from her stomach that the snacky dinner she and Eli had eaten the night before had long since worn off, so she'd put together an enormous meal of pasta, meat sauce, and garlic bread that had lured the men up to her apartment faster than any invitation.

While she cooked, Rick and Steve had spent a lot of time on the phone, Ben had returned with his donated medical supplies then just as quickly fled again, and Eli eventually appeared, looking calm and even a little subdued. He'd asked politely for the use of her computer and Internet connection, then planted himself in front of the machine and begun clacking away. He hadn't said another word until after dinner had been consumed and the mess cleared away.

They moved as a group to the living room, where the discussion naturally returned to the head of the NAH, who he was, what he could possibly have planned, and where he might currently be found. Rick's beta, as it turned out, was fairly certain that the answer to the last question was right nearby at a former Boy Scout camp on the Columbia River.

"He bought the place about a year and a half ago," Rick said. "The owner was retiring, and Huddlesford wanted a spot where he could not only hole up, but also turn into a meeting place for his cronies. A kind of mecca for maniacs. The camp came with a house, as well as a meeting hall, cafeteria, barn, storage sheds, and cabins with indoor plumbing and hot and cold running water. It's a pretty nice setup, and he's already hosted two conferences that saw upward of three thousand people each."

Josie shook her head. Why would anyone want to join up with such a man, she wondered briefly, but she knew history could provide more than a few answers to that question—Hitler, Stalin, Pol Pot, and on and on.

"He's also opened the place up to his followers who want to take 'advanced philosophical seminars' on his teachings." Steve consulted a page of notes and made a face. "My friends at the FBI tell me they may have started out as seminars designed to fire up the youth membership in the NAH so they'd go out and make demonstrations and launch protests like the ones in Stone Creek last summer. But these days, it's code for training camps in home-grown terrorism. They're open-minded about their tactics, too. They support everything from old-fashioned lynchings to airplane hijackings to bombings. And now, apparently, bioterrorism."

Eli frowned. "Yeah, and what did your fed friends say when you mentioned the part about the virus?"

One of Steve's eyebrows shot up, and his chin drew backward. "Do I look that stupid to you? If I whispered a word about why I wanted this information or what we planned to do with it, we'd have feebs crawling up our asses before we could so much as bend over. They'd love an excuse to take Huddlesford down. In fact, they're itching for one. But I see no reason to do all the work and then deprive myself of all the fun."

Josie darted a glance at Eli and found his gaze fixed on her.

"I can think of one," she murmured to herself, then raised her voice. "Why don't we just turn over all of our information to the FBI and let them raid the place and haul whoever they find there off to prison?"

Eli just stared at her. "Mainly because we lack what federal judges like to refer to as 'probable cause.'"

"You don't think that the virus and the attacks and the evidence from the campsite constitute probable cause?" she demanded.

"We can't bring any of that to the police," Steve reminded her, "except maybe for the newsletter, but by itself that doesn't amount to much other than a suspicion. None of the information I've provided can be substantiated without at least one of us going to jail, and I can tell you right now that I'd rather avoid that if I can."

She had forgotten about that. While Steve had been willing to take the risk of sharing what he knew with Josie and the others, she could understand why he couldn't do the same thing with the FBI. Even if he were willing to risk court-martial, prison, and a dishonorable discharge, he still couldn't guarantee that anyone would believe his claims. All the military had to do was deny the whole thing and no one without the proper clearance would ever know anything had happened.

It was the kind of thing that really made her wonder about space aliens.

"We've got no other choice." Eli spoke flatly, his expression blank, which Josie didn't like one bit. "We have to do this ourselves. Dr. Shad was able to retrieve the bullet, and I've got someone looking at it, but it had to have come from the same gun that shot Rosemary. If we can find the gun at this compound of Huddlesford's, I'll have more than enough to charge him with two counts of attempted murder. I can be satisfied with that for the time being as long as it gets him a prison term a long way from Stone Creek."

"What about the jurisdictional issues?" Steve asked. "Will that be a problem? The compound isn't here in Stone Creek, after all."

"No, but the crimes were committed here. And it wouldn't matter either way. The compound is still in the same county, and while officially the sheriff's office of Stone Creek acts as the town's independent police force, we're technically still part of the county sheriff's department. We'll be fine."

Steve nodded. "Good. In that case, I hope we find England at the compound, too. With him and any evidence of the virus on hand, I think we'll be able to upgrade one of those charges to premeditated murder. And tack on a few more besides, like treason. I'd like to do what we can to make sure neither of these bastards ever sets foot outside a prison again."

"Hear, hear!"

Eli turned to Rick. "What do you think some of your packmates would say to the idea of another short stint as honorary Stone Creek deputies?"

"I think they'd say, 'Hell, yes!'"

"Good. Ask them to come in and collect their badges. How long do you think before they can muster?"

"If I tell them what we're working on? An hour, tops. And the ones who are farther away from that are going to harass me for months for not waiting for them."

Josie watched, fascinated, as Eli transformed into a calm, efficient strategist in front of her eyes. She glanced from him to Steve and caught the look of amusement on the other man's face. It looked like she wasn't the only one thinking that her lover would have made an excellent general.

The sheriff glanced from the clock near the kitchen to his wristwatch and nodded briskly. "Dusk should be in about two hours. As soon as the Lupines get here, we'll go over the plan and start loading up. We can take my Jeep. Rick, make sure one of your men has a dark, smooth-running truck to transport the others. The compound is a little less than an hour's drive on back roads, so we'll move in after dark."

His eyes flickered to Josie and away. "Everyone suit up. Dress dark and sturdy. We'll be moving fast and quiet, potentially over rough ground. We meet in the back of the clinic at twenty ten hours. Questions?"

No one blinked.

"Good. I'll see you then."

As Josie watched, feeling a little dazed, Eli spun on his heel, strode to the door, and disappeared into the setting sun. Seriously. It was like watching something out of a modern-day Western. The hero barked out his orders and then marched out into the sunset, prepared to take on an army of villains to save the world.

All Josie really cared about was that he save himself.

CHAPTER TWENTY-THREE

Sandwiched in the middle of the Jeep between Rick and Steve, Josie felt a little like a mouse trapped in a herd of elephants. Not that any of the men in this truck or the one following it moved with anything other than lethally silent grace, she'd discovered, which only served to make her feel even more self-conscious. Maybe Eli had been right, and she should have stayed behind. She didn't have the experience with combat or self-defense or even just plain bare-knuckled fighting that every single one of them could boast, nor did she have the instincts of 99 percent of them. She was Josie Barrett, girl veterinarian, not girl wonder, and as they neared the location of the compound, she found herself hoping fervently that at the very least she just not get anyone hurt.

If she could avoid causing death or injury to herself and others, she would consider her participation in tonight's operation an unqualified success.

The thought of operations at least reminded her of the second reason why she had insisted on coming, the first being the stone-faced Feline currently steering the Jeep off the narrow country road and onto what looked like an old logging trail at the direction of Lucas Fairfield, beta and

second in command of the Stone Creek Clan. She clutched
a compact black satchel to her chest, reassured by its light-
weight bulk and the knowledge that she had packed it personally, choosing every item inside with utmost care. In it,
she carried saline, gauze, Betadine, waterproof tape, a fully
loaded medical staple gun, penicillin, lidocaine, morphine,
and two excessively lethal doses of sux, one for Bill and one
for . . . any number of possibilities, none of which she had
any intention of thinking about.

Josie would gladly pray no one got hurt. She would do
her best to ensure that no one got hurt, but if anyone *did,*
she intended to make damn sure that they still made it
back to their homes in one piece.

Eli guided the truck along the rutted, overgrown logging trail for a good fifteen minutes with the black Suburban behind them bumping steadily in their wake. Then
Lucas said something brief and quiet, and Eli slowed, killing the vehicle's headlights and glancing in his rearview
mirror to watch the Suburban do the same.

"Okay," he said in a low, surprisingly carrying voice
that Josie had no trouble hearing. "From here on out, we're
going dark, and we're going quiet. Remember the hand
signals we went over back at the clinic, and use those for
essential communication. If it's inessential, keep it to yourself. Everybody clear?"

No one said anything, which seemed to be the correct
reaction. Eli returned his gaze to the road and guided the
truck approximately another half mile using only the sliver
of crescent moon light and his own keen eyesight to show
the way. Finally, he pulled to the side of the road next to a
stand of young pine trees and cut the engine. The Suburban rolled in behind and followed suit.

Never in her life had Josie heard car doors open and close so quietly. Standing less than three feet away from the one through which one of Rick's packmates emerged, she barely even noticed a click. These men moved with unnatural silence.

She watched as the group of ten men gathered on the road beside the trucks. In addition to Eli, Steve, Rick, and Lucas, two of Eli's deputies had joined the mission, both of them Others. Mike Driscoll was a changeling, son of a human father and a Fae mother, and Will Chkalov an Ursal, a shapeshifter who could take on the form of a black bear. From Rick's pack, four other men had immediately answered his summons. Josie had met each of the Lupines before, but didn't know any of them well. Still, if they were Stone Creek, she knew she could trust them.

Back at the clinic, she had distributed the four air guns Ben had been able to collect that day, keeping the one from her storage room for herself, and provided each man carrying one with a supply of tranquilizer darts with instructions to use them on anything Other. She didn't want to see any more shifters die if there were even the remotest possibility that capturing Garrett England might lead to a cure for the virus. Bringing in anyone infected with LV-7 or -8 was likely a pipe dream, and she knew it, but it wasn't in Josie to give up hope until every last chance for success had been exhausted.

Her hands clutched the top of her med kit as she watched the men fall into formation, adhering seamlessly to the plan Eli, Steve, Rick, and Lucas had outlined on the large whiteboard in the back of Josie's clinic.

Thanks to the fact that the headquarters of the NAH had once served as a popular campground for Scouts, it had been easy to locate maps of the buildings at the site and even blueprints and written description of the major buildings. That had given their team a strong advantage. They had also benefited from the fascinated wariness with which Lucas viewed the supremacist group. On his own time, he had scouted the perimeter of the land twice and noted the positions of guards at the main entrance and at two additional points of access on opposite sides of the camp.

He, apparently, wasn't the only one who felt the need for an excess of caution.

With such valuable information in hand, Eli and the others had established the best point at which to gain entry into the fortified compound. They had also gone over the most promising places to search for Huddlesford, England, and any evidence of the possession of genetically engineered viruses for use in terrorist actions.

Once through the perimeter fence, their team would divide up into three search parties of three men (and/or woman) each, with one additional two-man pairing. Josie, it had been clearly established, would go with Eli and Steve and obey every command either one of them cared to give without hesitating or asking questions. And that meant *every one,* up to and including a potential order to stand on her head, blow spit bubbles, and sing "Battle Hymn of the Republic" in Swahili if that's what they told her to do.

When Eli made with point through tightly clenched teeth, Josie hadn't even had the heart to point out to him that she didn't actually know the words to that particular song. Nor was she certain she could stand on her head, considering that she hadn't tried to do so since she was seven years old.

She figured he already knew about her lack of fluency in the languages and dialects of the African continent.

Once one of the teams located either of their primary targets, an arrest was to be made as quickly as possible and with the least amount of required force (that had been the only point at which any of the volunteers for the evening's escapade had expressed their grumbling disapproval). The prisoners would then be escorted back the way the team had entered and returned to the Stone Creek jail for charging and processing. Unfortunately, given the assumed lateness of the hour at which this return would likely be accomplished, an judge would be unavailable to arraign the suspects until the following morning.

All evidence collected at the scene would be turned over to Sheriff Pace by the appropriate deputies immediately. The sheriff would provide this evidence in turn to the proper county, state, and federal district attorneys in order to substantiate the charges being leveled against the prisoners.

And once the trial dates were set, Josie vowed, she would sit in the gallery every day until the bastards paid for their crimes. She didn't care if she had to perform spay/neuter surgeries on top of a folding card table.

Just before the group prepared to move out, Josie felt an arm snake around her waist and found herself being pulled back against a firm and familiar body. When Eli's voice murmured almost soundlessly in her ear, she couldn't prevent the shiver that ran through her.

"Just remember these three things," he breathed, the current of air teasing her skin and sending a few short hairs at her temple wavering. "One, do exactly as I say.

Two, do exactly as Steve says. And three, if you get hurt, I will beat you so hard you have to stand up at our wedding dinner."

He slipped away before the sound of the last word reached her ear and took his position at the head of the line, leaving Josie blinking unsteadily after him. She had to hurry to catch up when he gave the gesture for the troop to move out. She slipped into place where she'd been instructed, sandwiched between Rick and Steve in front, behind Eli, and Lucas and Mike in back. The rest of the men followed in silent double file.

A short way down the logging trail, Eli guided the column to the right, off the road and into the dense woods. Around her, Josie could see little more than a couple of feet in front of her, just enough not to run into anything solid, and she heard even less. The only sounds came from the nightlife of the forest and her own boot-clad footfalls. The men around her moved like ghosts. She tried to make as little noise as possible, but she had no idea how they moved without even rustling the leaves underfoot. It should have been against the laws of physics.

In fact, she felt pretty sure it was.

The walk from the trucks to the rear of the fence surrounding the campground seemed to last for most of Josie's thirties, though she remembered Lucas saying he estimated they would reach it in approximately twenty minutes. They had to loop around fairly far to the west before doubling back in order to avoid where a trail from one of the camp's lesser-known exits wound back toward the logging road.

When they finally reached that first grand milestone,

Josie felt a sense of disappointment. Somehow, while they had been discussing this whole adventure, her mind had supplied a picture of a barrier something like the Berlin Wall. Or maybe a prison fence, something at least twelve feet tall, made of stone and concrete with broken glass embedded in the top and lengths of razor wire coiled above it. Maybe even with a few strategically placed guard towers built in for good measure.

Instead, they stopped in front of an ordinary chain-link fence, maybe eight feet tall. It had begun to corrode after years in the outdoor environment of the Pacific Coastal mountain range, and vines and creeping plants had curled their tendrils over and through it until it looked in places like a planter trellis in someone's back garden. Josie identified at least one of the climbers as honeysuckle and thought incongruously that if this were only a couple of months earlier, she could have plucked off a bloom and sucked the nectar from the bottom of the stamen.

None of the men seemed to share her peculiar reaction. In fact, only a couple of them actually bothered to look at the fence. The others watched the surrounding woods with wary, restless eyes, ensuring that no one stumbled upon them before they made their way inside and accomplished their mission.

Josie ran her gaze nervously over the shadows a single time, then turned her concentration back to the fence where Rick had begun to wield a set of sharp matte wire cutters on the weathered links. The whole group waited patiently, which struck Josie as significant, seeing that most of them could have jumped the fence with as little effort as if it were a small stone lying in their path. But since Steve, Josie,

Will, and Mike didn't have those sort of athletic gifts, they had decided to cut their way through.

It would also make for a faster getaway, as Steve had pointed out, if none of them had to swing up and over, but could instead move straight through.

This team of men and others was nothing if not thorough, she concluded as she studied the way in which Rick had dismantled the fence. He had cut through the wire in order to pull away a two-foot-wide section of metal, but at first he left it in place while he and Mike Driscoll quickly and carefully untangled the vegetation from its grid pattern. The flash of energy Josie saw from time to time told her that some of the stubborn plants gave in not to the men's coaxing hands but from a flash of Fae magic that asked the vegetation to kindly get out of the way so that the men could finish their task and move on into the camp.

When the section of fence came free, Rick moved it several feet away, laid it on the ground, and covered it with leaves, mulch, and soil until it blended completely with the forest floor. Then when Josie looked back at where the fence had once been, she realized that it took a moment before her eyes could relocate the area. By leaving the vegetation in place, Rick and Mike had created the illusion that the barrier remained intact, thus decreasing the chances that a sweep of the perimeter by guards or anyone else would lead to the sounding of an alarm. It was something Josie would never have thought of, but it was brilliant, which was probably why Josie didn't play chess. A strategist she was not.

Mike held the vegetation apart with a Fae touch while the others ducked through and into the shadows of the compound, slipping inside himself just before he let the vines settle back into place leaving little to no trace of their passing.

Josie stuck close to her two watchdogs and waited while Eli gave a series of hand signals to disperse the others in their teams. The men ghosted off in silence, leaving Eli, Steve, and Josie to head for the main house and, hopefully, George A. Huddlesford.

The three of them fell into the predetermined formation with Eli leading the way through the darkness with his superior night vision, Josie in the middle where she was least likely to get into any trouble, and Steve bringing up the rear to protect their flank. According to the maps they had consulted earlier, the main house of the old campground was situated in the southeastern quadrant some distance from the nearest other building. When the camp had been built, the owner and manager of the facility had wanted to live on site to make his job easier, but had desired not to live surrounded by pubescent boys, so he'd deliberately set himself up with a perimeter of privacy.

Convenient at the time, Josie was sure, but now she could appreciate that the remote location would make slipping in undetected a great deal easier. *Undetected* was her favorite word today, she decided. *Undetected* meant un-shot-at, un-maimed, and un-killed, and that was how she preferred to keep things.

They crept through the woods in a way Josie couldn't remember doing since her last year at summer camp when she'd been nine. The following year she'd begged to be allowed to stay home and help her father and his employees at the clinic for the whopping rate of a dollar a day, which she intended to put toward the vet school savings account she'd started on her previous birthday. But at nine, she had enjoyed her last summer of total freedom despite herself and even indulged in several spirited games of Hunt the Hunter. As she recalled, that game had consisted mainly of skulking through the forest by the light of flashlights pretending to be deer intent on revenge against the humans who had killed so many of their relatives. The campers she and her friends hadn't liked, of course, had been the hunters. Really, though, that was the last time Josie could recall skulking playing a part in her life. Wasn't it just amazing the way one's childhood began to repeat itself as one grew older?

Josie estimated that it took approximately another ten or fifteen minutes to walk around the outskirts of the compound to the rear of the three-story white house that sat atop a small hill about a hundred yards and several hundred trees away from the camp's main entrance. They avoided the fence line, of course, as well as any noticeable trails to minimize their chance of detection, but when the darkened house came into view, it remained one screened by several rows of trees and assorted underbrush. Eli halted them behind a particularly thick clump, and gave the signal for them to stay quiet and remain in place.

Not particularly pleased by this turn of events, Josie watched unhappily as her lover dropped into a crouch and began to pick his way closer to the building. She did appreciate that he at least refrained from shifting into his Feline form, something they had discussed that evening. Now that the LV-7 virus had become effective against Felines, Josie insisted that it was much too dangerous to risk Eli being caught in his lion form.

"I don't care if you turn furry occasionally," she had

informed him, "but I would care if you stayed that way permanently."

He had tried to argue that because his senses were keener and his presence much more easily explained in animal form, it could prove useful for reconnaissance, but Josie had put her foot down. On his toes, since they'd been standing face-to-face at the time. It was just not worth the risk.

As he neared the house, Josie rose on her toes and strained to keep him in sight. She felt Steve lay a comforting had at her back, and while it was a lovely gesture, she really wanted to let him know that it didn't help. She would feel comfortable when she, Eli, and all the others were safe back at home where they belonged, and probably not a moment before that.

No windows burned in or around the structure, so although her eyes had long since adjusted to the darkness, Josie began to lose track of Eli every time he ducked into the shadow of a tree or an overhang. When that happened, she would momentarily stop breathing until she saw him dart from one spot of cover to the next as he peered in windows and around corners looking for any signs of life.

Finally, after what seemed like days, he stopped near a low window at the back of the first floor and made a complex series of gestures with his hands that Josie understood not a flicker of. Steve, though, nodded and gestured back.

They had gone over hand signals earlier, back at the clinic, but Josie had concentrated only on the most critical ones: stop, halt, forward, wait, quiet, look, hide, and—her personal favorite—retreat. Or as she liked to call it, "run,

run away!" Steve had explained that the signals were a standard code used by all branches of the US military and could convey large amounts of information when necessary. Apparently, it had just become necessary.

Steve gripped her arm, gave her an apologetic look, and then pressed his mouth against her ear. "Eli's going in through the window. Once he gives the all-clear, we follow. We stay low, and we move fast. If you're not close enough that I feel you on my tail, I'll sic the werewarden on you. Ready?"

Josie swallowed, clutched her med kit closer, and nodded. Then she practically pressed herself up against Steve's back and waited with vibrating tension for the next signal. It wasn't long in coming.

Only seconds after pushing the window sash silently open and wiggling through the gap, Eli's hand reemerged with a beckoning motion. Steve didn't even glance back, just shot forward like an arrow with Josie at his back in a poor, ragged imitation of fletching. He halted under the window, turned smoothly, boosted Josie up and through before she even knew what was happening. Thankfully, she caught on in midair and was able to collect herself so that she slithered quietly to the floor and didn't land on her face with an echoing thump. Immediately she scuttled to the side next to Eli and waited for Steve to follow. When all three of them were once again crouched together in the darkness, Eli uncoiled himself in a smooth flow of muscle and made his indirect way to the door.

At first, Josie stepped where he stepped because she remembered that's what he'd ordered her to do when they left the clinic, but after only a few heartbeats she realized what he was doing. This house was an old one, built in the

1920s, with original hardwood floors throughout. Even if the men who'd constructed it, now long dead, had been master craftsmen, after decades of habitation the center of the floors—the most heavily used areas—would undoubtedly be the mostly likely to creak or groan when stepped on. By moving along the periphery, they might travel a few extra feet, but they would give far fewer unwitting signals of their presence.

A quick look around told Josie that they had entered the house in an old-fashioned study, sparsely furnished with worn antiques, faded upholstery, and walls lined with glass-fronted bookshelves. The only things that looked new were a few items scattered across the surface of an old-fashioned drop-leaf desk and the large flag of the Nazi party that had been hung above the stone fireplace. The sight of it made her grimace with distaste, but it served as a potent reminder of why she was here, skulking around someone else's house like a criminal.

She wasn't the criminal; George A. Huddlesford and his band of merry maniacs were the criminals, and Josie and Eli and the others had come here to stop them. The thought gave her strength and determination as they ghosted through the room toward the hall. As she neared the desk, she glanced down curiously and saw a pile of loose papers, an uncapped fountain pen, and a thread-bound theme book with a stiff black-and-white cover. In the dim light, she could just barely make out the heavy printing on the cover. It looked to be some sort of date code.

Josie had just reached out to flip open the cover when Steve nudged her sharply in the back. Jumping a little, she glanced over her shoulder and saw him jerk his head toward the hall door where Eli was already poised to slip through. Nodding, she grabbed the notebook and stuffed it in her medical bag. She'd told Eli she was coming for papers and information on the virus, and while she guessed she'd find them in a lab, it made a good excuse for snooping through what was probably someone's diary.

Stepping carefully forward, she and Steve made their way to the hall and halted while Eli scanned it for signs of their host's presence. As far as Josie could tell, the house was abandoned, which wasn't quite what she had expected.

Wouldn't that be a kick in the teeth, she thought, if they had come up with this elaborate plan and gone to all this trouble only to find out that Huddlesford was away on a pilgrimage to Berlin or something?

Apparently, she needn't have worried. No sooner had the thought crossed her mind than a huge thud echoed at the front of the house.

Eli shoved Josie, and she responded immediately, ducking back around to the inside of the parlor door, dropping to the floor, and pressing herself against the wall. Eli was flattened against the side of the center staircase that descended from the level above to end opposite the house's front door, and Steve stood over Josie, flattened into the shadows. Both men's hands had been free only an instant before, but even in the darkness she could see that each one now gripped the big black handle of a sleek and dangerous-looking semiautomatic pistol.

Suddenly Josie wished very hard that she'd been able to talk Eli into giving her a gun of her own. She would have no reason to use one, he had assured her, but right now she decided she would have felt very much better if she'd had something solid and reassuring in her hand. As it was, her fingers automatically dipped into her med kit in search of comfort.

For seven hundred years, none of the three intruders so much as breathed. At least, that's what it felt like to Josie. They were waiting to see if the source of the loud noise revealed itself as friend or foe.

In a scrabble of sound and air, the front door swung open. Josie hadn't been expecting the revelation that the source of the commotion was a Beatles fan.

"I ahm th' walrush! Iyum t' wahr'sh! Coogoog'shu," came the drunkest rendition of a classic rock tune that Josie had ever heard.

Turning her head, she realized that if she peered between the doorjamb and Steve's left kneecap, she had a decent vantage point from which to view the now wide-open front door and the swaying figure who stood on the threshold.

George A. Huddlesford, it turned out, stood only about five-foot-nine, and that was taking into account the thick-heeled cowboy boots he wore with his crisp white shirt and smartly ironed pin-striped trousers. He had a thick mustache that drooped along either side of his mouth, and shaggy gray-and-white hair that looked as if he spent most of his day dragging his fingers through it in agitation. His belly protruded in front of him like a six-month pregnancy, but he encompassed it with a thick belt of good Italian leather surmounted by a large silver buckle with the initials and logo of the NAH engraved in the front.

His right hand gestured to the supposedly empty hall

with hazy grandiloquence, and in his left he carried the explanation for his off-key, off-tempo, off-lyric rendition of one of the Beatles' immortal tunes: a fifth bottle of Kentucky bourbon with less than an inch of amber liquor left to its credit.

Lord, if he'd started on that new anytime today, it was a wonder he could still stand, let alone sing, albeit badly.

This had definitely not figured into their plans. Josie glanced up at Steve, who shook his head and looked across at Eli, who was staring at Huddlesford with an expression of baffled disbelief. The mastermind behind one of the most complex plots of biological terrorism anyone had ever heard of was a tone-deaf, middle-aged, overweight alcoholic with a fondness for classic British pop?

They had to be missing something.

"Dad!"

Josie's head almost snapped around as she strained to see where the new voice had come from. This one was decidedly younger, definitely sober, and more than a little hocked off, from the sound of it. It had also seemingly originated from somewhere above Josie's head.

A creak on the stairs narrowed the location, and Josie almost imagined she saw Eli's ears turn in the direction of the top of the staircase.

"Dad, you were supposed to be giving a lecture on the need for action from our younger members on the issues that are most important to them. We need to make a show of force at the International Summit of Councils in New York this spring. Do we have to do everything ourselves? Do *I* have to do everything myself?"

Josie looked up at Steve's face and saw a confusion to match her own. Nowhere in the information he or Lucas had provided to the group had there been any mention of George Huddlesford ever marrying or siring children. Who in the world would be calling him Dad?

Huddlesford tilted his head back to look up at the top of the stairs and nearly fell over backward at the change to his equilibrium. His shoulder slammed into the edge of the doorway, and he cursed.

"Garrett, my boy, I gave a mighty speech this fine evenin', yes I did," Huddlesford drawled after a moment, the injury swiftly forgotten in a haze of liquor. "While you sat down here in the parlor scribblin' away in 'at book o' yers, I drew fire on the mountain and lit it in the hearts of our younguns, that's fo' sho'. My ideas tonight were es-plosive, I guar-an-teeeeeeee-haw!"

"Oh, for God's sake," the younger voice snapped, "drop that nauseous good-ol'-boy routine, you old fool. You're from Scranton, Pennsylvania, and the closest you've ever been to Georgia is eating in a Krispy Kreme doughnut shop."

Stairs creaked and Josie's heart lurched as the young man began to talk down the stairs.

"And the only way you could cause an explosion right now would be to breathe near an open flame," the voice continued in disgust. "What you call my scribbling will make me immortal one day. Honest to God, I do not understand what form of insanity made my mother sleep with you, but I do thank heavens that she had the good sense not to marry you, at least. Imagine how much growing up knowing about you could have held me back."

Josie frowned. Obviously, Huddlesford did indeed have a son, but why had no one been able to dig up that information? Wasn't that what the FBI did, after all?

Collect information on people and put it in files that writers would then use in the coming decades to spice up your biography?

It looked like someone had been falling down on the job.

Craning her neck, Josie tried to get a glimpse of the figure coming down the stairs, but (a) the man's back was turned to the parlor, and (b) the beautifully carved and installed wooden banister kept getting in the damn way. Her curiosity nearly drove her crazy. She'd have killed for a better look.

"Come on, boy," Huddlesford sneered. Or Josie assumed it would have been a sneer if half the nerves in his face hadn't been numbed useless by the alcohol. "You wouldn't even be alive if it weren't for me. I gave you life! You're the fruit of my loins, the product of my superior breeding. You ought to be thanking me for what I've done for you!"

"What *you've* done for *me?* Don't make me laugh, old man." The mysterious figure proceeded to do exactly that. "All you did was pump out a few inexplicably worthwhile sperm. I *made* you! When I found out about my natural father and tracked you down, you were still planning to rid the world of the 'coloreds' one lynching at a time. I was only ten, and I already had a better grasp on the future of white humanity than you have today! I'm the one who showed you the path to the future. I gave you the cause of human supremacy. I created the Nation of Aryan Humans, and I created you, too, Frances, out of whole cloth. Without me, you'd still be getting into bar fights and running from Chicago mobsters. Without me, the LV virus series would never have existed. I created that virus, too, and I gave it to you, free and clear when the government tried to end my research. And I had to step in again and bring you the new strain when your inability to ensure that my step-by-step instructions were followed led to all those uncomfortable questions around my lab.

"I have given you more than you'll ever deserve, old man, so don't even try your pitiful attempts at paternal guilt on me."

There was another snide laugh, but this time Josie didn't wonder at the figure's identity. She knew it. Beyond doubt.

Mind reeling, she tilted her head back and looked to Steve for confirmation.

England? she mouthed, and received a terse nod in reply. But she already knew. The young man had given away enough information that he might as well have stepped forward and formally introduced himself.

No, what had taken Josie aback had not been the man's name, but the true story of what he had done. She and Eli and Steve and even poor paranoid Lucas had gotten it all wrong. The threat had never come from George Huddlesford. It had been Garrett England all along. The government might have wanted the LV-7 virus as a defensive weapon against enemy armies comprising Lupine soldiers, but the scientist they had chosen to achieve that goal had had something else in mind entirely.

The eradication of all Otherkind.

CHAPTER
TWENTY-FOUR

In the shadow of the stairwell, Eli listened to Garrett England spill out the story of his megalomaniacal plan for world domination and wished like hell he were getting this on tape. Unfortunately, recording equipment hadn't been part of the master plan. While the story unfolded, he had a very good look at the expressions on the faces of his mate and his friend, though, so he knew they heard every word. And would be happy to testify to the facts at trial.

He also knew that Josie had taken moral offense at the idea of a scientist and a doctor, any doctor, using his or her knowledge and skill in order to specifically destroy the life she had dedicated herself to fighting to preserve. So far, though, she had held steady, not leapt forward to confront the criminal mastermind single-handedly. He prayed for her to continue to show such sensibility.

The problem now was that the plans had changed slightly. Here his team had discovered the two highest-rated targets of their little mission but none of the evidence they needed to support the arrest. Since neither England nor Huddlesford had pulled the trigger on the rifle that shot Rosemary and Jackson, they couldn't be tied to the bullets. They could still be charged with murder if the DA could make the connection between their orders and the actual shootings, but that would require a lot more proof than a single statement overheard in the hallway of an NAH campground. So the question became: Did Eli step forward and make the arrest now in the hope that the other search parties had or would locate the necessary evidence against these men, or did he stand back and wait to see if England let out more rope for his own hanging?

Steve signed him that very question, and Eli hesitated for a second before he made the call—wait. Wait to see what else might come of the conversation, at least for as long as their presence remained undetected.

"I won't be dismissed!" Eli heard Huddlesford shout along with the creak of the stairs as England began to reascend. Another creak indicated that his father meant to follow. "I demand tha' you sshow me sssome respec', boy!"

"I show you just as much as you deserve. All you are is a front, Frances. I'm the real power in this organization, and I owe you nothing."

"Y'do so! Wivout me, you' still be sthinkin' yer firs' stinkin' virus w's some kina holy grail. I'm th' one foun' tha' Lupine'n brought 'im back here. I e'en told you the damn p'ple a' the refuge place gave 'im tha' rabies shot. I'm th' reason you know yer first bug was just a big frickin' flop!"

It took Eli a minute to piece together the meaning of that slurred and disjointed speech, but when he did, he felt his heart begin to race. Was Huddlesford right, or just drunk? Because if Eli understood him correctly, he had just said that a Lupine infected with the LV-7 virus—presumably, hopefully, Bill—had been picked up by a wildlife refuge and given a canine rabies shot, which had cured him of the infection. Was that even possible? He wanted desperately to ask Steve or Josie, but they couldn't take the risk of speech and this question was not one covered by the handy military hand signal code.

He also wanted to ask how a refuge had managed to pick up Bill in his wolf form and not believed he already *had* rabies, based on his last known actions. Had the violence worn off somehow? Shit, he needed answers.

Two bodies clashed somewhere on the stairs, and Eli heard a thud and what he assumed to be a moan of pain from the older man, because it was followed immediately by England hissing in contemptuous rage.

"Don't you ever speak that way to me again, you fat old bastard! All you brought me was a dead body. That virus was perfect in vitro! Indestructible! How were we to know that when the antibodies in a standard dose of vaccine combined with normal Lupine immune cells, it would spell disaster? Lupine immune cells aren't lying thick on the ground in laboratory supply houses, you know. But it hardly matters. The Lupine was one subject. A programmed loss. By now, there are dozens of infected Others out there, by tomorrow there will be hundreds, and within a few weeks, the virus will sweep across the continent. By the time anyone even realizes it's based on the rabies virus, they'll all be dead."

Eli's gaze flew to Josie's face and saw the dawning excitement written there. He watched as she fumbled in the bag she had slung over her shoulder and pulled out a black-and-white notebook, flipping quickly and silently through the pages. What had she found there? As long as it kept her occupied, he didn't care. He'd already half expected her to jump to her feet, run back to the clinic, and begin ordering massive amounts of canine rabies vaccine, but she didn't, and that was the important thing.

"I tol' you—" Huddlesford began, but the sound was cut off with another sickening thud.

"Shut up!" England yelled, sounding nearly unhinged at this point. "I don't want to hear another word, you disgusting waste of flesh! This is all. *Your*. FAULT!"

None of them anticipated what happened next. One minute the father and son were arguing on the stairway, and the next England gave a scream of inhuman rage followed by a grunt of exertion. Eli listened in disbelief to a series of three loud thumps, then the sickening crack of a melon splitting open on a wooden picnic table. Only the melon wasn't a melon; it was George Huddlesford's skull and the table was the parquetry floor of the house's elegant entry hall.

Eli couldn't see anything in front of the stairs, not from where he stood pressed up against them, but he saw the look of shock and distaste on Steve's face, and the abject horror on Josie's. Then his heart sank into his boots as he saw her throw herself out from between Steve's legs and scramble to her feet. She was halfway down the hall before the shout of denial had left his mouth.

His Josie just had to be the hero.

He sprinted after her in a panic and collided with Steve doing the exact same thing. Like something out of the Keystone Kops, their chests bounced off each other, sending both of them to the floor in a tangle of limbs and weapons, but neither felt like being amused. Over the roar of panic in his head, he heard Josie calling the old man's name over and over, and after a week of medical mishaps, he could picture her clearly pressing her fingers to his throat, looking for a pulse. He knew already that she wouldn't find one. Underlying the smell of fear, rage, and blood was the smell of the waste released at the instant of death when all the body's muscles went simultaneously limp.

George Huddlesford was already dead. Dr. Josie Barrett, he thought, wouldn't be satisfied until she had checked for herself. Then she would know for certain.

Eli scrambled to his feet with a sense of urgency he'd never experienced before. Time seemed to distill into something like slow motion and sound reverberated in his head the way he remembered from the old television shows about people with bionic limbs, only the sounds Eli heard were his own footsteps on the wood of the hallway floors and Garrett England's footsteps as he raced down the stairs intent on destroying the witness to his father's murder. They seemed to fall simultaneously to Eli and with every step he took the length of the hallway beside the stairs seemed to grow in comparison with the number of stairs on the way down.

Panic surged inside him and he feared he wouldn't make it in time. If England reached Josie first, all it would take was one blow and he could crack her skull against the floor as easily as he had his father's. The height of the stairway was entirely superfluous.

"Bitch!" Eli heard, and he wondered oddly if this was what it would feel like trying to move through quicksand. "Who are you? What are you doing here? What did you see?"

"He's dead."

Josie's voice sounded oddly calm and unconcerned for

someone about to be attacked by a proven murderer still not recovered from his last homicidal rage. As Eli plowed forward, he saw her come into view, crouched beside the body of George Huddlesford with one hand in her medical kit and the other still poised on the pale skin of the man's throat. She didn't seem to notice the spreading pool of blood slowly encroaching on the spot where her left knee touched the floor.

"You killed him," she said levelly. "You hadn't done enough? You had to kill your own father, too? Why? What drives a monster like you?"

She couldn't have been more than seven feet away, but to Eli it seemed like miles.

"You won't wonder about that when you're dead!" England screamed and dove off the bottom stair with his arms outstretched and his finger curled into grasping claws.

Eli shrieked in rage and completely disregarded his promise to remain in human form. He shifted as he leapt, wanting fangs and claws with which to tear limb from bloody limb the man who dared to threaten his mate.

His foolish, brave mate, whom he was going to beat for breaking her promise to him, just as soon as he got her to safety. His mate who didn't even flinch away from the madman bearing down at her. Instead, Josie twisted at the waist, her hand coming out of her kit and swinging toward her attacker's chest in one smooth motion.

England, it turned out, was the last one to scream. His mouth opened and rage and pain poured out for a single instant before he went limp and crashed to the floor at the feet of his dead father.

Eli was left with no target and nothing to slow his

momentum. He sailed through the space England had recently occupied and caught his hip against the decorative ball on top of the newel post. The wood cracked under the force of a seven-foot lion fueled by momentum and rage and the ball popped off, bounced against the floor once, and rolled through a doorway on the other side of the hall. Eli crashed into a wall and slid down into an undignified heap, his hip throbbing and his head spinning, since that had been the part of him to hit the wall first. Thankfully, the old plaster had been replaced with drywall, which had enough good grace to give under the impact, leaving the wall scarred but Eli's skull intact.

He watched in a daze as Steve reached Josie just seconds behind England and hauled her to her feet.

"Are you okay?" the colonel demanded, scanning her for injuries. Luckily, he wasn't sufficiently lost in the moment to run his hands over her to check. "Did he hurt you? What happened?"

"I'm fine," she reassured him. "He barely touched me, but he's probably dead. I need to make sure Eli is okay."

As she hurried to his side with gratifying speed, Eli watched Steve walk up to the second body and use his boot to nudge it over onto its back. In the center of its chest, a hypodermic needle protruded at an odd but clearly effective angle.

Eli shook his head again, felt it actually clear this time, and shifted just as Josie laid a hand on his chest. He heard her gasp and saw wonder flicker through her sweet chocolate eyes as she got a little feel of his transformation spreading through him.

"I'm fine," he reassured her, taking her hand in his and raising it to his lips. "I've got a pretty hard head."

Josie laughed, then gave a little sniffle. "See, I've been telling you that all week. It's nice to finally hear you admit it."

"What did you give him?"

"Sux. Succinylcholine. The stuff I used to knock Bill out that morning in the clinic, but it was a dose calibrated for a crazy Lupine with a built-up tolerance for sedatives. I imagine it stopped his heart immediately."

Eli was happy to hear not a single note of regret in her voice. He was even happier to confirm with his own hands and eyes that she really had not been hurt.

"You shouldn't feel bad about it, Josie," Steve said, clearly less attuned to the nuances of the woman's tone than her mate was. "He would have killed you. You just used the weapon at hand and made the only decision you could have made: Kill or be killed."

Josie sighed. "Well, I didn't actually mean to kill him. When I put my hand in the bag, I could feel a needle, but I wasn't sure which one it was. I have a couple of other preloads in there in case of emergency. I was kind of hoping that I'd grabbed the morphine and it would be enough to get him off me and give Eli time to get to him. I would have preferred for him to live so that we could find out more about how he worked with the virus and whether or not he'd already started any more modifications. Now we'll have to hope we find out when we search the rest of the place. I hoped the notebook I found in the study would be the key, but it's mostly megalomaniacal self-congratulations. His real notes are probably in his lab, wherever that is."

Eli felt the room spin and saw his life flash before his eyes. He squeezed his mate's hand, not letting up until she squealed in discomfort.

"Are you telling me," he began weakly, "that instead of running away from a demented killer, you faced him thinking that you had nothing to defend yourself with aside from a needle full of painkiller? Josie?"

He saw her eyes searching his face and knew she was looking for anger. He hadn't bellowed the question, after all. In fact he'd asked it quietly and politely and with a sort of dawning wonder that must make quite a contrast from the other times they had discussed her right and ability to take care of herself. He didn't waste words trying to reassure her, just let her see the truth on his face.

Finally, she nodded, still looking a little wary. "I am. Are you going to lecture me?"

"No."

"You're not?"

"No. I'm going to congratulate myself for having such a clever, resourceful, quick-witted, and courageous mate," he murmured, smiling into her eyes. "And then I'm going to thank my lucky stars that she belongs to me."

Slowly and beautifully, a smile began to curve her lips. It actually started in her eyes, making them glint and glow; then it spread outward bit by bit, crinkling the corners of her eyes, rounding her cheeks, and finally blooming into a perfect expression of joy.

"I think you should also thank this mate of yours," she whispered back, leaning forward until her forehead rested against his and her body melted against him in perfect intimacy.

"I should?"

"Mm-hm. Thank her for having the incredibly good sense to fall in love with you." She brushed her lips over his, more a promise than a kiss. "Thank her by telling her you love her, too."

Eli smiled and wrapped her arms around her, realizing that nothing ever felt to right as the moments when he touched this woman; on the hand, on the cheek, on the breast, it didn't matter. All that matter was her and him, joined.

"I love you," he whispered and watched her joy turn to exaltation while the same feeling rose warm and perfect in his own chest. "I will always love you, Josephine Barrett. And I will always be thankful to you for loving me."

Behind them, a completely forgotten air force colonel cleared his throat and tilted his head toward the ceiling, making a big show of studying the intricate detailing of the plasterwork there. Between them, they continued to ignore him.

Josie laughed softly and her smile took a slightly wicked turn. "Well, if you're going to thank me for loving you," she murmured as she raised her lips to his once more, "you're going to have an awful lot to be thankful for."

And he did. Every day of his life.

Don't miss out on the new Others novel!

Coming soon from
New York Times bestselling author

CHRISTINE WARREN

PRINCE CHARMING DOESN'T LIVE HERE ANYMORE

ISBN: 978-0-312-94794-1

Available in Fall 2010 from St. Martin's Paperbacks